THE
COMPANY
OF SAINTS

THE COMPANY OF SAINTS

EVELYN ANTHONY

G. P. PUTNAM'S SONS/NEW YORK

Library of Congress Cataloging in Publication Data

Anthony, Evelyn.
  The company of saints.

  I. Title.
PR6069.T428C6   1984   823'.914   83-23019
ISBN 0-399-12895-6

Printed in the United States of America

To Blanche and Isidore

with my love

THE
COMPANY
OF SAINTS

1

VENICE. The Queen of the Adriatic. The four golden horses and the pigeons in St. Mark's Square. The gondolas gliding like painted swans down the lightly ruffled waters of the lagoon. The Lido, with suntanned bathers splashing in the waves. All the tourist claptrap came into his mind as the plane landed at Marco Polo Airport. It was an internal flight from Milan; most of the passengers were foreigners ending their Italian tour with a visit to the most beautiful city in Europe. Some would say, in the world. He had never been there before. He was born in the Dolomites and his hair was fair and his eyes blue. He didn't look like an Italian. He had been given money and false papers. He had booked himself into a modest pensione some ten minutes' walk from the Grand Canal. He lined up with his fellow passengers for the water-bus that would take them out into the lagoon and land them by the Rialto Bridge. It was a warm May afternoon, and the first thing he noticed was the smell. A musty smell with refuse as its base, hinting at rottenness beneath the surface of the blue-green water. For him, it symbolized the modern world. The excited people craning forward, pointing out the sights as they came into view, filled him with contempt. He saw no beauty in the splendid buildings, no romance in the extraordinary phenomenon of a city built on water. He would welcome the day when it crumbled and fell into the encroaching sea.

He heaved his suitcase up and disembarked. He had a map of the city; he walked through the dawdling crowds, a hurrying figure intent on finding refuge. The pensione was down a dark, cobbled side street, where the overhanging houses closed out the light and the twentieth century. He went to his room and unpacked. His equipment was concealed in the handle of the suitcase. His instructions were to leave the pensione but not the city after it was done. He was to go to a house on the Street of the Assassins. Nobody would think of looking for him there.

"I feel like a schoolgirl," Davina said. "If I had a satchel I'd swing it and start skipping."

"You look like one," Tony Walden said. "A very desirable fourteen-year-old. Now aren't you glad we came here?"

She took his arm and squeezed it. "You know I am. It's more beautiful than you said, and you did a pretty good PR job! All those Canalettos and Guardis coming to life in front of our eyes. I promise you, darling, from now on you choose where we go for a holiday. I'll never argue again."

He guided her through a group of students clustered in front of the Basilica of St. Mark and steered her to the right. The canal gleamed in the sunlight ahead of them.

"The day you don't argue, I'll know there's something very wrong," he said. "Let's catch the water-bus back to the hotel."

She turned to him, disappointed. "Why? I could wander round here for hours."

"Because I'm expecting a call," he said.

"I thought we were supposed to be on holiday," Davina protested. "The trouble with you is you never stop thinking about business."

They boarded the big water-bus and took seats in the stern. "Can you honestly tell me," he countered, "that you haven't given thought to your office or what's happening since we got here?"

Davina looked at him and smiled. She did look ridiculously young, he thought, with her hair red in the sunshine, tied back like a teenager with a twist of blue elastic and a silly bobble on the end.

"You win," she said. "I did speak to Humphrey yesterday when you were having your hair cut. And he was delighted to tell me that everything was running perfectly without me. What's your call?"

"A client in Milan," Walden said. "Mobile Internazionale. Very big in the European market. They make marvelous modern furniture; I believe we could do a major promotion in the States." He put his arm round her. "If I get the account I'm going to buy you a keepsake."

He knew immediately that he had made what people called a Freudian slip. He might have known she'd pick it up. If only she wasn't so incredibly alert; but then she wouldn't have got the job . . .

"Why a keepsake? You're not going away somewhere you haven't told me?"

"I meant a present," he said it quickly and was saved because the bus bumped gently into its mooring and they had to get up.

"I don't want presents," Davina said as they walked toward their hotel. "I have enough trouble with you trying to pay my own way as it is."

They went up in the elevator to the first floor. His insistence on using an elevator rather than walk up the shortest flight of stairs slightly irritated Davina. She thought it was lazy of him and she said so. He still used the elevator.

"That's only because you're afraid someone would say you were being bribed," he said, unlocking the door of their suite. "The head of the SIS is banking Gucci bags in Switzerland! Come here." While he was kissing her he began to undo the jaunty ponytail. Davina knew that he liked her hair hanging loose when they made love.

She said, "What about your call from Milan?"

"I conned you," he murmured. "It's not due for two hours."

Humphrey Grant left the office in Anne's Yard twenty minutes early. It was a quiet time of year, a gentle May, as his deputy, Johnson, described it, meaning that apart from the continuing crisis of East–West coexistence, there was little fluctuation in the Intelligence graph. He was having his biweekly lunch with his former chief, Sir James White, at the Garrick Club, and over their long association, Grant had learned to be early rather than late. Since Sir James's retirement, Humphrey Grant had grown closer to him than ever before. Close enough to confess one day that he was living with a young man. He would never forget James White's reaction. The bushy white brows raised a little and the blue eyes showed the merest flicker of surprise. He hadn't known whether to expect shock or, worse still, the older man's lacerating scorn. The response caught him off guard.

"How very brave of you to say so," White had said. "I admire you for this, Humphrey, although I disapprove. Are you proposing to resign from the Service?"

"If you think I should, Chief," Humphrey had said.

"I'm not the Chief anymore," Sir James had reminded him. "My opinion doesn't count. You have to contend with Davina, my dear chap. But I can give you my advice on how to deal with her if you like. And still keep your job."

Humphrey had taken that advice. He had gone to see her and told her that he was a homosexual and had a lover. Sir James had been right about her too. It took her twenty-four hours to make up her mind. It was a decision taken after consultation with the prime minister, she told him, and he winced, expecting the worst. His private life was only relevant if it exposed him to blackmail. He had forestalled any possibility of that by telling her the truth. He had agreed to a security vetting on his lover. His confidence in the boy was justified. He was exactly what he appeared. A simple young man of working-class background without any affiliations, political or homosexual, to anything or anybody, before he came to live with Humphrey. In no way could he be regarded as a risk.

It was strange that he couldn't feel grateful to her. Strange that he actually hated her for letting him remain, when he knew that she despised him for adopting a mode of life that put him and his career at risk. She had been promoted to the post that should have been his; now he owed his position in the Service to her and he would never be able to forgive her.

He enjoyed his lunches with Sir James. Ironically, although he had recommended Davina's appointment, Sir James displayed a veiled malice toward her that Humphrey identified very quickly. He resented being out at grass, as he called it, and his natural bent for mischief and intrigue focused on the woman he had elevated to his former job. He lunched with Humphrey to hear the gossip and to slip in odd suggestions that might cause his protégée discomfort. It kept him amused and it allowed Humphrey to be thoroughly spiteful and disloyal.

On that pleasant May midday, after a glass of sherry in the splendid room on the first floor, Humphrey leaned his long body toward Sir James White and said, "I must say, it's quite a relief to have her out of the way. She wants everything done *yesterday*. It's not the way to get the best out of people."

"And does Tim Johnson feel the same?" Sir James inquired. He watched Humphrey with a kindly twinkle. He had recommended Johnson to Davina. A very clever, ambitious young man, endowed with formidable talent. Here too, Sir James had a quirky motive. A young lion like Johnson would keep Davina Graham on her toes. And goad poor Humphrey if he was tempted to sulk or turn complacent. Just because he had retired, Sir James reflected, he wasn't obliged to be bored. Humphrey made a grimace; his ugly face contorted, as if a skull had become a gargoyle. He could have sat high up on a church as a waterspout, his Chief thought at that moment. What on earth motivated the lover . . .

"Johnson," Humphrey said, "would like it the day before yesterday. They don't like each other, of course. Too much of a muchness."

"Well," Sir James said, "you're in the driving seat, my dear Humphrey, while she's on holiday. Enjoy it: make Johnson run a few circles. It'll be good for him."

"There's nothing happening at the moment," Grant said. "Very quiet. He said so himself. I think he'd love an international incident; he'd be quite capable of engineering trouble if he thought he could promote himself. The Eastern desk hasn't reported anything except routine for the last month; April was dead and it looks as if May will be the same."

"Perhaps our friend Borisov is on holiday too?" Sir James suggested. "I know Franklyn is touring Europe."

"He's the only American I've ever had time for," Humphrey said primly.

"Because he takes a hard line?" Sir James raised an eyebrow. "They all do, in the administration. They wouldn't last long if they didn't."

"Franklyn knows the Russians," Grant countered. "He's quite different from the crewcut goon you had to deal with. He was three years in Moscow and he has a very sensitive political nose. Even Davina admits that. How do you know he's in Europe?"

"Oh," Sir James said lightly, "I have a few contacts, I keep in touch. Shall we go down to lunch?"

They were drinking coffee when he said, quite casually, "You know Humphrey, there's something that's been bothering me for some time. I think I ought to mention it. Alfred, would you bring me the cigars?" He knew how much Grant hated people smoking. As he lit it and puffed, Grant didn't seem to notice. Maybe the boy friend liked the odd fag. He chuckled to himself at the bad joke. "It's Davina's good friend, Tony Walden," he went on. "Has anyone run a security check on him, do you know?"

Humphrey nodded. "It was the first thing she did," he said gloomily, "after she got the job."

"I might have known," James White remarked. "Davina's not exactly sentimental. Or rather she's more responsible than sentimental. Which is a great compliment to her, of course. However," he played with the cigar, examining the tip for a moment, "she's been at the top for eighteen months. What was a clean sheet when she started might read differently by now, a lot of doubtfuls slipped through the vetting system at that time. Think about it, Humphrey. I'd run a second check on Walden if I were you. Davina needn't know unless you find anything."

Humphrey looked at him; the cigar smoke made him want to cough. "Do you have any particular reason for suggesting this?"

"Only an instinct," Sir James said softly. "I met him once; I didn't like him."

No, Humphrey Grant thought, you wouldn't. A Polish Jew who made a fortune out of an advertising agency; a flamboyant self-made man without an old school tie in his wardrobe. Not your type at all. But Davina Graham's type, it seemed. On holiday together in Venice. They'd been together for nearly three years. But James White wouldn't suggest a check on the man just because he didn't like him. In twenty-five years his instinct for something wrong had only failed once. And that particular failure was drinking himself to death in Moscow.

"I'll take a look at Walden," he said. "I'll let you know what happens."

They got out their diaries and fixed a date in two weeks' time.

He had been given the code name "Italy." They were all known by the country of their birth. He had been well briefed on how to melt into the background. The great mistake was to arouse curiosity. In a city that delighted in gossip and lived the best part of its life in cafés, the recluse would cause comment. He must talk to his fellow guests and to the *padrone* in the pensione. He must tell them about his interest in architecture, paint the false picture of home and family that had been created for him, and he would be absorbed and forgotten. He was not gregarious by nature. Talking to strangers was an ordeal. But the time was short enough, and he spent the mornings walking the route, and going up and down by bus and gondola past the hotel on the Grand Canal. Finally he went into the hotel itself. The famous Gritti Palace, once owned by a Venetian nobleman, had been adapted to provide every luxury for those who could afford it.

He felt conspicuous going into the bar that overlooked the canal, but his clothes were expensive and there were numbers of young men like him drinking Camparis or Scotch. He didn't expect to see the target. Familiarize yourself with the background, get to know how people move in and out, when the vaporettos pull in for the evening runs, for the morning expeditions to the Cipriani out in the lagoon. Stand on the landing stage, sink yourself in the atmosphere so that nothing can take you by surprise. You won't need any of the things you'll observe and memorize if the plan goes well. But you may if it doesn't.

When the target came through the door and into the bar, he glanced up briefly, then finished his Scotch and left the hotel. If the planned method failed, then the bar at the Gritti could provide an alternative. He had seen the man accompanying the target. A bodyguard, naturally. He would keep the alternative as a very probable reserve.

Walden was asleep; he looked older, Davina thought, when the curtain came down and the extrovert retired out of the spotlight. His energy, his enthusiasms, his diversity of interests might exhaust at times, or tempt her into argument, but she had never been bored. As he lay beside her in the golden sunlight, he was a tired man in his late forties, with a vulnerability that touched her deeply.

She knew him better than anyone else, including his former wife and the present incumbent, or the numerous women he had had as lovers. Davina had seen him almost broken once, and quite alone. A man with everything and nothing, except her. That was when she had fallen in love with him, long before they became lovers. They were so different outwardly that they should have been incompatible. But he made no demands. She lived her professional life as a single woman, unencumbered by personal ties. She couldn't have done the job otherwise, in spite of feminist arguments that men married and ran high-level careers. She couldn't have and didn't want to try. And equally she stood aside for Tony Walden. His business commitments, his family duties came first. What was free in their lives they reserved for themselves. He had wanted to buy her an apartment. She refused; she could afford a comfortable co-op in a sedate area near Sloane Square. She wouldn't let him give her expensive things like furs and the car that had been delivered last Christmas and had to be sent back. He had made a joke about her vulnerability to bribes. But it was based on hard fact. She couldn't take and she couldn't give, except on a modest scale that suited her much better. Minks and Mercedeses reminded her of her sister Charlie. She didn't want to think about her. Or her parents, with their chilly response to her approaches. That hurt as much as ever, and Walden had stopped trying to bring the family together. They wouldn't let him. They hadn't forgiven Davina for ruining their daughter's life. And contrary to her past form, Charlie Kidson had stayed at home with her baby son, and there wasn't a man in view.

According to the reports coming from Moscow, it wouldn't be long before she was a widow. Davina sighed and turned onto her back. The ceiling was painted; centuries of sunlight and modern pollution had faded the erotic nudes and the lascivious cupids. They were a soft blur in the painted sky, a suggestion of the silky, sensual figures that had aroused the passions of dead men and women.

Walden had insisted upon staying at the Gritti Palace. Davina would have preferred somewhere less ostentatious, less formidably expensive. But he had a childish love of luxury. He enjoyed being pampered, wallowing, as she unkindly put it, in red plush; he disarmed her by an innocent reminder of his hungry, hunted boyhood in Poland. He had earned the fleshpots. He wasn't an upper-class Anglican with a guilt complex about spending money on being comfortable. They were going to the Gritti for their holiday. When they went to Paris they stayed at the Ritz, and in New York, he took a suite at the Plaza. She had learned to live with it. And, she admitted to herself, to like it too. She got up, careful not to wake him. He worked at a ferocious pace; he wouldn't admit it, but he needed the break. He was actually very tired. She looked at her watch. The phone call from Milan wasn't due for another forty minutes. She went into the bathroom, showered, and put on one of the long, uncrushable shifts that were a godsend to travelers. Their bedroom opened out onto a balcony not wide enough to stand on; she perched on the window sill and leaned out. The panorama fascinated her. The faint smell of tainted water rose from the canal, the swish of waves following the water-buses and the motor cruisers lapped against the walls below; to the left the exquisite Church of Santa Maria Della Salute gleamed whitely against the darkening blue sky.

London seemed a million miles away; the pleasant room on the first floor of the town house in Anne's Yard might have been on the moon. She had talked to Humphrey Grant, needing reassurance that everything was well; then she had forgotten him, and Johnson, and the excitement and the problems of work. That was the real purpose of a holiday. To escape from reality, to refresh the mind and the body for a return to the real world. She loved her work. She loved the challenge of it and the sense of personal achievement. She had succeeded and confidence glowed inside her. And she was confident in her own feminine nature too. It was a Russian who had given her that. After his death she had taken off the wedding ring. She would never put another in its place.

She didn't hear Walden approach. He moved very quietly, which was surprising because he was stockily built, and could run to fat if he wasn't careful. He put his hands on her shoulders and was pleased to feel her start.

He loved his little victories. They made him feel good. He enjoyed telling her something she didn't know, creeping up on her unsuspected, proving that in spite of everything, she wasn't always on an equal footing.

"You'll catch cold, sitting in that draft."

"Don't be silly, it's beautifully warm. Why don't you go and have a bath before your Milanese call comes through?"

"Why don't you stop being bossy?" He kissed her neck.

"What shall we do this evening?"

He reached over and pulled the long window shut. "If you get a cold," he said, "you'll give it to me. So you mustn't be selfish.

19

There's a marvelous restaurant off the Piazza San Marco. Why don't we go there?"

"Why not?" Davina got up. "We can have a drink in the bar first."

When the man called "Italy" went back to his pensione for dinner, the girl who sat behind the desk called out to him. His brother had telephoned. Would he call back as soon as possible? The young man said thank you, yes. Could he use the phone in the *padrone's* office?—it would save him going out. She opened the office for him and he dialed the number he knew by heart. The contact was on schedule; he hoped the message would confirm his plan. The door was closed, but he was certain the girl would try to listen. The Venetians were as curious as their colonies of cats. After five rings the number answered. For her benefit he wasted a full minute asking about his parents and nonexistent nieces and nephews, and then he opened the real conversation.

"Venice is a miracle," he said. "I've never had such a good holiday."

The voice on the line responded. "They're going to the Cipriani for lunch tomorrow. Proceed as arranged. If there are difficulties have you an alternative?"

"Yes," "Italy" answered. "I've already provided for that. But I think the original route will be the best one. Kiss the family for me." He rang off. He said to the girl outside, "I've left a hundred lire for the call."

She looked up at him with an expectant smile. "Everything well at home?"

He nodded. "I should have sent a postcard—my mother worries."

"All mothers worry," she said.

He ran up the short flight of stairs to his room. They had a contact in the Gritti Hotel. It was wonderful how well informed they were. Little links in an enveloping chain, and all along the line the connections were broken so that the links couldn't lead to other links. Who was working for them in the Gritti? A waiter, a chambermaid, one of the switchboard operators . . . someone with sharp ears and a telephone number to ring with information. A tiny link in the human chain that was known to its members as the Company of Saints.

The target was lunching at the famous Island Hotel the next day. The motor launch left the Gritti just before noon; he had already timed it, followed it in a hired motorboat. Everything was planned on his part. But if anything went wrong, then he would use the alternative plan and attack in the hotel itself. There would be innocent casualties—his shoulders lifted unconsciously as he dismissed the qualm. Individual lives were not important compared to the objective. He didn't rely on reaching his haven in the Street of the Assassins. Nothing mattered but the target and the plan. He pulled his suitcase out from under the bed. The handle unscrewed and the small metal cylinder, insulated in rubber against metal detection at the airport, fitted into his hand. It looked like a short cigar tube. He checked it, replaced it, and went down to the crowded room where the clients ate their dinner in the evenings. He paid his bill, had a glass of wine with the *padrone* and his wife and said how sorry he was to be going the next morning. His next stop was the ancient city of Padua, where he wanted to study the cathedral. Such a pity that so much industry was creeping round the coastline. The *padrone* agreed, but then he shrugged. Without industry there was no work; Venice in the winter was cold and dead, shrouded like a widow in her gray sea mists. They talked well, the man called "Italy" admitted, with an ear for a poetic phrase. They'd be talking about something else this time tomorrow. He nodded, agreeing with the old man's nonsense. Industry for the benefit of the few at the expense of the many. Pollution for profit, exploitation for the sake of those already bloated with money like gas-filled corpses.

They said goodbye to him and sent a present of a bottle of wine to his table. They liked him; he despised them for it. If they remembered him at all, it would be as one of themselves. He drank the wine and called them names under his breath. He went early to bed and slept very well. When the morning came he was fresh, and only the slightest flickering of a nerve near his left eye betrayed his excitement.

The temperature had risen unexpectedly; the sun blazed off the canal as he walked to the Rialto Bridge and the stage where he had found his hired motorboat. Business was brisk already; he pushed and shoved his way to the front and hailed one of the two empty boats remaining.

"Go to the Gritti Palace," he said. He stripped off his jacket;

the heat was lapping over them. "Slowly," he said. "Just idle along, I don't want to miss anything. Then pull up by the Gritti; I want to sketch the façade."

"Can't do that," the boatman said. "There's no mooring place on the other side and you can't tie up there; it's a concession and I don't have it." He said something in dialect that sounded, and was, a very vulgar curse.

"Never mind," "Italy" said. He had known about the mooring and the concession. "Just go there and take your time." He checked his watch and reckoned they would reach the hotel just as the Cipriani boat pulled out. He sat crouched forward slightly as they made a leisurely way up the Grand Canal; the boatman pointed out a few landmarks and then gave up when he saw that his passenger wasn't listening. He wasn't taking much interest in the *palazzi* on either side of them either; his jacket had fallen off the seat and was lying in a patch of water at the bottom of the boat. He must remember to mop it up when this sullen craphead got out. He could get his feet wet, so far as he cared.

The Cipriani boat was just ahead of them. He could see the target very clearly, wearing white, sitting forward by the bow.

"Why don't you have the concession?" He asked the question suddenly.

The driver turned to look at him. "Because I can't pay for it," he said. "In Italy, you want something, you have to grease the other man's hand. You're an Italian, you ought to know that!"

"I think the practice stinks," the young man said. "Get up close, give the rich bastards a few waves."

"I'll lose my license," the Venetian said.

"No wonder they get away with it," "Italy" sounded contemptuous. "You looked as if you had balls. But still . . ."

It was a challenge no Italian could ignore. The accelerator drowned out the richness of the language, remarkable for its scope and imagery. The little boat cut close to the cruiser. He slipped the cylinder out of his pocket, leaned slightly over the side and trailed his hand in the water. It was a technique he had practiced over and over again in simulated conditions. When to activate the magnetic device. The wash from the little *vaporetto* gently rocked the bigger boat. As they sped past, "Italy" pressed the tiny homing button and released the cylinder. The waves carried it backward and the metal hull of the cruiser drew it inexorably through the water. He had seen the hurried screening of his target by the security men pretending to be passengers, when his little craft came close. Much good that human shield would do him now.

The Venetian said sullenly, "Where do you want to go?" No balls, eh . . . he'd charge the pig double for that remark.

"Get a move on," the man said abruptly, looking over his shoulder. "Go to the Lido." He hoped they'd get clear, but he had taken no chance of the mine going astray. He had released it within the distance of maximum accuracy.

What was the saying—the only reliable assassins are Bulgarians, because they blow themselves up as well? He checked his watch; they had gathered speed very quickly, partly because the Venetian was hoping it would upset his passenger. The little *vaporetto* was skimming out toward the lagoon. "Italy" felt a surge of panic in those last few seconds when he turned again to stare after the cruiser. Thirty seconds was the timing after the mine attached itself. He had turned round when the explosion boomed out, shaking the air and convulsing the water. A pall of thick black smoke rose into the air, shot through with piercing tongues of orange flame.

"My God," the Venetian swung the wheel and cut the engine; the little boat curved into a semicircle and then lost speed. "My God, what was that?"

"I don't know," his passenger said. "It sounded as if something blew up."

"We should go back," the driver said. "If it was a boat."

"What can we do? I want to go to the Lido."

"Then swim!" The Venetian's temper blazed. He wasn't going to drive off and leave the accident. Seamen didn't desert one another. Also he was curious.

He didn't get time to start the engine. The passenger killed him with a blow that broke his neck as if he had been a dangling rabbit.

The body slumped and he climbed over, pushing it aside, shoving it down and out of sight. He had exceeded his instructions. But never mind. There had been too much incident to let the man live. He would remember cutting in on the other boat, remember the jibe that had made him break the law of the canals. It was better to kill him. Sirens were wailing close astern. There were boats converging on what lay behind him; nobody even glanced at the little taxi boat as it began its journey through the waterway. He saw a beach near the Lido; it was stony and uninviting. Nobody swam or sunbathed there when the gleaming sands of the huge public beach beckoned only a few hundred yards further on. He cut the engine and took his time. He tied the dead man down with his own anchor; he found a box with a few tools, and kneeling on the floor, he smashed a hole through the deck below the waterline. The sea gushed in. He switched on the engine and wedged the dead man against the wheel, her bows pointing out to sea. She began to move forward, as he dived off the side. He idled in the water, watching her make way, listing as the hull filled up. She'd be well out from the shore by the time she sank. There were no craft in sight. Luck was on his side. *La Bella Fortuna.* He turned and swam toward the empty beach. When he reached it, the boat had vanished. He stripped and lay in the sun while his clothes dried. A shirt, trousers, canvas shoes. The jacket was ruined. He bundled it over his arm when he set off. He caught a water-bus back late in the afternoon. Everyone hurried to see the signs of the disaster that had happened on the Grand Canal. Bits of blackened debris still floated, and the smoke and fumes hadn't cleared. Someone, God knows who, had dropped a wreath of red and white flowers onto the water, where Henry Franklyn, United States secretary of defense, had been blown to pieces just before one o'clock that day.

"Well," Humphrey Grant remarked, "You were complaining about things being too quiet. We'll have enough excitement now."

Tim Johnson tried not to look pleased. Ever since the news came in on the telex, the adrenaline had been pumping through him. He had hunted with his uncle in Galway as a boy; the love of excitement and challenge had been born in him as he flew over jagged gray walls and galloped across the wild terrain. He still hunted on odd weekends, but it was not the same. Now he pursued human quarry.

Davina's telex had followed within an hour. Johnson was to fly to Venice immediately; Humphrey was to contact the Agenzia di Sicurezza and ask for full cooperation with their British colleagues. An explosives expert was to follow Johnson as quickly as possible.

"I think Davina's pushing this too far," Humphrey grumbled. "The Agenzia people are notoriously touchy about outsiders."

"They're notoriously inefficient too," Johnson retorted. He detested the Old Boys Network attitude. Davina Graham didn't care whose toes she stepped on and he admired her for it. "I think it's a good idea."

Humphrey didn't look up from his desk as he answered. "When you've worked with the Italians as long as I have," he said, "you'll find they're as good in their way as anybody. What time's your plane?"

"Six-thirty," Johnson said. Patronizing old prune, he said to himself, looking at the balding top of Grant's head. Never looks you in the eye when he's giving out.

Grant's head came up and stared at him as if he'd spoken out loud. "Then why don't you catch it?"

Johnson didn't bang the door. He didn't care about Humphrey. Humphrey had nowhere to go but the green fields of retirement.

His wife was waiting at Heathrow with a small bag; they'd been married for seven years and had twin boys. Johnson loved his family; his wife was very understanding about his job. They kissed and he said, "Darling, I don't know when I'll be back. I'll bring the boys something." Four hours later he was met by a senior officer of the Italian anti-terrorist squad and driven by private launch to the Gritti Palace hotel.

"I'm sorry about this," Davina said. "I'm afraid our holiday's gone up in smoke."

Walden held her hand. "Of course it has." He looked shaken, sallow under the suntan. "I can't stop thinking about it," he said. "We could have been on that launch."

"Not a chance," Davina answered quietly. "Everyone on board was part of Franklyn's security guard. Nobody got a place on any boat when he was in it. They saw to that."

He looked up at her suddenly. "You knew he was staying here?"

"Yes, I knew. I recognized him when he walked into the restaurant last week. He had his daughter with him. The wife died last year."

"Why didn't you say anything?" He sounded subdued.

Davina was surprised at how much the tragedy had shaken

him. She said very gently, "Darling, I didn't say anything because I couldn't. What was the point? Franklyn was traveling incognito, showing the poor girl round Europe. The whole thing was being kept as quiet as possible to give them a chance to enjoy themselves. He's not a well-known face; he never went on TV like a lot of them. They were very tightly screened, and it might well have worked."

"But it didn't," Walden countered. "Somebody knew who he was all right and the so-called bloody screen didn't stop them being blown up in broad daylight on the Grand Canal! Why can't you go home and let this Tim Johnson take over out here? What good can *you* do?"

"I don't know," she admitted. "But I was on the scene and Johnson wasn't. You're not worrying about me, are you? Tony, for God's sake, don't be silly. I'm not in any danger."

He said angrily, "If they knew about Franklyn, what's to stop them having a go at you?"

"Nothing," she admitted. "Except it doesn't work like that. The bosses don't attack one another. That's the unwritten law. I don't worry about Borisov having a crack at me, Brunson at CIA doesn't either, Borisov doesn't worry about us. Nobody has ever broken that rule. It's understood."

"In other words Franklyn was murdered by the KGB?" He had turned away from her, looking out of their window. It was dark, but the flashlights of the river police were playing over the water outside. The area where the boat had blown up was roped off up to a hundred yards on either side. Water traffic passing by was limited to three knots. No flights had been allowed out of Marco Polo Airport; the railway link with the mainland was closed. "The radio said it was a terrorist organization."

"That's a pretty good description of the KGB," Davina answered. She came up to him. "Tony, you mustn't let this get on top of you. You've always known what I did. You know as well as I do that there are risks involved. But not for me. That's the irony of the damned job. We're the generals; we don't get into the firing line. Now please, come on. Let's go down and have a drink and wait for Johnson."

"It'll be crawling with police," Walden muttered. "The place is full of them. I'd like to move."

"All right, we will, as soon as I've seen Tim."

He put his arms round her and held her for a moment. "I love you so much," he said. "That's the trouble."

"The trouble," Davina said, "would be if you stopped. One day, I'll tell you just how pointless my life would be without you. Now let's go down, shall we?"

The bar was full; the trade in drinks had been brisk ever since the police said the hotel could function normally. Statements had been taken from the guests and staff. Davina and Walden were excused after she identified herself. They would confer with the head of Sicurezza. He had set up his headquarters in the Agenzia Polizie in the Via Leonardo Da Vinci. There was only one topic of conversation among the American, British, and German tourists; the Italians kept themselves in a group, embarrassed and shamed by what had happened. Davina and Walden were drawn in in spite of their efforts to tuck themselves into a corner.

"How dreadful," a pretty young English girl kept saying, "How ghastly . . ."

"It's the Red Brigade," her husband insisted. "Just like the way they killed that poor devil—the politician—what's his name?"

"Aldo Moro," Davina suggested.

"That's right—bloody savages, that's what those people are. The Germans had the right idea. . . . They knew how to deal with Baader, whatever it was, Group."

"Baader-Meinhof," Davina spoke again.

"That's right," he repeated. "They hanged themselves in prison, or so the Germans said."

"We were out when it happened," the pretty girl was saying to Walden, leaning close toward him as if they were all conspirators. "I don't think I want to stay here now. I keep thinking about it— did you see all those awful bits floating around on the canal . . ."

"There's Tim," Davina interrupted. She smiled briefly at the couple. "Excuse me. Goodnight."

It surprised her how well Johnson and Tony Walden got on. They talked about the flight, Johnson made a joke at the expense of the local carabinieri, which made Walden laugh, and after that he seemed to relax. They went upstairs to the suite, where Johnson opened the window and leaned out. The lights were playing over the black water; a gondola with a load of tourists came close enough for the serenade "O Sole Mio" to float like a lament over the hum of passing launches.

"I don't know what they expect to find by now," Johnson remarked. "I gather there wasn't much left to bury. Analysis would tell us what sort of explosive they used."

"Does it matter?" Walden queried.

"It could be a pointer," Johnson explained. "The more sophisticated the device, the easier to eliminate groups that couldn't get hold of it."

"But it has to be the Russians," Walden said. Johnson glanced at Davina.

She answered the question he hadn't asked. "It's all right," she said. "You can talk in front of Tony. This is only routine stuff. Later," she reached out and touched his hand, "We'll have to go into a huddle. When our Italian friend arrives."

The house on the Street of the Assassins had a small television set. The man whose name was "Italy" ate his meal of spaghetti alle vongole sitting in front of it. He listened to the commentators, saw TV replays of the scene on the Grand Canal, watched the night cameras relaying the continued activity in the area. There was a young woman in the house; she had opened the door, and given him a kiss as soon as he was inside.

"Congratulations," was all she said. It was a small, very dark house, low-ceilinged and with narrow windows; it belonged to a Venetian antique dealer, who relished the historical significance of his address, and enjoyed himself filling the sinister little building with early furniture and some rare Renaissance bronzes whose owners didn't know what they were selling. His shop was closed for renovations; part of the lower floor showed subsidence due to the waters of the canal. He had moved his stock upstairs, called in the builders and gone off on a buying expedition with his wife to Rome. His daughter had stayed behind.

The girl came and stood behind his chair, watching the screen in silence. Messages of outrage were coming in from world leaders. The pope's image appeared, and the girl laughed. "You've made quite a stir, 'Italy.'"

The man looked over his shoulder at her. "Shut up," he said. The report returned to the Grand Canal; there was nothing new to tell the audience. The taxi boat had not been found. He leaned forward and switched the TV off. He felt the girl's excitement coming at him like electric waves. Some of the women were like that. Death gave them an orgasm. As soon as someone was killed they wanted to fuck. He didn't feel like it. "I'm going to bed," he said. "And not with you. So cool off."

She shrugged. She was very slim, very dark-eyed, with the olive skin of the true Venetian. Somewhere, centuries back, there had been a Moor in the bed of a Valdorini. "Suit yourself," she said. A pity. She liked men with his coloring. But he might feel different tomorrow. Then so might she. She took the tray away and washed the dishes by hand. She had been brought up to be economical. They didn't use the machine unless it was full. By eleven-thirty the lights were out and the house was a blind face in the crumbling wall of ancient houses. The water ran close to the edge of the narrow street outside, and a sinister humped bridge, too narrow to cross except in single file, spanned the sluggish flow. And in that flow, carried by the unseen tides that crept in from the sea, floated the remains of the boat, and of the people who had died that morning.

Alfredo Modena was in his sixties. He was a quiet, rather dour man who could have been an academic. He spoke excellent English, also German and French. He joined Davina and Johnson just before midnight. Walden had excused himself after dinner.

"I'm sorry to be so late," Modena said. "My headquarters is like a madhouse. There are times when I'd like to shoot every media man on sight!"

"I don't envy you," Davina said. "The last thing you need in a situation like this is outsiders getting in the way." Be tactful, Humphrey had advised on the telephone. You have a unique opportunity to get in on the investigation, but remember how touchy the Italians are. . . . She decided to be tactful, as he'd said. "Signor Modena, I hope you don't put me in that category. As I happened to be practically on the spot and staying in the same hotel, I felt you'd understand my request for information." He wasn't going to respond. She saw the resentment in his eyes as he looked at her.

"The United States is principally involved," he said, "I am expecting a planeload of their people. I have to give them priority, as far as any information is concerned. All I can make available to you, Signorina Graham, are the preliminary reports." He handed a thin file to Davina. "There's nothing much there. We're waiting for the forensic reports and laboratory tests. Then we'll have a clearer picture of what happened. But it's definitely murder. The gas tank exploded, but only after a primary explosion of great force set it off."

"That would be pretty obvious to anyone who saw the boat go up," Davina said. "Nobody suggested it was an accident at our end."

"But accidents occur," Modena's tone was sharp. "And not only in Italy."

"Prunehead was right," Johnson said to himself, "they certainly don't like outside interference."

Davina said, "What most concerns us, Signore Modena, is whether this is an Italian organization or an international one. What is your view?"

"Until I have studied all the reports and collated all my facts, Signorina, I don't have a view." He detested abrasive, abrupt women who squared up to men as equals. But then he was old-fashioned. The English had made a woman head of their government. It wouldn't happen in Italy.

"But you must have a private opinion," Tim Johnson decided to take it up. "Is it the Red Brigade?"

Modena shrugged. "It could be. It could be the Dutch Red Hand, or what's left of the Baader-Meinhofs coming back into the picture. Or the PLO. After all, Franklyn was a Jew."

"But not a Zionist," Davina said. She glanced quickly at Johnson. We're wasting our time, the signal said. Let's cut it short.

She stood up, "Thank you for coming to see us. Mr. Johnson will be here for the next few days and anxious to consult with you. I'll be on my way to London tomorrow. As I said, I don't envy you. Especially when the CIA arrive in force."

There was anger in his voice. "They are already blaming us for lack of protection. I believe my government will point out that you can't protect someone unless you know they're in your country. I can't think how our American colleagues could have taken such a risk with a public figure."

"Perhaps they thought it was less of a risk than letting other people know," Davina answered. "We mustn't keep you; goodnight, Signore Modena. I hope you catch whoever did it."

He shook her hand without enthusiasm. "I shall do my best. Goodnight."

When he had gone, Johnson said. "That was below the belt, wasn't it, Miss Graham? He didn't like that last crack at all."

"It happens to be true," she said. "The country's so bloody riddled with Mafia and corruption of every kind that nobody would trust them with anything. But there wasn't any reason why Franklyn couldn't take a private holiday with his daughter, using another name. Whoever got him has contacts at the highest level. Which rather answers my question, don't you think?"

"Borisov," Johnson nodded. "If they had a go at the pope through a Bulgarian terrorist outlet, why not this? Why not?"

"He's very good at getting people killed," Davina said quietly.

It was a long time ago, Johnson remembered, but she hadn't forgotten. Her husband had been murdered in Australia. Igor Borisov had planned the assassination. He was a junior officer then; now he was the head of the KGB, the exact counterpart to Davina Graham. What would happen, he wondered, if those two ever met?

"I don't think we'll get much help from their lab people," Tim said after a pause. "Or the autopsy. I don't think Sicurezza's going to share anything with anyone."

"They aren't," Davina lit a cigarette. She had tried to give up the habit, nagged by Walden; her resolution was forgotten then. "And if they don't like us asking questions, I wish the buggers joy when the CIA get here."

Johnson paused by the door. "Are you going back tomorrow?"

"I'm leaving here," she said. "It's supposed to be our holiday. I'll have to see."

He went down the corridor, humming the gondoliers' sugary serenade. O Sole Mio. Oh, my soul. "Our holiday." She didn't miss a trick and she didn't give a damn what people thought. He admired her for it but he didn't find it attractive.

Walden was sitting up reading when Davina came in. "How did it go, darling?" There was no resentment for being left out, thank God. No macho nonsense. He understood the job and its demands upon them both. She came and kissed him gratefully.

"You are a love," she said. "Sorry I was so long. I needn't have bothered, actually."

"Why not?" He put his book aside. He knew that stubborn look and the set of her chin.

"The Italians aren't going to give us anything," she said flatly.

"I can see why, of course, but it doesn't make it any easier in a case like this. They're acutely embarrassed and on the defensive. They'll protect their own reputation even if it means letting the killers off the hook. I could have hit that bastard tonight. All he was thinking of was his own side!"

"Wouldn't that be true if it had happened in Britain?" Walden asked her.

Davina looked quickly at him. "You have a talent for saying the bloodiest things, don't you? Yes, of course it would, but not if I could help it. If this is what I think it is, there's no room for national pride or inter-Service rivalries. We're just cutting our own throats in the West if we don't work together."

"What do you think it is, or can't you tell me?"

She undressed and got into bed beside him. "I think we're at the start of a chain of assassinations," she said after a moment. "I don't know why I think so, but I do. I think it's Borisov behind it, but it'll be impossible to prove."

"But what's his motive?" Walden asked her.

"I don't know," Davina admitted. "And I won't know till a pattern starts emerging. And that means another murder."

"Italy" had done well. It was interesting to consider, in the words of the Christian Bible, how many were called to do his kind of work, but how few chosen. A very special talent was needed to kill in this way. Take away the profit motive—there was no shortage of mercenaries—substitute an ideal with which the killer could make his impulses respectable and there was a deadly weapon in the right hands.

There was a spectacular view from his window; he never tired of looking out over the changing skies, the variety of sunsets. And he liked the tranquility of being alone and able to think. The vagaries of human nature concerned him more and more; he had long ago learned to despise it and to capitalize upon its weaknesses.

Whoever had said that Man was made in God's image had a poor opinion of God. But God was a myth, one among many that mankind needed to combat the fear of death and nothingness. In the East they had made a virtue of Nothingness; pretending that the darkness and the worms were the ultimate form of human achievement. He had made a study of comparative religions; it amused him to test them intellectually. And from that study and the need to utilize human psychology, he had evolved the organization that he called the Company of Saints. It amused him to equate his band of death-dealing disciples with the great host of Christian souls grouped round the throne of God in Majesty. There was a magnificent canvas depicting the Last Judgment with all the scope and imagery of the Italian Renaissance. The blessed chanted praises round the dispenser of final justice, while the wicked were sucked into a fiery hell. He had reversed the roles. "Italy" had done well, he said again. It was a perfect operation, meticulously planned and executed with maximum impact. One less enemy and all the repercussions from his death would benefit them. He turned away from his contemplation by the window.

It was time he took up the other burdens of his public life.

2

THE weather was so mild that the Grahams were having breakfast out on the terrace. Marchwood faced south, so that the front of the old house was bathed in sunlight. The front terrace was Captain Graham's innovation; he liked to eat breakfast there and read the morning papers. He was reading *The Times*, exclaiming over items of news; Davina's mother usually made pleasant noises during this ritual and thought about her flowers. But not that morning. The dreadful murder of the American politician had upset them both. Captain Graham was reading excerpts aloud to her, and instead of thinking about spraying the roses, Betty Graham was paying full attention.

"And that poor daughter," she said. "Only nineteen—how could people do such a thing!"

"They're the scum of the earth," her husband retorted. He put the newspaper down. "Where's Charlie?" Having his favorite child living at home again was a marvelous bonus for him. He adored his little grandson, and he was always asking where Charlie was, or wandering off to peer into the carriage. His wife thought it was touching and sweet. It had never entered her head to be jealous of his love for their younger daughter. She pitied Davina because she had minded being second-best so much. "I think Charlie's coming now," she said. "I can hear Fergie—he's such a bundle of energy, isn't he? We were so lucky to find Pat, otherwise Charlie would have been worn out."

They had engaged a local girl to help look after the little boy. Fergus Graham felt that a boisterous toddler was too much for his daughter to manage; he worried because she looked tired and too thin. He often said to his wife that Charlie had never recovered from the awful shock although it was two years ago.

"Darling," Mrs. Graham said. "The coffee's still hot, I'll make you some more toast."

Charlie Kidson thanked her with a kiss. Her father beamed. Really she was a lovely girl, and still so young-looking. Nobody would have given her a day more than, say, twenty-eight. Not thirty-seven, not three years from forty. That abundant red hair, the too-thin figure, the girlish laugh. Not heard so often now, not since she found out about her husband. It grieved him to think that she was sad. And she wouldn't apply for a divorce. He couldn't understand it. It wasn't like Charlie to sit still and let life pass by.

"Pat's going to take the monster for a walk," Charlie said. She referred to her son by the nickname; it rather shocked some people who didn't realize that she adored him. She picked up the paper and glanced at the headlines. They had watched the late news together the night before. She had gone up to bed rather abruptly, her parents thought.

"That ghastly thing," she said. She drank some coffee. Then she looked at her father. "I expect Davina will be reveling in it. I couldn't stop thinking about her last night. I didn't get to sleep for hours."

"You shouldn't let it get on your nerves," her father said. "Forget about her, Charlie. I've said this over and over to you. She doesn't try and come here anymore. She's stopped writing. Put it out of your mind."

"I do," Charlie insisted. "But something like this brings it all back. I thought of her last night, sitting in her bloody office, queen of the heap at last, while the poor little monster grows up without his father and John sits in Moscow, drinking himself to death. Do you know, Daddy, I've thought about going out to join him?" She saw the alarm on her father's face and then shook her head quickly, "No, not seriously, just when I felt so fed up and angry about what happened . . . when I thought about Fergie. Of course I wouldn't go. I'd loathe it and I'd loathe John too for ruining everything. I shouldn't have said that, I'm sorry." She got up and put her arms round him.

"It would kill us if you went," he said. "Remember what he did. You couldn't live with that."

"I know I couldn't," Charlie went back to her chair. "Maybe I should get a job, Daddy. Pat can cope with Monster during the week. All I do is drip around here and he doesn't need much now. Mother won't let me near the kitchen."

"As you can't boil an egg, darling," Mrs. Graham came back with the toast, "it's not surprising. What's she grumbling about, Fergus?"

"She's not," he said rather testily. "She's had a bad night and she's upset." He got up and shuffled back into the house. He was far less active than a year ago; age had suddenly encroached upon him. He had never moved like a man of seventy before disaster struck Charlie. Mrs. Graham looked after him for a moment.

"You mustn't worry him," she said quietly. "He hasn't been well lately. *Are* you upset, Charlie? What's the matter?"

"I was talking about Davina," her daughter said slowly. "She's in her element with this Venice nightmare, isn't she, Mum? I can just imagine her, can't you?"

"No," Mrs. Graham said, "I can't. And that's a terrible thing to say. I know you're bitter and you've every reason, but I won't let you talk about her like that."

"If it wasn't for Daddy," Charlie remarked, "you'd still see her, wouldn't you?"

Betty Graham rarely asserted herself, but when she did, her family listened. "Yes, I would. Davina's my daughter just as much as you are. I think it's time you pulled yourself together, Charlie, and stopped feeling sorry for yourself. Perhaps you should do some voluntary work. Helping other people is the best way of taking one's mind off oneself. I'm going into the village to do some shopping. Do you want to come?"

"No thanks, Mummy." Charlie had flushed. For a moment her eyes filled with tears. She wasn't used to being chided and she reacted like a child. Resentful and uncertain. For Christ's sake, can't you grow up even now? And back the answer came to her. No you can't and you never will so long as you nestle under Daddy's wing. Just as you did with your husband, with every man you've ever known. Poor, helpless, beautiful little me, I must be taken care of. It's time you stood up on your own two feet. She got up and gathered the crockery onto the tray. "I'll put these in the dishwasher," she said.

"Thank you, darling." Mrs. Graham had said what she felt, and it wouldn't be repeated. She wasn't a woman who created atmospheres.

Charlie went into the kitchen, loaded the dishes, poured the powder and switched the machine on. She went upstairs to her room, not because there was anything to do. Pat cleaned the nursery. Charlie was meticulously tidy about her own surroundings. She went up to be alone and to cry if she felt like it. Her reflection was a comfort; looking at herself diverted her attention from less pleasant things. Still beautiful; not a line, not a blemish on the perfect skin. Damn it, if she cried, it made her eyelids swell. She'd cried enough. Davina wasn't crying. As she had said to her father, her sister was on top of the heap, successful, carrying on an affair with a very rich man, living her life exactly as she wished. The tables had certainly turned for both of them. She had achieved it all at the price of Charlie's happiness. It was easy enough for her mother to reproach her for being bitter. She had the same cool quality of detachment as Davina. Her father understood because he and Charlie felt the same. Voluntary work, her mother had suggested. Charlie addressed herself in the glass.

"You're not just miserable," she said aloud. "You're bored to death as well. It's time you did something about it."

Later that day, when her parents were lulled by an afternoon sitting in the sun and she had set out to be particularly thoughtful and sweet to them, she announced that she was going up to London to buy some clothes and look up her old friends.

"Why don't we go down to Sicily for a few days? It'll be perfect, not too hot."

Davina shook her head. "I can't, darling. I wish I could. I can't leave Humphrey in London and Tim coping out here while I swan around finishing my holiday. I've got to go back." She slipped her arm round him. "I may have to fly to Washington; I was thinking about it last night."

"To see Brunson?"

"To see somebody; I'm sure this isn't an isolated assassination.

We've got to get together with Langley and try to work out who could be next and why."

Walden had insisted that they leave Venice. He looked as strained and preoccupied as she did. "Davina," he said, "spend one day with me in Paris. One day and a night won't make any difference."

She didn't hesitate. "Of course it won't. You've put off things for me often enough. We'll go to Paris; can we fly direct?"

It was part of the balance in their relationship that Walden always made the travel arrangements, chose the hotels when they went away and took over the organization of their lives. She said to him, "Why Paris, Tony? Any special reason?"

"I'll tell you when we get there," he said. "You've started smoking again. I wish you wouldn't."

She didn't answer; ever since the tragedy the day before Walden had lost his exuberance. He seemed weighed down and uneasy, quite unlike himself. She stubbed out the cigarette. Something was wrong; something more than the revulsion of a sensitive man from violent death. Knowing him so well, she couldn't account for the sudden change of mood. Paris, for twenty-four hours. Why?

"We can fly direct," he said. His smile was tense.

While she lay awake, he hadn't slept either. "And I suppose you're going to book into the Ritz again?" Davina tried to make it sound lighthearted. "No good me suggesting some nice little pensione on the Avenue de l'Opéra?"

"You always suggest it," he answered. "Just because you stayed there once and there weren't any lumps in the mattress. And I always say no. If we can't get a decent room at the Ritz, we'll try the Crillon. Or the George V. Go and pack while I get on the telephone."

Tim Johnson took a launch out to Marco Polo Airport. The explosives expert wasn't staying at the Gritti; Johnson booked in with him at a more modest hotel and they went over the routine report Modena had given Davina. "We're seeing the boss lady after lunch," Johnson remarked. "See if you can dream up a theory or two by then. Our gallant Italian allies are going to tell us fuck-all. So I picked up these odds and ends for you." He put a plastic bag on the table.

The expert, a genial man inappropriately named Moody,

opened it, sniffed at what was inside, and then probed gently. "Wood, metal and—er—something else. I know what it feels like ... where the hell did you get this, sir?"

"Out of the canal; near enough to where it happened. About a hundred yards away from the actual explosion. I just fished up what I could in the dark. Felt a bit messy. It may be just ordinary garbage and flotsam."

Moody put his nose to the bag again. "I don't think so," he said. "I think you've got something for the lab and the forensic boys as well."

"Good," Johnson said briskly. "We'll go and see Miss Graham at three. She's flying back today."

They arrived at Charles de Gaulle Airport at eight o'clock. There was a car to meet them and as they drove into Paris, she slipped her hand into his and said, "The Ritz or the Crillon?"

"The Ritz," Walden said. "Luckily someone had canceled. We have our nice suite. I also ordered dinner there. You look tired, my darling."

"I am," she admitted. "But I'm curious too. I asked you why Paris, remember?"

"I know you did," he glanced out of the window. "Isn't it the most beautiful city in the world? And look—how marvelously, typically French. Look at that tricolor! What a sense of theater!"

The Arc de Triomphe was bathed in floodlights, and between its arches, fanning out in the breeze, there blazed a vast tricolor flag.

"Now we would never do that," he said. "Only the French have the self-confidence to be so magnificently vulgar."

They had a small suite on the first floor overlooking the Place Vendôme. There was a huge bowl of red roses in the bedroom.

"Tony," Davina said, "don't tell me they remembered—"

"No, I did."

There was a card with the flowers. "With all my love always, Tony." She held it in her hand, and suddenly the luxurious bedroom felt cold.

"Darling," she said. "What's wrong?"

"I was going to wait till we got back to England," he began slowly, hesitating. The bedroom wasn't cold; she shivered and knew that the chill was in her own tense body as she listened. "I've been so happy with you, Davina. You're the only woman

I've ever loved in my life, do you know that? Darling, don't look at me like that. Sit down, sit down. Come here beside me."

His distress was making it worse. He took her hand and held it tightly between both of his, while she sat close to him, frozen and sick with anticipation. He stumbled over his words and suddenly Davina couldn't bear it. "You're leaving me," she said. "For God's sake, why?"

"I can't tell you why," he said. "We just can't go on being together anymore."

"I love you," she protested. "You love me, I know that. Is it your wife? Tony, for Christ's sake, you've got to tell me the reason! It's just not good enough to say we can't go on and I can't tell you—I won't accept that!"

"No," he answered. "It's nothing to do with Hilary. That would be simple." He didn't look at her, he kept his head down, gripping her hand in his. "I've known for months now, that we had to break up. I couldn't face it and I lied to myself. But not now; not after Venice."

She said, "But why? What happened in Venice couldn't happen to me! I told you, I'm safe—you're talking nonsense."

"Not nonsense," Walden said quietly. "I'm just finding saying goodbye to you difficult, that's all. Will you listen to me and not interrupt? Please, Davina?"

"I'll listen," she said. "What else can I do?"

He went on, slowly, dragging the words out until she could have screamed. "You know I love you. You're the most important person in the world to me. And that is why I wanted to spend our last time together in Paris. I wanted to make it beautiful for you. I wanted to tell you in the place where we've been so happy and had some wonderful times."

She pulled her hand away and got up. She walked away into the sitting room. Such wonderful times. That suite held memories; stolen weekends when they left their responsibilities behind, the joy of exploring Paris together, the sweetness of their nights. She broke down and wept. Not since losing Ivan had she cried aloud as she did then.

She heard him say, close to her, "Even the roses—they were waiting for you the first time we came. It was a mistake, my love. I shouldn't have told you here."

She turned round to him. "Then why did you?" she demanded. "Why choose this of all places to tear us both to pieces? You and your bloody roses—you like a bit of theater yourself, don't you? How could you do this, Tony? How could you hurt me like this?"

He tried to take her in his arms, but she fought fiercely, pushing him away. She saw the anguish on his face and suddenly her anger disappeared. She felt sick and cold and unbearably empty.

"All right," she said. "You say it's over. I can't argue—I won't beg either, thanks very much. But I want to know why. You owe me that, Tony. I want to know the reason."

"I can't answer that," Walden said.

"Because you don't love me and you don't have the guts to say so?"

"You know that's not the reason," his voice rose. "You know I love you! Christ, I need a drink—where do they keep it in this goddamned place?"

Her voice stayed level. "In the cupboard over there. You ought to know, it's always in the same place. If it's not because of your wife, and you still love me, what else could it be?"

She watched his back, listened to the awkward clatter as he fumbled with glasses and swore in Polish. "I didn't want to get mixed up with you," she went on. "I had a good man who wanted to marry me; you were the one who chased me. You were determined to start something up between us. Now you say it's over. What am I supposed to do, Tony? Shake hands and say it was fun while it lasted?"

He swung round on her then. He changed color, turning very white when he was angry. She saw that he was angry now. He came up close to her and said, "I'll tell you what you do. Give up your job with SIS. Resign, and there will be no problem. I'll get a divorce and we'll get married!"

Suddenly Davina was calm. "What has my job got to do with it? Are you saying that if I resign we can stay together? Tony? Is that what you mean?"

"Yes," Walden said flatly. "And now, my love, you can answer your own question. And think about it seriously. I meant what I said. I'll marry you and we can be together for the rest of our lives."

She sat down and after a moment said, "Get me a drink, will you?"

He brought her a glass, hesitated, and when she held out her hand, he sat beside her. "I didn't think you'd be so bitter," he remarked. "Maybe I didn't realize how much you loved me."

"When you're hurt," she said quietly, "you lash out. Anyway I do. I'm not going to leave my job, but you're going to tell me why it matters. And by the way, you might try trusting me a little bit. Pass me a cigarette, will you? You can't nag me about smoking now."

"I've never hit a woman," Walden said, "but Davina, if you needle me—just shut up and drink your drink, will you!"

She lit her cigarette, sipped the brandy. The lights were twinkling in the Place Vendôme outside their windows. "At least I've stopped shaking," she said. "That's something. It's blackmail, isn't it?"

There was silence for what seemed a long time to Davina. Then he looked at her and said simply, "Yes."

The man called "Italy" stayed on in Venice till the end of the week. He became very bored, watching television and reading the art books and magazines. The girl hadn't given up trying, even on the last night she approached him. She wanted to sleep with what he'd done, not him. He told her so. She banged her door and he left the house early next morning without seeing her again. There were checks at the airport. He bought a train ticket to Pisa and the carabinieri passed him through the barrier. From Pisa he boarded a train to Innsbruck. It was a very long and tiring journey, but the train was full of people like himself, sleeping all night in the uncomfortable second-class carriages, some dozing on their luggage in the corridors. Nobody noticed him. From Innsbruck he took the bus to his village at the foot of the mountains. He ate a meal with his parents and gave them the souvenirs he had brought back from his holiday. Then he went to bed and slept through till the next day. He would never see or hear from his comrades again. That was the rule, and it guaranteed their safety. And his own. He was back at work in his father's chemist shop. He had made his contribution.

The device used, Humphrey told James White at their next lunch, must have been some kind of mine, either laid in the path of the cruiser, or attached in some way. Considering the vigilance of Franklyn's bodyguards, it was difficult to see how it had been done. White nodded. Details bored him now; he liked to hear the broad issues, the personal gossip. He had never been a technical man. Humphrey sensed that he was impatient. "Everyone seems to think it's a terrorist group," he said. "Except Davina."

James White looked up and said mildly, "And who does she say did it?"

"Borisov's people," Humphrey sounded impatient. "She's got that man on the brain, you know, Chief. She sees his hand behind everything. I said to her yesterday, 'He isn't God, you know. He can't be blamed for every crackpot killing in Europe.' " He didn't repeat her reply, because it stung. 'If the person who killed Franklyn was a crackpot, what the hell is a professional?' And he knew she was right. It was a supremely professional job, its operator equipped with the kind of technology that ruled out the splinter groups of political fanatics. His choice of word had been a slip of the tongue. Crackpot. She had swept his theories aside because of it. Tim Johnson supported Humphrey's view that money and expertise were at the disposal of the assassin, but he didn't believe it came from Moscow.

Davina was flying to Washington on Tuesday, Humphrey told Sir James. "Needless to say, they're having a fit over there. The president himself has told Longley to go ahead and find the killer, and let the Italians argue about it afterward. I suggested Johnson should go with her instead of me."

"Don't let him take over too much," White remarked. "You could find yourself eased out, my dear Humphrey. He's a thrusting young man."

"I have plenty to occupy me," Grant replied. "There's nothing to be gained in Washington for anybody but Davina. She's the boss lady, to use Johnson's awful phrase. He'll be a glorified aide, that's all. And by the way, Chief," he leaned across the table slightly. "I've started some inquiries about our friend Walden. One of our chaps in West Berlin has some good Polish contacts. He'll report back in a week or two."

"What are they going to look for?" James White asked.

"Old associates," Grant answered. "Family, friends, anyone in official circles who knew him before he came here. Anyone who's been in recent contact with him. We know he has a mother and sister living in Cracow. Our German friend says if there is a lead his people will find it."

"That's good, Humphrey," Sir James said. "I don't think

you're wasting your time. I think something will come out of this. By the way, Charlie Kidson has decided to set herself up in London. It seems she's out of mourning. Perhaps one shouldn't call it that, since Kidson is still alive."

"He's in a clinic," Grant said. "Drying out. I can't think why they bother."

"It wouldn't look good if he died," White remarked. "It wouldn't encourage others to claim their reward in Moscow. God knows how they kept Burgess going for so long. A thought occurred to me, Humphrey. See what you think of it; now that I'm out to grass, I don't want to step on anybody's toes. I thought I'd ask Charlie to lunch. See what she's up to—would you agree?"

Humphrey hesitated. Out to grass my foot. He had picked up odd vulgarities like that from Ronnie. He decided to play the innocent. No come-backs from Davina if the Chief was caught meddling. He must stop thinking of him as "the Chief," even though White liked him saying it. "Why think about it," Humphrey countered. "You've been a friend of the family for years. Why shouldn't you see Charlie, or any of them?"

Sir James smiled his bland smile, famous for its lack of meaning. "Exactly. Such a beautiful girl, and so full of charm. I can't think she'll be alone for long, now that she's come back into circulation. It's a pity there's this feud with Davina and the family. Perhaps I can do something to help mend the fences."

Humphrey looked at him bleakly. Fence-mending was not Sir James's specialty. He had never healed a rift between other people in his life. He wouldn't have found it amusing. If he wanted to be mischievous, that wasn't Humphrey's business. Personally he thought Davina Graham's sister was a spoiled little tart. Women like her made him shudder. He turned the conversation back to serious things. "Davina is convinced there'll be another murder," he said suddenly. "That's one of the reasons she's going to Washington."

"Does she think it'll be another American? Good God, if she starts running that one, the CIA will go berserk."

"I don't know, nor does she. She just insists that Franklyn wasn't a lone target."

"Well," Sir James said cheerfully, "only the next few months will prove it one way or the other. Now, I must get the bill."

"No," Humphrey said. "I insist, Chief. This is my lunch."

The smile enveloped him again. "Very well, don't let's argue Humphrey. And you must," he said gently, "break that habit of calling me Chief."

"I'll try," Humphrey Grant promised. "But it isn't easy."

The house in the Rue Constantine had been recently redecorated. The minister was famous for her taste and elegance; being a distinguished lawyer and a feminist, Isabelle Duvalier had earned her place in the new government, which declared itself committed to women's rights. The fact that the new minister for the Interior was married to a rich man twenty years her senior and bought her clothes from St. Laurent didn't detract from her brilliance and her flair for publicity. Her enemies nicknamed her Evita; passionate concern for the underprivileged and jewels by Boucheron. It was a jibe that bounced off the lady like a toy arrow. She was impervious to her critics; her style carried her above the jealous sniping of the press. She gave lavish parties but she worked a twelve-hour day. And she was a conscientious, enlightened mother of two teenage daughters. They attended the lycée, and the elder at eighteen was having an affair with a student from the Sorbonne. Being progressive parents, they approved after she assured them she was on the Pill. The girls had their own quarters on the top floor of the house; there they played records, cooked themselves the junk food that was in fashion and entertained their friends without interference from their famous mother.

That evening found the family together; the minister was at home, free of social commitments. Her daughters and their friends joined her for dinner. Her husband was in Munich; in spite of his age he led a very active business life. The murder of the American statesman had been their major topic during dinner.

"I met him when he came to Paris two years ago," Isabelle Duvalier remembered. "He was most amusing. His wife was a chic Californian, you know the type, darlings, Nancy Reagan, but not so pretty. I couldn't believe that she died just a year later."

"It was so terrible to kill his daughter," the elder girl, Louise, remarked. "Don't you think so, Helene?"

There were eight of them round the table; cigarette smoke hung in a cloud above the lights. The talk was quick and uninhibited. The minister loved the conversation of the young. She waited for Helene's answer. Helene was Louise's closest friend, and, in Isabel's eyes, almost an adopted daughter.

"Such bad luck she was with him," Helene agreed. "But they'll never catch the people who did it."

"What do they hope to gain? That's what seems so crazy about the whole thing." The young student who was Louise Duvalier's lover was a committed pacifist. A nice boy, the minister felt, sure to come to his senses when he grew up a little.

"Violence achieves nothing but violence," he went on, aware of his lover's admiring looks. "Whoever these terrorists are, they've activated a new chain of violence against themselves. They've killed innocent people along with Franklyn, his daughter, the bodyguards, the boatman . . . for what?"

"If we knew the motive," his hostess said, "we might have some idea who they are."

"They're the same lot under some other name," Helene volunteered. "I agree with you, Raoul, violence doesn't help. But wasn't Franklyn violent too, in his way? Didn't he support nuclear arms?"

"There's no comparison," Diane, the younger daughter entered the argument. Like her mother she was articulate and competitive. "The Americans want nuclear weapons as a deterrent. Having them stops wars—"

There was a general outcry of disagreement. Helene didn't join in; she was a little out of her depth when the talk became too involved with politics and dialectics. She regarded her own views as clear-cut, even basic.

She didn't want her clever friends to see her limitations, so she knew when to drop out of a debate, like now. She watched the adroit way in which Isabelle Duvalier steered them from one point to the next by asking a pointed question. She noticed the genuine interest and enjoyment she displayed in the company of the group of students. And she had always been especially kind to Helene.

Helene had come to Paris to get away from home. And at the lycée she had met Isabelle Duvalier's daughter and become friends. That friendship soon extended to the whole family. Isabelle spent every summer holiday with them in Normandy. There were definite advantages to being a politician with a rich husband. The delightful château built on a lake was one of them.

Helene liked going there. She heard her name and started; her thoughts had drifted far away.

"Let's go into the salon," the minister suggested. "Come along, Helene, let's lead the way before they all start coming to blows. Tell me, how is your aunt?"

Helene's aunt was the widow of a doctor; she lived in modest style on the Left Bank, and disapproved of all the things most dear to Isabelle Duvalier. She was a devout Catholic and a fierce admirer of ex-President Giscard d'Estaing, and she loathed the feminist movement. However, she had been invited to tea with the minister and been charmed by her.

"She's very well," Helene answered. "A bit cross with me at the moment."

"Oh? Has she any reason?" Isabelle Duvalier slipped her hand through the crook of the girl's arm.

"She says I spend too much time fooling about," Helene admitted, "and not enough time working."

"Which is true, isn't it?" There was no reproach, only a smile. Helen nodded. "Yes, Madame. Quite true."

"Then don't stay upstairs too late tonight," the minister advised. "Otherwise your aunt won't like you coming here so often. Go home and do some work. And ask if she can spare you for the weekend after next. We're going down to Blois to stay with my sister-in-law. Louise is in love and is sulking, as you can imagine—I dare not bring Raoul, they don't sympathize with peace and ecology, I'm afraid. Diane is staying in Paris and Louise will be bored to death unless you keep her company. Would that suit you?"

"Oh, Madame, I'd love it. How kind of you to think of me."

"I'm very fond of you," the older woman said. "I'd like you to come for me, too. So don't be late tonight."

"No," Helene promised. "I certainly won't." She kept her word. A weekend at the home of Albert Ferdinand Duvalier. Old and rich and hated by so many people. She didn't mind making an excuse and leaving the records and the marijuana on the upper floor. She took the metro to the Station Malakoff and went into the public telephone. She dialed a number and tapped her foot impatiently. When it answered she said quickly, "This is 'France.' I've got important news."

* * *

Tony Walden was away when Davina got back from Washington. He had a trip booked to Australia; it would keep them apart for three weeks. She arrived on a Saturday morning, feeling mentally and physically exhausted. Consultations had gone on nonstop for the full four days of her visit. She and Johnson had been flown by helicopter from the capital to Langley. Eric Brunson, the CIA's director, was a pleasant man under normal conditions, but the pressures building up made him peremptory and suspicious.

Davina showed Tim Johnson that she could be patient and tactful, qualities he hadn't thought were in her. And he saw Brunson warm to her as to a friend. A very clever boss lady, Tim decided. She's mentally holding the man's hand, sympathizing with his predicament. And by the end of the visit, Davina and Brunson were committed to a joint investigation. The SIS would contribute anything that came its way through its private Intelligence sources and send the information direct to the States. And the CIA would share its findings with London. Between them they should circumvent the deliberate blocking tactics of the Italian government and its Security Service. They were more concerned with proving that the assassin had come to Italy from outside than finding him. As Brunson said on their last evening together, "They don't want to find the bastard because they think he *is* Italian!"

Davina didn't disagree.

Johnson was met by his wife at the airport. Davina spoke to her briefly; she felt a sickening pang of loneliness when she saw them drive off together. She was going back to her empty apartment.

It was a lovely June day; the surburban gardens were bright with flowers on the way into London. She longed to get into the country, to breath some clean air and walk with a dog running alongside her. Marchwood. Marchwood with its famous garden rioting with color; her mother's loving care rewarded by the splendors of that perfect English flower, the rose. She missed the house terribly; she missed the summer evenings with a drink on the warm terrace, and the scents drifting on the faintest breeze. She missed her mother, even her father's awkward welcome. For a while she had been friends with Charlie. Now that was finished. There was no welcome for her at home. They had exiled her as completely as her brother-in-law was exiled. She in her lonely London apartment, he in his KGB apartment in Moscow.

She unlocked the door, left her suitcase unopened on the bed. There was a stale atmosphere in the place, although it had only been empty for a few days. Davina opened the windows; there was little traffic and the quietness grated on her nerves. When the city fell silent it was unnerving, as if everyone in the world had gone away for the weekend and only she was left behind.

She chided herself irritably. There were people she could ring up. If Tony Walden wasn't available she stayed at home, content to read or watch television, feeling relaxed after the week's work. But not this time. Not after Paris. Now that she was alone this day, Davina felt despair. She couldn't counter it with argument, because instinct and logic told her that their relationship could not survive. And there was no one in the world she could confide in. She remembered Sir James White's remark when she moved into his office.

"It's a lonely spot to be in, my dear. Especially for a woman. But I think you'll come to terms with it."

Until that night in Paris, Davina believed that she had faced the problem. Now she knew the real test was just beginning. She didn't ring Australia. She made coffee, unpacked her clothes, had a hot bath and dialed the number of James White's house in Kent.

His wife, Mary, answered. Yes, of course he was in—would she hold on? Davina said briefly, "Chief, can I drive down and see you?"

His voice was full of pleasure. Very warm. "My dear, of course! And stay the night—we haven't a thing to do the whole weekend. We'll expect you in time for tea." He rang off and slowly Davina put the receiver back.

Of all the men in the world, he was the last she ever expected to go to for help. But of all the men in the world, now he was the only one that she could trust.

Four thousand miles away another lonely man prepared for his weekend. He had a dacha outside Moscow, nestled in the pine forests above the Moskva River. It was a luxurious house, secluded from the other dachas that gave the members of the Politburo their retreat from the city. It was smaller than the magnificent residence of the president himself. But not much smaller. The shadows moving discreetly round the grounds belonged to the KGB militia; they guarded Igor Borisov, director of State Security, head of the largest network of intelligence in the world, with a quarter of a million men under arms at his command. The second-most-powerful man in Russia. Some said the first, because the president was old and ailing, kept alive by the doctors at the Ushenkaya Clinic.

Borisov had sent his wife on a Crimean cruise. She didn't want to go. There had been the usual scene when he suggested it. In the end he had simply told her she was going. He needed the dacha to himself and she couldn't stay in Moscow.

He retreated from his offices in Dzerjinsky Square to the peace of the woods and the empty house. He had wanted to get a divorce for a long time. It wasn't easy, because the president was a family man, married to the same woman for forty years. He wouldn't like his protégé to cast his wife off, like an old shoe that pinched. But how she pinched, Borisov complained, how she bored him and nagged him and froze him into impotence whenever they shared a bed. But he would have to wait. It couldn't be too long. The old man's heart was laboring, the slightest chill turned to a lung infection. And while he walked along the riverbank, or sat in the sunshine on his porch, Borisov made plans. They occupied his mind from the time the snows of winter melted, when the life of his friend and mentor, President Keremov, entered its final term. The old man knew that he wouldn't see another winter, but he had faced the future with typical stony courage and set himself the task of finding someone suitable to care for Russia. He had the mentality of a tsar and the jealousy of a hereditary ruler for his heirs. No old men, he declared to his wife while she sat by his bedside. No bald heads living in the past. Russia needed a man of vision, a man who was young enough to lead her into the next century. Igor Borisov was his choice. That choice could be his guarantee of supreme power or cause his humiliation and ultimate fall. He had more enemies than friends. And he would need friends. Friends inside the all-powerful Politburo and the support of the army. The army and the KGB were natural rivals. No former director of State Security had been liked by the generals. The troops with the red shield badge had provided the firing squads too often for the regular armed services to trust them. Borisov was determined to change that attitude. He agreed with Keremov; Russia needed a diplomat to guide her into the future, not a hard-liner living on the dicta of the past. Borisov had disposed of the worst specimen not long ago. A very convenient stroke had carried him away, with the assistance of a certain drug.

The prize was enormous. The power staggered the imagination. He had no precedent behind him to give encouragement. No man of his age had ever been elected. No holder of his unpopular office had ever stepped up to the throne. But there was a first time for all things. Sooner or later change overtook the most entrenched institutions. Even in Russia. Borisov ran his own personal empire of repression and subversion with his habitual skill and dedication, but the grander scheme preoccupied him more and more.

He hadn't really concentrated on the situation outside Russia until after the assassination of Henry Franklyn in Venice. And it was high time that he did.

Venice had soon returned to normal. The tourists flocked like the famous pigeons; the shops selling leather and cheap jewelry did a handsome trade, the hotels were full, and the summer season looked like booming. The antique trade was better than the previous year, but the recession still hit the market hard. Work on the lower floor of the shop in the Piazza San Raphael had been completed. The owner installed the two Renaissance pieces he had bought in Rome and hung a little primitive gem of the Crucifixion in his house in the Street of the Assassins. He had come home to find his daughter in a foul mood. She was surly enough anyway. Her mother tried to make excuses, but Valdorini had begun to dread his daughter's presence in the home. She was spoiled, he insisted, spoiled and typical of her generation, which had no respect and no aim in life. Her studies were a joke; her exam results were consistently poor, and it seemed to him that she was merely wasting time and money staying on at the university.

The perpetual student was becoming an Italian phenomenon. There were graybeards of thirty still lounging around on government grants and their families' allowances, achieving nothing. And of course her aggressive left-wing politics drove him mad. According to his daughter, everything was wrong, he declared one evening when they had friends to dinner and the girl was out. The world was being destroyed by industry, which was turning the good earth into an ecological desert, the Third World starved while the affluent threw food into their dustbins and the threat of nuclear war hung over humanity, denying the children the right to grow up. She had an answer for everything, Valdorini complained, but it was always the same answer. Everybody else was wrong and only she and her friends were responsible and caring.

His child had become a hostile stranger. He had drunk a lot of wine and he became maudlin, blinking back tears. No son, only this angry girl who looked at her parents as if she hated them, and while they were away in Rome she'd had someone staying in the house and never said a word. Among the friends round the table was a member of the quinta, the city's governing body. He was a Venetian whose ancestors had elected the doge in centuries past. He loved his great city and took his responsibilities very seriously. He had been summoned to a meeting with Signore Modena, the head of Security; the meeting was composed of members of the city's public bodies, and its most influential citizens. The problems arising from the assassination of the American and his daughter had been put to them and their help was solicited. The killer must be found. If the Red Brigade was mounting a new terrorist offensive, no one in public life would be safe. If, as Modena confided, they faced a new menace, then the prospects were horrifying. He wasn't asking anyone to inform, or to do anything that placed themselves at risk. But just to listen and use their judgment. Venice had harbored the assassin. Somewhere, he or she had left a trace behind. And that meeting took place before the body of the dead man was washed up on the public beach at the Lido. The fish had eaten through the anchor rope, releasing the bloated corpse. But the remains of that rope were still knotted round his waist and the post mortem showed that he had died from a broken neck and not from drowning. Identification had done the rest. Modena had a related clue that tied in with the other crime. The boatman had disappeared on the same morning. He was last seen at the public mooring by the Rialto Bridge. But nobody remembered who had hired him. There it rested, until the evening when Valdorini had too much wine and started talking about his daughter.

3

"**I** MUST say, I'm surprised," James White remarked. He gave Davina a kindly look. She recognized it. It meant as little as his smile. "I never thought you'd turn to me for help, my dear."

"I never thought so either," she said. "But needs must, Chief, when the devil drives."

"And are you quite sure who this devil really is?"

They were alone in his study; Mary White had slipped away so they could talk in private. Davina's head came up. He in turn recognized her mannerism.

She was about to challenge him. "What do you mean, the real devil?"

"Well," he leaned back in his chair, crossed his legs and dwelt on the word. "Let's go over the facts. You are having an affair with a man. You know his background, you had him thoroughly vetted as soon as you took over at Anne's Yard. He's clean. Or nearly two years ago he *was* clean. Mother and married sister living in Poland, but no problems there. No affiliations with anything suspicious since he set himself up in England. He did run one or two refugees out of Eastern Europe, but they were personal friends and he did it by using his money and bribing the necessary officials. In this role he came under Humphrey's notice and Humphrey introduced him to you. When you were both playing spies behind my back," he added. "I must say now that I don't like your friend Walden."

"You don't have to tell me that," Davina interrupted. "You proved it once."

"If you say so," he murmured. "I don't like the type. It's not a good situation for someone in your position, but you've taken all possible precautions and you can't see that your private life can impinge on your job. But out of the blue, in the middle of a holiday, Walden tells you it's all over. He makes a heroic renunciation for your sake and then allows you to persuade him to go back on it. Am I being accurate, Davina?"

"You're being a bastard," she answered quietly. "But I expected that. Go on."

"He's a very sophisticated man who's made a lot of money out of manipulating people. Playing on their credulity. Wouldn't you agree that defines top-level advertising? He's been your lover for two years or so. He knows you very well by now. He sets the scene and writes the lines. He knows perfectly well that you're not the type to accept his noble gesture without wanting to know how and why. Very few women would, I imagine. Certainly not you. So he gives in and tells you that he's being blackmailed. And what a story! His brother-in-law was arrested as a sympathizer with Solidarity. He's in the Ministry of the Interior, didn't you say? He's been interned ever since martial law. He doesn't say whether his brother-in-law is innocent or guilty. I find in my experience that civil servants have little sympathy with workers' movements like Solidarity, but that's beside the point. The point is, his sister is pregnant, living with her mother. That paints a picture of two frightened women, one old and feeble, the other having a child. Helpless and under siege by a ruthless military regime. By now, you're probably running ahead of him, Davina, filling in the gaps. It's the penalty of a quick mind. The blackmail is his brother-in-law's release? But no. It's crueller than that. The brother-in-law isn't interned as his family think. He's been taken to Russia, because the KGB knows about Walden's relationship with you. They believe they hold a hand of trumps. Walden is to pass on anything you tell him and to pump you for secret information. In exchange for his brother-in-law's life. If he refuses, the poor chap either gets a bullet, or a ticket to the Gulag camps. Now, is that accurate?"

"It's accurate," Davina admitted. "If I ignore the interpretation. That's what Tony said. They're holding this man as a hostage. The only way out that he could see was to break off with me."

"Saying that you'd left him, of course?" Sir James said. "For what reason, I wonder? Our friends in Moscow are difficult people to convince. He'd have to have a strong story that could be checked. Davina, my dear girl, don't you know the answer to all this yourself? Didn't you just come down to have it confirmed by an outsider?"

"You don't believe it," she stated. He shook his head gently. "I think it's a pack of lies and so do you."

She got up and stood looking down at him. "That's what it looks like," she admitted. "Except for one thing. If Moscow dreamed this up, they ought to be ashamed of themselves. It's so full of damned holes it doesn't make sense. Unless it's true. That's what I don't know. That's what knocks your theory sideways."

"Only if his story can be confirmed," Sir James said. "If it can't then the answer's simple."

She said, "I haven't any cigarettes; I've been trying to give them up. Could I have one of yours?" He handed her the case; she took the fat Turkish cigarette and lit it. Sub Rosa; his trademark.

"How was it left between you?"

"I said I'd think of something. I wanted to believe him. And I had the Washington trip. I couldn't think straight till that was over."

"What a true professional you are, my dear girl," he said. "Just what I'd expect of you. So he's in Australia, selling high-powered advertising and waiting for a word. He must be chewing his nails, don't you think?"

"Not if he's genuine," Davina said quietly.

"It's rather a big 'if,' " the old man added.

"Tell me something," she asked the question abruptly. He knew that mannerism too. She was on the defensive when she appeared to attack. "Tell me, if you'd *liked* Tony, would you be quite so certain he was rotten?"

"It wouldn't make the slightest difference," he declared. "I've never let my personal feelings affect my judgment. I've had people working for me that I couldn't stand the sight of. But I trusted them. And in all my years as Chief of the Service I never gave anyone the benefit of the doubt. Nor should you. Now, I hear Mary calling—shall we have dinner and put it out of our minds till the morning?" He opened the door for her; he had beautiful manners. Davina went ahead into the pleasant dining room. The Whites had simple taste in food and wine. The house was comfortable, conventional, with Lionel Edwards hunting prints, shabby sofas where dogs had slept, pieces of very good furniture rather disregarded in odd corners, and a portrait of Sir James White in army uniform, which Davina thought was crude and badly painted.

There was nothing to suggest that the couple who had lived there for so many years were quite extraordinary people. They had been friends with the Grahams since Davina was a little child; an odd friendship between her straightforward father and the Machiavellian head of SIS. And over dinner, Mary White asked how the family were.

"I haven't seen them for a long time," Davina admitted.

"They're not still sulking over that wretched John, are they?" Mary White exclaimed impatiently.

"Sulking is hardly the word for what they feel," Davina answered. She felt Sir James watching her. "They think I ruined my sister's life. They won't have anything to do with me."

"How perfectly ridiculous," Mary snapped. "I've never heard of anything so unfair, have you, James? What did they expect—that you'd let a traitor get away with it because he was your brother-in-law?"

"People do bend the rules for their families, my dear," her husband objected, "even for brothers-in-law." He didn't let Davina catch his eye when he said it.

"Besides, if I know Charlie, she'll find someone else, if she hasn't already," his wife said. "If I get the chance, Davina, I shall say something to your mother."

Davina shook her head. "Don't bother. It's my father who's taken against me. You know how he worships my sister. It wouldn't do any good and it might make trouble between you."

"It's because he worships her that she's made such a mess of her life and other people's," Mary White said firmly. "She's a lovely girl, but spoiled absolutely rotten. And it's your parents fault, I'm sorry." Under the light, her cheeks had flushed pink with indignation.

"Mary," Sir James said, "You're not to go into battle! I always said I'd rather face a regiment of Gurkhas than my wife when she thinks something isn't fair."

They had coffee and Davina went up to bed early. She was still suffering from the five-and-a-half-hour time change; she felt tired and desperately low. "Put it out of our minds till the morning." Easy for James White; impossible for her. He hadn't allowed her to deceive herself. Without waiting for the morning, Davina knew the explanation White would give. Confess yourself a spy, allow yourself to be turned and you were practically invulnerable thereafter. You could meet your Russian contact, pass the doctored information and other secret material with it. It was an old ruse. She got up, pulled back the curtains and opened the window wide. She felt stifled, as if she couldn't breathe properly. And after that conclusion there was the worst suspicion of all. Walden had never loved her. He had been a plant from the beginning. She'd said it herself in that awful moment in Paris. "You were the one who chased me. You were determined to start something." He had pursued her with singular purpose. And she had let herself be caught. She closed her eyes against the cool night air. She shivered for a moment, as she had done in the centrally heated bedroom at the Ritz.

If his love for her was an act, then she had no right to stay in her job. Anyone capable of being taken in like that was unfit to sit in James White's chair. But there was one way to prove it. She wondered what James White would say. She shut the window and went back to bed. Exhausted, she fell asleep immediately.

"Davina looked well, I thought," James White said to his wife. "A bit tired after her trip to Washington."

Mary poured out the remains of the coffee. "Damn, I'll have to make some more—don't talk nonsense, dear, she looked utterly miserable. Now you can tell me why she came to see you. She's never liked you, so it must be something very urgent."

"Not very," he smiled at her. "Because I'd already foreseen it and the thing is in hand. She doesn't know, of course."

Mary looked at him. "You're retired," she said. "But nobody would think so. Anyway you can tell me about it." While he was head of SIS she hadn't asked a single question concerning his work. As soon as he became a private person, his wife's curiosity was insatiable. She asked him about everything, even the most insignificant detail. What was in his mail, who was that on the telephone, why was he so long in the village. . . . It must have been a great strain keeping silent for all those years, he reflected, and loved her for it.

"You remember that advertising chap, Tony Walden?"

"The one with the yacht and the stupid blonde wife?"

"That's right. He and Davina have been having an affair for quite some time."

"Good Lord," she exclaimed. "I am surprised. I can't think of him as her type."

"There's no accounting for women's taste in men," he answered. "That's what makes them such bad security risks. It appears that the wealthy jet-setting Mr. Walden is being blackmailed by the KGB. I don't have to fill in the details for you, dear, but it's put Davina in a very difficult position."

"You can give me the details in a minute," his wife said firmly. "Just let me make some more coffee."

When he had finished she frowned, thinking hard. "What a blow for the poor girl," she said at last. "She's had so little happiness. What will she do about it?"

"I hope she'll take my advice," he answered. "If she's tough enough, and I believe she is, she will."

Mary White got up. "By tough, James dear, you mean heartless. And there you're wrong. The heartless one is the other sister. It's quite late, look at the time. Let the dogs out and lock up will you?"

"You say that every evening," he remarked gently. "Knowing I always do both."

The call from "France" was reported to him direct. He listened, nodded, smiled and said, "Good. Better than we hoped. Make certain 'France' is psychologically ready and that all the details have been finalized. This is one of our most important targets; impress that on her."

The assurances came through. He remembered the file on the girl Helene Blond. Repressed, feelings of profound inferiority and aggression, brutally ill-treated as a child; a personality geared toward megalomania. She had been found like a jewel among the dross that came to them. And like a jewel she would soon shine among the Company of Saints. He put the telephone down. If anything went wrong, there was a fail-safe. The Nothingness that all were sworn to embrace rather than betray their organization. Those who killed had to be prepared to kill themselves. It was a logical conclusion to the disturbances they all had in common. A hatred of life and themselves transposed into a hatred for others. Death was the solution to all problems. They were taught to accept that, even to enjoy the acceptance. He felt refreshed and optimistic. His plans were going well, and in spite of other setbacks, other anxieties, his Saints were giving praise.

It was 10:00 P.M. in Sydney. The dinner given in honor of Walden by his Australian associates had finished early by local standards. He was booked into the Gazebo, a glittering glass-fronted hotel with breathtaking views over the harbor. The dinner had been all male, and in different circumstances Walden would have enjoyed every moment of it. Australian hospitality was as rich and individual as the national sense of humor. The dinner was uproarious; his two partners were in excellent spirits and the fifteen guests, all very substantial clients, talked business and sport and would happily have extended the party to a nightclub.

Walden laughed and talked, gave every appearance of enjoying himself. He was careful not to match them drink for drink. He needed a clear head that night. Watching him no one would have guessed that every nerve was taut and a headache of symphonic proportions battered his brain. When the dinner broke up, he excused himself. "I have an important call to make." His smile was conspiratorial.

"The lovely lady, eh?" The manufacturer of Australia's best selling lager nudged him and grinned. "Pity she isn't with you this trip."

"Next time. She made me promise," Tony Walden said. They had met his wife two years ago. So blonde and beautiful, so stupid that she passed for being delightfully feminine. She had made many conquests among the robust Antipodean males. He had a call to make and a caller to see. But neither had anything to do with Hilary Walden. At this time, nearly eleven on a Sunday morning in England, his wife would be waking up in the country mansion he had bought her, with her boy friend sharing the breakfast tray. Walden didn't think of her for more than a few seconds.

He had a fine suite on the eighth floor, overlooking the harbor and the extraordinarily beautiful Opera House that had once caused such a furor. That night, looking out over the harbor, fiery with lights, flanked by glittering high-rise buildings, Tony Walden tried to find an answer to his life. He had achieved every goal; success hadn't been easy. He knew what failure meant, and disappointment. Grinding anxiety was just as familiar as the exhilaration of success. Two marriages, two sons, money, a tremendous business bursting with expansion. And Davina Graham.

There was a knock on his door. It was very soft and the thudding of that dreadful headache was very loud. He opened it. The man outside didn't say anything, he just walked past Walden through the hallway and to the sitting room. He stared at the view for a moment and then turned round. He was smaller than Walden, thin; with a beaky face and bright blue eyes.

"That's bloody spectacular, isn't it?" The man spoke with a broad Australian accent.

"Yes," Walden said. "How did your party go?"

"Well. They enjoyed themselves." The man looked round him. "You keep any booze up here?"

Walden said, "Help yourself. I won't be a minute." He went to the bathroom and took two painkillers. His face looked sallow and lined in the mirror.

His visitor made himself at home. He had a glass of whisky in his hand and was perched on the edge of the sofa. "Any news for me?"

"No," Walden said. "I'm putting a call in later tonight. But you can report back that I don't think it's going to work. I never did think so, and I want to make sure you understand. The whole scheme is a bloody waste of time."

"But that's your problem. It's up to you to make it work. Nobody gives a shit for opinions, old sport. It's action we want. You better get cracking." He finished his drink, and wiped his mouth with the back of his hand. He grinned at Walden, showing uneven teeth, with a gold crown glinting in the cavern of his mouth. "You look a bit worn—we work and play hard over here. Find the pace a bit hot, eh?"

Walden ignored the remark. He had hated the snide little bastard the first time they made contact. A dockside rat come up in the world. God knew what he'd had to do to get there. "I've booked a call," he said. "I want you out of here before it comes through."

"Okay. Keep your pants on. You know my room number?"

"I know it. I'll be in touch before I go to Melbourne."

"Okay," the man said again, and grinned again. He let himself out. Walden looked at his watch. He sat down beside the telephone and waited. Nothing eased the headache. At 1:20 his phone rang. He picked it up. The operator said, "I'm trying your call to London, Mr. Walden." Amazing how clear it sounded; he could have been calling from across the road. Amazing how good the lines were. Phoning Italy was like dialing Mars by comparison. "I'm sorry," the operator's voice cut in, "there's no reply."

He said, "Never mind. Goodnight." Davina was due back from Washington on Saturday morning. He'd calculated the time changes, included her stress after a grueling session with the Americans and a night flight. She didn't sleep on planes. As he well knew. She would need the whole of Saturday and a good night's rest. Sunday morning she would wake to his call. But she wasn't in the flat. He should have canceled the Australian trip, but he'd never ducked out of a business commitment in his life. He couldn't change a schedule that had been worked out three months ahead.

He checked his watch again. He'd rung at a stupid time, too late to catch her if she'd woken and decided to slip out. He undressed slowly, asked the operator to try the number again in an hour, and lay on the bed waiting. The headache had lost its thunder. The painkillers were working. There was no answer when they tried the second call.

He shrugged aside his fears. She hadn't come back from Washington. As soon as he decided that, he fell asleep.

While the telephone shrilled in the empty apartment, Davina drove down to the village with Sir James to fetch the Sunday papers. "Did you have a good night? Mary thought you looked tired," he said.

"I slept very well," she answered. "I always do, when I've seen my way clear."

He glanced quickly at her, and then switched back to the road. "And what have you decided? About your friend Walden?"

"I've decided to take him at his word." The car stopped outside the village paper shop. The days of delivery were long past. "I'll get the papers." Davina opened the car door.

"They're ordered and paid for," he called out. "Take him at his word." How irritating of her to say that and then go into the shop, while he had to wait outside. Irritating and yet enjoyable, like a tooth that threatened to ache. Retired be damned, he was still sharper than any of them. And in due course he'd let his clever protégée find out exactly how much. "*Telegraph, Times,* and the *Mail* on Sunday. There; one color supplement missing, I'm afraid."

"That won't worry me," he retorted. "I never read them. They're full of rubbish pretending to be bargains. Mary's an absolute child when it comes to this mail order thing. She sends off for saucepans and electric waffle toasters and God knows what. Do you ever read the *Mail?*"

"No. *Telegraph* and *Times.*"

"Don't be such a snob, my dear. It's very lively. And I wouldn't miss Ivor Herbert on racing for anything. What do you mean, take Walden at his word?" They stopped in the front drive and Davina got out. They walked into the house together, Sir James calling to his wife.

"We've brought the papers, where's the sherry?"

"In the decanter." The voice sounded tartly from the kitchen. "And don't sit there hogging it, James, bring one out to me!"

"Now," he said pleasantly, eyes shrewd under their thatch of white brow, "now tell me."

Davina sipped her sherry. "Tony said if I resigned there'd be no problem."

"Good God, what a bloody cheek!" Two red spots flared on his cheeks.

"It makes sense if you think about it for a second," she said. "If he's being blackmailed to get information out of me, then the best solution is me giving up the job. Surely that's true love's answer?"

"You can call it what you like," he said shortly, "but I call it a bloody impertinence. Resign? Just to keep him? It's the most conceited thing I've ever heard in my life."

"He said he'd divorce his wife and marry me," Davina went on. "I'm going to take him at his word, Chief. If he's genuine he'll jump at it. If it's a bluff, I'll have called it. That way I'll know."

"It is a bluff," James White insisted. He frowned, tapping his fingertips together. "But it can work two ways. He can play it back to you. You realize that?"

"Of course—but not for very long. I know him; he's not the type for a siege situation. If he's what you think he'll back away, and pretty quickly. Then I'll know."

"And no investigation?" he inquired softly. "Why not let Humphrey get his people in Germany to dig a little." He paused and coughed slightly. "I can suggest it for you, if you'd find it awkward. That way it doesn't have to go on the records. You don't want to be implicated on file."

Davina nodded. "I'll tell him myself, thanks, Chief."

James White let a silence develop. She had given him a bad shock for a moment. His whole life had centered round Intelligence, from the time he was a young officer after the war. His twenty years at Anne's Yard were the happiest in his career. He loved the Service, and it filled him with rage to suspect, even for a moment, that his successor could value her private life more. A bad fright, but not for long. He sighed with relief. He hadn't made a mistake when he broke with precedent and recommended Davina Graham over the heads of experienced men. She had been shaken the night before, but she was quite recovered now. He relaxed. He would ring Humphrey up as soon as she had gone and forewarn him. Life would be full of interest in the coming weeks. "Changing the subject," he said, "what is the CIA view of that affair in Venice?"

"The same as mine," Davina said. "Borisov's people took Franklyn out. Just to throw a monkey wrench into American relations with Europe. To stir up a political storm in the States and get a very able opponent out of the way."

"If they start using left-wing groups to do their killing for them it's going to cause a lot of problems," he remarked. "I don't see Borisov's hand in this, myself." He paused for her reaction.

"Nor did Humphrey," Davina answered. "The attempt on the pope was Soviet-inspired."

"It's not proved yet," he countered. "And besides, it was an exceptional circumstance, because of Poland. Borisov may have given it a tentative blessing, but they usually make certain of their victims. I've never known a KGB target recover, have you?"

Davina shrugged. "Maybe it was prayer," she suggested. "There was enough flying around."

James White gave a little chuckle of contempt.

"If you believe in things like that, my dear, you disappoint me. Damn, there's the telephone. Oh, Mary's answered it."

The call was for Davina. It was Tim Johnson. "I've been trying to contact you since yesterday evening," he said. "I've been going up the wall."

"Well, you've found me," Davina was brisk. "What's the panic?"

"They've picked up Franklyn's killer. The news came through from Rome yesterday. Nothing official but they've got her."

Davina said slowly, "You did say 'her,' didn't you?"

"Yes; it's a girl. She must be a real blossom. Rome aren't issuing any invitations, but you could bring pressure to bear if you want someone to sit in."

She could tell by his tone of voice that he was hoping to go himself. "I'll think about it," she said. "I'll be in the office by four. Get Humphrey along too. Sorry about your Sunday."

"Can't be helped." He didn't sound as if he minded. "See you at four."

"A woman—how appalling," Mary White exclaimed. "A woman planted a bomb and killed all those people?"

"Women are just as violent as men," her husband countered. "They haven't got the physical strength but they've got the will if you give them the weapons. I haven't had any illusions about your sex for many years."

"You haven't had any illusions about anyone, Chief," Davina said. "You'll forgive me if I rush back after lunch?"

"Of course. They haven't got the name of the organization, I suppose?"

"Johnson didn't say. But they'll get it. The Italians can play very rough."

"I hope they do," Mary White said. "She'd jolly well tell if I got my hands on her!"

Sir James raised his sherry glass. "To the gentle sex," he said, and laughed his mirthless laugh.

"You can stuff yourself!"

Alfredo Modena wasn't troubled by insults. The prisoner could spit at him as she'd done at his colleagues, and unlike the less experienced, he wouldn't have hit her. She had a cut and swollen lip. "You're being very stupid, Elsa," he said calmly.

"We know you threw that bomb. You were seen. We've got wit-nesses."

"You're lying," the girl shouted. She wasn't frightened; she was defiant and sustained by anger. He knew the type; he also knew how hard they were to break. And the women were often tougher than the men. "You haven't got a witness. I was nowhere near the canal that day!" Modena didn't look at her; his office was air-conditioned, but he'd taken off his coat and loosened his tie, making himself comfortable. He had iced water on his desk and a supply of cigarettes. He didn't offer anything to Elsa Valdorini. She was standing, because after she spat at the first interrogator, they'd removed the chair. She stood with legs apart, arms akimbo, glaring at him. She had been in detention for forty-eight hours, without food or sleep, and with only a few sips of water.

Very tough, Modena decided. But I have all the time in the world and she knows it. She would be more than capable of kill-ing. "You took a boat," he said, "you hired one of the little taxi boats, and as you passed the launch Franklyn was traveling in, you threw the bomb. Did you see his daughter? She was only nineteen. Didn't you mind killing her?"

"I didn't kill her," she sneered back at him. "But it wouldn't bother me if I had!"

"Any more than murdering the boatman afterward?" The flash of surprise was his first breakthrough. She hadn't known about that. Which he had gambled on. He leaned a little towards her. "You broke his neck, the poor bastard," he said slowly. "Just a poor working man, hiring his boat out on the canal, and you murdered him. What kind of socialist revolutionary are you?"

She had recovered her nerve, and managed a chilling smile on her swollen mouth. "Too bad about him," she said. "I'm going to piss on your floor."

Modena pressed a buzzer on his desk. The door opened imme-diately. "Take Valdorini to the lavatory," he said. The man caught her arm and dragged her out. Modena poured himself some water. She hadn't killed the boatman. The blow needed a man's strength. She hadn't thrown the bomb, either, but she had sheltered the man who did. And that was the pearl he intended to prize out of this particular oyster. Even if he had to crack the shell to pieces. He was smoking when she came back. "Feeling better?"

"Fuck off," came the reply. He thought of her parents, respectable Venetian traders, the mother weeping, the father's stricken face when his daughter was arrested. How do we breed them, these children of violence, he wondered? How can a pretty girl like this one become a merciless little savage? He put the question aside. "After you murdered the boatman, you sank his boat and swam ashore."

She glared at him in triumph. "I can't swim," she said. "You'll have to think of another lie."

"I can think of any lie I like," he remarked. "I say you took the *vaporetto*, threw the bomb, killed the boatman, and swam ashore. I can prove it."

"Then go ahead," she snarled at him. "Charge me; just let me get to court and I'll prove every word you say is a lie! I've got witnesses who'll swear I never left the house that morning!"

"They won't be believed," Modena answered. "But my witnesses will swear to anything I tell them." He took a cigarette out of the packet and lit it. She stared at him. "You look surprised, Elsa. Did you think you and your friends had the monopoly on violence? I won't do violence to you, and I'll reprimand the officer who hit you. But I'll kill the truth as surely as those unfortunates in the launch were killed. There are many kinds of violence, not just physical. I'll charge you with the crime, and I'll see that you're convicted. Although I know for certain that you didn't do it."

She hissed a long Venetian obscenity at him. And for the first time he sensed that she was afraid. "I know you're not guilty, and you know that when you go to the Isola Santa Magdalena, it will be for the rest of your life, for something you didn't do. I think it'll send you mad, Elsa, after a few years."

"You," she said, "I can't think of a word for you—"

"Pig? Swine? Policeman? I'm indifferent to insults. Haven't you realized that? Jews are insulted from the time they're born. I don't care what you call me. I'm only concerned with one thing. Who stayed at your house after the assassination?"

"Nobody," she shouted back. "Nobody."

That was her first mistake, he thought, and decided to goad her with it. "There were traces of a man," he reminded her. "He used a disposable razor—you forgot about that. Your mother found it; you changed the bedsheets and forgot to empty the wastebasket in the bathroom. Very careless of you. Why didn't you just say it was a lover? Why did you lie and pretend nobody was in the house?"

"All right then," she jeered back at him, "it was a boy friend."

"Then all you have to do is tell me his name," Modena suggested gently.

Tim Johnson arrived on the afternoon flight; he was met and driven direct to Modena's office. The Italian was cordial and much more relaxed than at their first meeting in Venice. He's got a suspect, Johnson thought; that always makes them happy. He wondered whether he'd be allowed to see her.

"I don't think it's advisable," Modena explained. "It'll only make her feel important. At the moment she's on a kind of 'high,' a sort of exaltation, like the martyrs. About to die for the cause, you understand what I mean? It's necessary to bring her down to earth. To make her feel that she's forgotten, that nobody knows or cares."

"Have you established that she's part of an organization? How much has she actually admitted?"

Modena shrugged. "Nothing," he said. "And it's the organization that's important. It will take time, I'm afraid, but we'll break through in the end."

"But how much time have we got?" Johnson asked curtly. "What happens if these people hit again and we don't know anything about them? I don't think you can treat this with kid gloves, Commissioner."

Modena gave him a look of smooth dislike. "I don't wear gloves," he said. "Valdorini will tell us what we want to know. I have had experience of these terrorist types; I don't think you have, as yet. Ordinary pressures don't affect them. They like nothing better than a challenge; they actually welcome violence. I shall get my information by a different method, and when I do, you can be sure it will be the truth."

Johnson looked at him. "And this girl blew up the boat?"

"Yes," he said. "Until she tells us what we want to know, that will be the charge against her. How is Signorina Graham?"

"She's fine," Johnson said. He didn't mention Washington. Langley had people already doing their own investigation in Italy. One of their best men was in Venice, poaching delicately upon Modena's preserve. Modena could play his cat-and-mouse game with the girl, but his allies weren't going to sit around waiting for the outcome. Johnson decided to round off the interview. He wasn't going to see Valdorini, let alone sit in on the interrogations. He might as well take a trip round Rome and catch an evening flight back.

"I've got two kids," he said. "I wish I knew what makes them turn out like that girl you've got. Middle-class background, good education, enough money—what the hell makes them want to tear society to pieces?"

"If we knew that," Modena answered, "we wouldn't have the problem." He wanted the Englishman to go; he had no intention of expressing his own opinions and encouraging a discussion. He didn't like the Anglo-Saxon type. He liked the American equivalent even less. What did they call themselves—Wasps? White Anglo-Saxon Protestants. He was a Jew by race and an Italian Catholic since his grandmother converted. If he did discuss his views on the moral vacuum in modern society, a man like Johnson wouldn't understand them.

He shook hands and rang down for his car. It would be at Johnson's disposal until he caught his plane back to London.

"Davina? Darling, it's me. I've been trying to reach you since Sunday morning—where have you been?"

The phone had been ringing when she got into the apartment. She knew who was calling because she'd avoided the last two attempts to reach her at Anne's Yard. Mr. Walden on the line from Sydney. "I'm not taking any personal calls, tell him I'm not in the office and can't be reached." Her voice had sounded cool and impersonal when she gave those instructions to the switchboard. No one would guess what it cost her. There were times in those three days since she came back from the brigadier's house when Davina was tempted to pick up the phone and call Sydney.

If he was lying then she wanted to know for certain, and to be able to face up to it. If he wasn't—she hadn't dared think that far ahead, because since she came back from Kent the doubt about Walden had almost become a certainty. His story wasn't true; there was another motive, a far subtler trap being set for her. All she had to establish was whether he was a willing party to it. Afterward she could decide what to do.

In the early hours when she woke, and the dawn hadn't even

touched the windows, Davina thanked God for the escape she found in her work. Johnson had come back from Rome; the visit had established nothing but the existence of Elsa Valdorini, buried in the headquarters of the Italian Anti-Terrorist Squad. According to Modena, she wasn't believed guilty of direct assassination.

And all they talked of was time. As Johnson said, she didn't think they had any to spare. When the phone rang it was one in the morning, her time. She picked it up, and knew she'd hear his voice. It was so close and so damnably familiar that she winced. It hurt like a blow when he said Darling, and she didn't know how to answer.

"I was away," she said. God, let me keep my voice normal, don't let the feeling show. And, "Yes, yes I'm fine, just tired, that's all. You know how I hate traveling."

"So do I," Walden's answer was quick. "Especially when it keeps me away from you. I know we can't talk about anything, but I've been going crazy worrying. You do still love me, don't you? You haven't had second thoughts while I've been away?"

She felt her throat constrict; it took several seconds before she could say, "I love you, Tony, you can be sure of that." And the hell was that she meant it. The lie followed afterward. "I've thought of a way out. No darling, I can't. It'll have to wait until you get back. I think you'll agree it's the best solution. For both of us. Yes. Yes, I think so. Of course I miss you. . . . How's your trip?"

"Bloody lonely." Lonely for me too, she thought, with the worm of suspicion burrowing into my guts. Yes, his voice went on, it was very successful, he'd tied up a big contract and he was on his way to Melbourne. "I've decided to cut it short," he said. "I've canceled the trip to Perth." Part of her wanted him home, longed for an end to the uncertainty. Part dreaded the discovery that he was lying, and wanted to put it off as long as possible. "I want to get back to you. Darling you've got me sick with worry now; what the hell is this solution? It sounds so bloody clear-cut. Can't you give me *any* hint?"

"No, Tony, I can't. I told you, you'll be pleased. So there's nothing to worry about, is there? You'll be back when?"

"Friday the twenty-ninth. We'll have a weekend together—I'll fix it, somewhere nice."

"Not Paris," Davina said. "I don't think I want to go there for a long time."

"All right, sweetheart."

She could hear the eagerness in his voice. "If it's an act," she said to him silently, "you're the best actor I've ever met. You deserve an Academy Award if you can make it sound like that."

"I'll call you before I leave. Maybe you can meet me at the airport?"

"I'll do my best," she said. "Goodnight, Tony."

"Goodnight, my love."

She put the phone back; her chance of sleep had gone. She had brought a briefcase back with her. The contents were not classified; she never took anything confidential out of the building and forbade even Humphrey to do so. The monthly intelligence data compiled from their European and Eastern European desks were prepared in précis form for her to study. She made herself a thermos of coffee, and went back to bed with the file.

It stopped her thinking about Tony Walden. Until she reached the section on Soviet Russia. It was the largest and most detailed, originating from the embassy in Moscow. Keremov was in very poor health, and the usual internal maneuvering was starting among the candidates in the Politburo. When there was a new leader what would it mean for Igor Borisov? Her old enemy; the enemy whose face was a blurred photograph taken fifteen years ago. The man who had reached the top of the most sinister organization in the modern world, after he'd arranged the murder of her husband, the defector Ivan Sasanov. When the leadership changed, they were often replaced. In the case of Beria, Stalin's bloody-handed executioner, he had been shot. What would happen to Borisov? Who would her opponent be then? She sat with the file open on the bed for a long time, before she took it up again.

The next morning she sent for Humphrey Grant as soon as she got into her office. She looked haggard, he thought with satisfaction. She certainly wasn't aging well in the job. She looked up and saw him watching her. It didn't surprise her to know that he hated her. After all, he owed her quite a lot. What was surprising was his inability to keep that hatred hidden. He was going to love what she had to tell him. That couldn't be helped. "Humphrey," she said quietly. "You came to me once about your private life.

Now I have a personal problem, and I need help. I want a security check carried out on Anthony Walden."

He said, "You've already had one done."

"I want another," Davina said. "I want information on his family in Poland. Particularly his sister and her family. Can you get this going right away?"

Humphrey nodded. "Yes, no problem. Is anything wrong? If there is, Davina, it would be better if you told me." Interesting to see whether she trusts you, the brigadier had said. My guess is, she'll keep back, but you mustn't mind that, my dear chap. After all, you've been doing your own investigating on the fellow behind her back. She wasn't going to trust him; James White had judged correctly.

"If there wasn't a problem, I wouldn't ask for the vetting," she said. "If it turns out to be important, you'll be the first person to know, Humphrey. So let's leave it like that for now. Right, what's on the agenda for this morning, apart from these bloody appointments with Treasury and the Min. of Defense. God, how I hate having to ask them for money!"

"So did all your predecessors," he remarked. "It's the only way the Civil Service can get back at us for flushing out some of their pinkos. Shall we go through the stuff now? I can put this other business in hand with a telephone call."

"All right," Davina was bent over her desk. "Thanks, Humphrey." She didn't look up.

"No problem," he murmured. He had so nearly added, "It's a pleasure."

4

THE Duvaliers traveled down to Blois in two cars. The minister used her official car and her husband went with her. She had work to do during the drive. Louise took her friend in her own little car. She talked all the way but Helene wasn't listening to a word.

She'd packed her only long skirt and a change of frilly blouses. Albert Duvalier and his wife expected their guests to change for dinner. It was a bore, the minister said, but they were old and very set in their ways. Anything pretty would do. She knew that Helene had a limited allowance and wouldn't have spent it on formal dresses. She was so tactful, so thoughtful of her young friend's feelings. Helene told her aunt where she was going. Her aunt was impressed; Helene had expected she would be. She fussed and fretted over her niece's clothes, suggested she have her hair cut; she hoped that perhaps there might be some eligible young men invited. Helene knew what she was thinking, she understood the mentality that saw nothing degrading in women selling themselves to men and calling it marriage. She let her aunt chatter on, no sign of her searing contempt was evident. Helene was such a pleasant girl, her aunt would say. A little reserved, but genuinely sweet-natured.

Helene kissed her goodbye; she enjoyed making a fool of the old woman, showing her affection and respect. Taking her in with every word and action. If she had only known—shock horror, Helene laughed to herself. It was the "in" slogan among her friends the Duvaliers and Louise's boy friend, that simpering idiot Raoul. Peace and love and vegetarianism. He sickened her. She hated him more than she did Louise, who was chattering like a silly monkey all the way to Blois.

How long had she worn that sickly smile? For two years, nearly three? But not for much longer. Sweet little Helene, such a nice girl. Oh, it was going to be shock horror for real this time. She was shivering with excitement when they reached the château. Huge, gray stone walls, the classic French fortified house of the fourteenth century, with its protective moat surrounding it. A pair of milk-white swans floated disdainfully past. They sickened her too. Money and enormous wealth, a wall of privilege as thick and impregnable as the house they lived in—financed out of legalized slaughter. Albert Duvalier manufactured arms. Nothing could touch him, or punish him. He could topple the government of France if he chose. Helene had heard that said and she believed it. And his brilliant liberal-minded sister-in-law was a part of that government.

Helene didn't meet him until she came down with Louise to dinner. She didn't know a lot about art; she didn't have to, because the pictures on the walls were the originals of postcards people bought as souvenirs.

Renoir, Manet, Gauguin—the great impressionists bloomed on green silk walls in the salon, and a tall old man with a face like an Apostle came forward and kissed her hand. The minister was beside him, smiling, looking elegant in one of her viciously expensive dresses. And then there was Albert Duvalier's third wife. She was a retired film actress who had been more than just a sex symbol. She was famous for her intelligence; the fading beauty was preserved by plastic surgery, but the acute brain was what had captured France's richest man. He had formed a partnership as much as a marriage. She had a cold, dry hand like a snake's skin, too thin for the massive sapphire ring; Helene was repulsed by the touch of her when she shook hands. Like a beautiful mummy, with huge black eyes that went through her and beyond. Nobody of importance, just a friend of that tiresome girl

Louise. All she had was youth, and to Irena Duvalier, that wasn't a recommendation.

Helene felt herself turn red, and looked quickly away. They'd think she was shy. They wouldn't know that hate and fury were making her choke. But they'd know later. They'd look at her and stare and see her for the first time. She said very little during dinner. She was the poor little bourgeoise, befriended by the rich important Duvaliers. Brought along like a Spanish dwarf to amuse the Infanta Louise.

She went upstairs after dinner and listened to the sounds of the household going to bed. The footsteps of the servants; the yapping of Madame Duvalier's little terrier, its topknot crowned by a silk bow. The creak and murmur of an ancient house settling for the night. Helene was sleeping in a room next to Louise's. She had been tactful but firm about not letting her in for a gossip when they came upstairs.

She didn't expect to sleep. The program for Saturday was as rigid as a military exercise. Breakfast downstairs. Tennis before lunch. After lunch, which was at two precisely, they would go and see the royal château at Blois.

Tea was at five, and dinner at eight-fifteen. The Duvaliers would play bridge, and the young guests could amuse themselves. Bridge. That was perfect. She could imagine it in her mind. The tables set out, the cards, the scores, the paraphernalia she had seen in the minister's Paris drawing room. A ritual as meaningless as everything else that generation did, except grow rich at the expense of life itself. She wasn't nervous. Just excited, as if she had gone back to being a child and it was the night before a special treat.

"Where did Louise find that girl?" Irena Duvalier asked her husband. They were dressing before dinner the next night. Both had excused themselves from the trip to the château; they rested for an hour and a half every afternoon, and spent an hour before tea discussing the day's newspapers.

Irena loved jewels, and her husband had amassed a rare collection of historic pieces. She chose an antique necklace of turquoises and diamonds, part of the French crown jewels.

Albert Duvalier shook his head. "I don't know. She's Louise's best friend, that's what I was told. Rather dull and middle class. Why?"

"Because there's something funny about her," his wife answered, examining herself from different angles in the mirror. "If she's Louise's best friend I wonder why she looks at her as if she hates her? I shall have a word with Isabelle about that girl. I don't think she should be encouraged. Should I wear the earrings?"

He considered for a moment. "No, just the necklace. The dress is exactly the right color. Why do you say that girl hates Louise?" He frowned, feeling suddenly uneasy. His wife had an instinct for people that was never deceived.

"Because I've been watching her," Irena said. "And I've seen something in her eyes that I don't like at all. She must never come here again."

They went down to dinner, and afterward drank coffee in the small salon where the bridge table had been set out. A red velvet cloth, fringed with gold; two unopened sets of cards, cigarettes in a Fabergé silver-gilt box, score cards set into velvet pads with the initial "D" embroidered on them.

Helene refused coffee. She gave an anxious glance toward Isabelle Duvalier, who leaned over to her and said, "Helene?" Helene blushed. "Madame, I've got an awful headache. Do you think I could go upstairs and go to bed?"

"Of course," the minister smiled sympathetically.

"Irena, Helene's not feeling very well. You'll excuse her if she goes straight to bed?"

Irena's black eyes were cold as pit water. They examined Helene for a moment, and froze the apologetic simper off her face.

"If you're not well do you want a doctor?"

Her tone implied that it would be a great nuisance if she did.

"Oh, no, no thank you. It's just a migraine. I get them sometimes."

"Really? You shouldn't at your age. Perhaps you eat too many sweet things. Louise, can you amuse yourself while we play?"

"Oh, yes, I'll watch. I've always wanted to learn, but Mother says she hasn't the patience to teach me."

"That's because you've no card sense, my darling," her father teased. They laughed, the little family group of five, and Louise said, "Poor Helene—have you got aspirins? Shall I come up with you."

"No, no—it's just a headache. Madame Duvalier is right—I had too much chocolate cake at tea. I'll be fine in the morning. Goodnight everyone."

"Goodnight," they said in chorus, and forgot about her.

Helene went back into the dining room. Two maids were preparing the table for breakfast. "I left my purse in here," she said. "Have you found it?"

"No, Mademoiselle." They swept under the table; there was no purse.

"I must have left it in the salon, then," Helene said. "I'm not feeing very well, don't lay any breakfast for me. I'm going up to bed."

"I'm sorry," the senior parlormaid said. "Would you like me to bring your purse upstairs?"

"Would you? They're playing bridge and I won't want to go back and disturb them . . . thanks so much." She did look sickly, the women thought, with a patch of bright red on each cheek and the rest of her face a pasty white.

Fifteen minutes later the younger maid knocked on Helene's bedroom door. There was a mumble and she went inside. The room was in darkness, and a voice from the bed said thickly, "What is it?"

"I've brought up your purse, Mademoiselle."

"My what? I've taken a sleeping pill. Oh, yes, thank you . . ." the words trailed off. The maid put the little purse on the dressing table and went out.

Albert Duvalier, with Isabelle as partner, won the first rubber. Louise was talking to her aunt, who was dummy for that hand. They didn't hear the door open, and it was the minister herself who looked up from her cards and saw Helene.

"Helene? What are you . . ."

The first bullet hit her square in the chest. The second and third killed her husband and Albert Duvalier instantly, bursting their skulls like eggshells. Louise didn't manage a scream before she was cut down and Irena's strangled cry was choked off by a bullet in the throat. Helene stood very still. There hadn't been a sound in the room except for the pop-pop of the silenced gun. She stepped forward to the table and shot Isabelle through the forehead. There was no need to worry about the two Duvalier men. Louise, eyes open, was twitching slightly. Helene made sure of her. She paused for a moment by Irena and emptied the gun into her body, although she could tell she was dead.

Then she threw the gun on the floor. Blood was dripping everywhere, forming pools on the polished wood, soaking into the magnificent rugs. She stepped carefully back to the door and opened it. She could see into the hall and to the stairs. There was nobody about. She didn't worry about touching anything. She was wearing a pair of Louise's gloves. When the household went to bed, an elaborate security system was switched on. She had been warned not to come out of her room and wander about during the night because the alarms were set until morning. The time was just after ten o'clock. The butler locked up and set the outside system at ten-thirty. Routine was inviolate in that house. The internal system closing off every room was operated by him as soon as the Duvaliers and their guests had gone to their rooms for the night. She had twenty minutes in hand, unless someone came through the hall. She turned and ran up the stairs. She put the gloves back in Louise's drawer in her room. She was already undressed. She hung her dressing gown over a chair, put her slippers neatly by the bed. She didn't switch on any light; the light from the corridor was enough and her door was ajar to let it in. She had prepared everything in advance. There was a carafe of water beside her bed. Two Mogadon sleeping pills were by the glass. A tube of tablets for the treatment of migraine were also in place; one dose was missing. Helene swallowed both pills, shut her door and got into bed.

When the butler began his routine of locking up and setting the first stage of the alarm system, he knocked and went into the salon. By midnight the news of the massacre of the Duvalier family was on the TV and the radio stations. The French nation woke up to read the appalling story of mass murder, and the incredible escape of the young student who had been found deep in a drugged sleep in her room upstairs.

Davina switched on the television news at eight o'clock. She watched and listened, and ate no breakfast that morning. When she reached her office Humphrey and Johnson were already in conference with their colleagues on the French and Italian desks. Davina didn't waste any time on saying good morning. "Have you got through to Rome?" she asked.

Humphrey nodded. "I couldn't talk to Modena, he wasn't available."

"Goddammit," she exclaimed. "The American secretary of state and the French minister of Justice! Within a month of each other."

"Larue wants to talk to you, Davina," Humphrey said. "I explained your view about what happened in Venice; he wasn't convinced that there's a connection."

"Then he's a bloody fool," she snapped.

"Anything more on the telex?"

"They're still questioning the servants and the student, Helene Blond. The theory is that the assassin walked in while they were playing bridge and gunned the lot of them, and then just walked out again."

"Shall I put the call through to Larue?" That was Johnson, and she said, "Yes, right away. And we'd better ask Washington to put us in touch with their operator in Venice. We're not going to get anything from Rome. Unavailable! God Almighty!"

They took the staff and Helene up to Paris. She was bewildered, still dopy after the heavy drugs. The escorting police felt sorry for her. One of them kept saying how lucky she was. On the journey she said she felt sick, and they took her into a country lane where she retched and retched by the side of the car. Shock, they agreed. Delayed shock. Lucky girl though. The salon on the ground floor of the Duvaliers' château smelled like an abattoir. Helene made her statement to the chief of the Sûreté, and had to be taken out in the middle because she felt sick again. He sent her home to her aunt; she was already a public heroine. The modest little apartment was under siege with reporters and TV crews when she arrived, white as a winding sheet and shaking all over. Her aunt's doctor hurried over, prescribed tranquilizers and complete rest. She got into bed and lay under the covers, sallow and shivering while her aunt fussed over her, and she promised to take the tranquilizers. Just let her be alone for a little. Please?

When her aunt went away Helene waited for a while and then slipped out of bed. She went to the dressing table and looked at herself in the mirror. Her friends had known what they were doing. Pills to make her sick, to turn her into a pasty wreck. She smiled at herself in the glass. She knew the police believed her. The two maids would corroborate everything, even to finding her half-asleep in bed. She had to keep calm, play the part of Helene

Blond, the simple student and friend of the family who had so nearly shared their fate. Even that stupid doctor who'd just gone away would confirm that she suffered from migraine. She'd complained of it as soon as the plan was worked out. She put her hands together as if she were going to pray. The Company of Saints used that as their recognition sign, like the secret signal of the brotherhood of Masons. She wasn't Helene Blond. She was "France." Her part was over. All she had to do was prove their faith in her. Prove that her nerve was as iron-hard as her heart. She smiled at herself once, slowly, and then got back into bed. She dozed peacefully, tired out. Her aunt came into the room and cried over her as she slept.

Davina went for a walk that lunchtime. There had been a message from the prime minister's private secretary. Would Miss Graham please make a personal report at five-fifteen? Miss Graham left it to Humphrey to draft and set out to walk round St. James's Park. Isabelle Duvalier, shot dead, with every member of her family. But why had the killer chosen to go into the house to murder her? Why not an attack in the street, during her public appearances? She was always lecturing, performing official functions. The woman was exposed to the assassin's bullet or the bomb a dozen times a month. Yet the venue picked was particularly horrible, involving the murder of her husband and young daughter, and her brother-in-law Albert Duvalier, the arms magnate, and his wife. Davina stopped and sat down on a seat by the edge of the lake. A young man was reading a paperback; he glanced up without interest as she joined him. Children were feeding the greedy ducks that swam in flotillas round the water's edge. Duvalier was a hate figure for a variety of people. People he had ruined in his quest for monopoly inside France, the pacifist and anti-nuclear organizations reviled him as a merchant of death. Had he been the target? She got up abruptly, and began to walk rapidly back along the path leading out to Birdcage Walk. A platoon of guardsmen drilled in the square of the barracks as she walked past. The drill sergeant's voice barked incomprehensible commands. Was Duvalier the real objective and the others a bonus? Killed because they were there and had to be silenced. Or was the minister for Justice the prime target, as at first supposed.... She'd better have a clear idea about that before she faced the formidable list of questions at five o'clock. Inside her office she spoke to the army colonel who was head of SEDECE, the French equivalent of her own service. A service to be feared and treated with respect. He was a dour, monosyllabic man, who didn't like women. It was whispered that he had lost his testicles in a shooting during the Algerian war, but nobody knew. He was no friend to Davina Graham. However, he set his prejudice aside. France was in an uproar over the killings.

The press and the media were stirring things up as usual, the wildest accusations and rumors were flying round. He answered her queries truthfully and briefly. The gun was a Walther XP 45, fitted with a small silencer of the latest design, giving maximum accuracy and negligible noise. The gun bore no serial number, it had been acid-burned off, and there were no fingerprints. There were no fingerprints anywhere in the château that didn't match the family, their servants and their guests. The shooting had been done by a trained marksman. It was accurate and, except for the multiple bullet holes in Irena Duvalier's body, economical. All the bullets came from the same gun. There was no sign of forced entry, no evidence of a car being used, or of footprints on the lawns. The killer had kept to the gravel paths and simply walked into the house, performed his ghastly task, and left. Interrogation of the indoor staff and the three gardeners and the chauffeur had not produced anything. All were being closely vetted now. "Tell me," Davina cut in, "looking at the murders as an operation, properly planned and carried out, do you see any signature?"

"I know what you're suggesting," the colonel's nasal voice was sour. "The answer's no. It isn't the far leftists or the right-wing Fascists. And it doesn't fit in with Moscow's methods. They don't go in for public mayhem."

"Venice?" she cut in.

"We don't see a connection," was the curt reply. "Well I do," she answered. "And maybe you should look very closely into this Helene Blond."

The listener curled his narrow mouth into a sneer. He was not going to be told what to do. "We have," he said. "Her story checks out. She is not a suspect."

"If there are any developments," Davina said, "will you keep us posted?"

"Of course," he answered. "I see no reason to expect a third assassination."

"I believe there will be," she said. "And it could be we're next on the list."

"And you think there is a list?"

"I'm certain of it."

"I don't agree."

"You don't have to," she retorted. "You've had your turn." She rang off.

The president hadn't attended the weekly Politburo meetings for over two months. His colleagues were surprised to see the papers and the carafe of vodka in place at the head of the table. Borisov knew he was coming down from his apartment on the top floor of the Kremlin. He knew because he had already been up to see him, long before the others were setting out in the motorcade that swept through the traffic in the center lane of Moscow's highways. Keremov looked better than usual; his face had a healthy pink tinge and his hooded eyes were bright under their heavy lids. Borisov knew that the color was skillfully applied, and the brightness due to eye drops. The doctors had spent the early morning upstairs, checking and giving a last-minute injection to stimulate the faltering heart. They stood up to welcome him, the eleven most powerful men in the vast Union of Soviet Socialist Republics. Men responsible for every facet of life within the borders of an empire that stretched from the Caspian to the North Atlantic, and from Europe to the mountains of Afghanistan. Education, Communication, Internal Affairs, the Army, the Navy, the Soviet Air Force, Agriculture, always a festering sore in the Russian economy, Foreign Affairs, particularly important in the nuclear age, and—the most vital of all—the director of State Security, Igor Borisov.

It amused Keremov to look round at his colleagues and make them uneasy. Which ones were plotting to take power as soon as he was dead? He knew their names. Which were the hard-liners who had kept very quiet since the death of their spokesman, Rudzenko, the year before? A stroke, the official story called it. Keremov knew better. His protégé Igor had a versatile medical team who worked for the KGB. They could simulate anything with drugs these days. The disciples of neo-Stalinism had said very little since Rudzenko died. What a magnificent funeral he had been given. The obedient crowds had lined the streets to honor what Pravda called a champion of Soviet communism. A narrow fanatic, bigoted and lusting for conflict. Borisov had killed him because whatever happened, Keremov wasn't going to let Russia fall into the hands of men like him again.

There were three men in particular who worried Keremov. His old friend and colleague Nikolaev, Soviet foreign minister, a bulwark of the Russian Establishment, a survivor who had trimmed to the winds of Stalin and Khrushchev. But in his heart he flew the colors of repression and eventual nuclear war at the masthead. A powerful, clever, very experienced politician who had a hunger for power. He had been a Rudzenko man. And then there was Marshal Alexander Yemetovsky, who controlled the army. Tall, imposing and built like a tank. He had risen through the Great Patriotic War performing acts of great daring behind the German lines, graduating to commands and then to the General Staff. A brilliant young man; almost too brilliant, because Stalin's paranoia had singled him out as a potential rival. Once the war was won, the marshals and generals were pushed out of the limelight. There was no room for more than one Hero in Soviet Russia. Luckily for Yemetovsky, Stalin had died before he had ordered his removal. Like all soldiers, Yemetovsky was not a man who saw peace as a solution. The massive arms build-up that was draining the Soviet economy was his guarantee of safety from attack. Yemetovsky and Nikolaev. And Mishkogan, a cunning Armenian, greedy for power, a merciless persecutor of dissidents and Jews. These three could strike at Borisov, together or singly, and win the power struggle. Listening to the ministers' reports, item after item on the agenda, Keremov's thoughts drifted away from them. He had lived long, fought hard for his power, and served his country well. He didn't mind dying. His body was tired, and the cold he had caught at Rudzenko's funeral in Red Square had made a home in his lungs. There were would be another more magnificent procession through the Moscow streets before the summer ended. Borisov would stand among the mourners around the coffin. Keremov knew that dead men took their influence to the grave with them. Igor would have to fight the final battle for himself.

The Soviet foreign minister was going to visit the president of East Germany. From there he would make a trip to Poland. Keremov listened to the discussion about how hard the Polish military government should be pressured. He interrupted, and immediately the rest were silent. "We are waging a propaganda war against the defense systems of the NATO alliance and the Western world," he said. "And for the moment we're winning that war. The controversy over nuclear deterrents has pushed the Polish question off the center stage. We don't want to bring it back."

"The West has accepted the situation there," Foreign Minister Nikolaev pointed out. "They made a lot of noise, as they did when we took action against Afghanistan. They were never going to help Poland."

"Afghanistan is different," Keremov grunted impatiently. "Nobody cares what happens to a pack of brigands. But the Poles are a very sensitive issue. Not least because of the pope." There was a murmur round the table. Some glanced furtively at Borisov. Had he instigated that attempt? Was it a KGB failure? Nobody had ever put the question. Only Keremov knew if the rumors were true, and he had imposed a silence on the subject.

"I shall impress the general with our views," the foreign minister said, "but the visit can be cut short, if necessary. That will minimize its importance. I need only spend a day and a night in Warsaw after I leave East Berlin."

Keremov smiled slowly. "Just long enough to threaten a little," he said, and they all laughed. "He's a good man; he's got the situation well under control. You'd know best about that, Comrade Borisov?"

"The activists are still in custody," Borisov said. "And the sting has been taken out of Walesa. He knows if he steps over the limit, he will be removed from public activity again. I think we can feel confident about Poland now. On our advice they made no martyrs, and a revolt can't sustain itself without them."

Keremov turned to the foreign minister. "You leave on the twenty-first—that coincides with the visit of President Hauser to London. Comrade Mailsky—" The man in charge of Internal and External Information said, "Yes, Comrade?" Deferential, but not genuine, the old man knew. Too soft, rather than too hard. That would be equally dangerous for the future. "I think we should make a gesture that will embarrass Bonn," Keremov suggested. "A speech in Berlin—a call for reduction in American arms in Europe, specifically the Cruise missile deployment in West Germany. We can imply that our S20s will be reduced." There was a mutter of agreement.

Marshal Yemetovsky said, watching his civilian colleagues, "But without making any commitment."

"You don't have to worry, my friend," Keremov said. "We want them to disarm. We aren't going to make that mistake ourselves. You'll have your missiles."

He reached out and poured the vodka. Just a little, not enough to make him sleepy. He sipped it slowly. Another half an hour; he didn't want to cut the meeting short. He saw Borisov watching him. He trusted the man; in his way he loved him. He was no fanatic, no Savonarola preaching the purity of ideas and baptizing in blood. He was a realist, a pragmatist, a man in touch with the modern world. He had learned English and he spoke very good French and German. He was young and strong. He could rule Russia for twenty years or more, and bring her safely through the coming power struggle with the rest of the world. The massive machinery of Soviet government would function by itself for quite a time. Nothing could be changed quickly, but changes must come.

The half-hour was up. He gave a signal to Borisov, who stood up, and within a few minutes the meeting ended. Keremov walked to the door, and managed not to stumble till it was closed behind him. The nurse waiting outside took his arm, and the stalwart young soldier who shadowed him everywhere supported him. They had a collapsible wheelchair waiting, and he was lowered gently into it and taken upstairs in the elevator.

After the meeting Borisov returned to his own office in the Lubyianka building on Dzerjinsky Square. He didn't try to concentrate on work immediately. He called for a glass of tea. Keremov was facing death like a lion. His only concern was for his country. He would weep for Keremov, who'd been more of a father than his natural one. And like a father, he had willed him his vast inheritance. But Borisov would need time to scatter his rivals, and to gather allies before the vital election took place in the Kremlin. The leader was always elected. But the days when the votes came out of a gun barrel were gone. Now it was the man who could muster support with promises of power-sharing who won. Borisov would have to deal in ministries and promotions, before he could defeat his opponents. Russia was civilized now, as Keremov remarked; nobody was shot for disagreeing. We have become bureaucrats, he told Borisov. Men in serge suits, with ties and pocket handkerchiefs. Nobody wears the Stalin tunic anymore. But there are those who'd like to, and he told him again who he thought these men were.

And then the doctors came in with their injections and the nurse began reapplying the false tinge of health to his sallow skin.

Borisov pressed his buzzer. He had a male secretary now. Once, there had been a girl. A girl with gold hair and a skin that was smooth as silk. For a long time after her death he imagined that he saw her shadow pass along the corridor or even heard the quick tapping of her heels outside his door. He had loved her, and she had betrayed him. The man who answered his call had held her down while another poured vodka and barbiturates down her throat. "Alexei," Borisov said, "I want to talk to you. Sit down."

Alexei did as he was told. Sometimes, in spite of his loyalty and his efficiency, Borisov disliked him for behaving like a robot. The girl had smelled of apple blossom, a scent he gave her when they became lovers. He put her out of mind.

"Comrade Nikolaev is going to East Berlin on the twenty-first. I want you to make the arrangements for his safety. He is also paying a visit to Poland, just for a day and a night." Borisov reached out for a cigarette; the lighter was in Alexei's hand a second later. "I want a special detachment to look after him," he went on. "Maximum coverage wherever he goes."

"What about his regular protection, Comrade?"

Alexei's eyes never quite held the gaze of his superior. But he was a faultless killing machine, as well as a most efficient secretary, trained in all the skills. I wish I could like him, Borisov thought suddenly. I can trust him as I can't trust any other person, but I'm uncomfortable having him near me for long. "You have my authority to replace them," was the answer he gave. The bodyguards for all the members of the Politburo were provided by the KGB. Only the president had his personal squad, his Preobrazhensky Guard, as Borisov privately called them, remembering the guardians of the tsars. "No criticism is intended, make that clear to Colonel Varvov. But after what happened in France, we can't take any risk." He drew hard on his cigarette.

"They haven't caught anyone, then?"

"No," Borisov said quietly. "And I don't think they will. Make the arrangements, Alexei. Pick your men."

* * *

She knew that Humphrey had something to say as soon as he came into the office. He had an unctuous expression on his lugubrious face, and a gleam of malice in the eye. Davina was on the telephone; she said, "Sit down, I won't be a minute," and went on talking. By the time she had finished her conversation and turned to him with a friendly smile, he looked less self-satisfied.

"Sorry to disturb you," he said, "but I thought I might as well tell you what I've discovered about that other business."

"What business?" she asked him. She knew very well.

"Your personal business," he said acidly. "The inquiries you asked me to make."

"So I did," Davina said. "With all the fuss going on before Hauser's visit, I forgot all about it." The lie didn't deceive him. He saw the nervous reaction when she reached for a cigarette. For some months she'd stopped that revolting habit. If it was due to the lover's influence, that was one good thing Humphrey could say about him. The only good thing. He leaned forward and put a thin file on her desk. "There's not much new in it," he said. "Except the parts I've underlined. I hope it'll be a help."

It didn't take long to read. She didn't linger over the passage Humphrey had scored for her attention in his green ink. She could study that later. It was concerned with money. Large sums of money. "Thanks, Humphrey," she said. He didn't get up and leave. He wasn't going to let her slide out of it. He had a homosexual lover, and she was bedding down with a crook.

"He's put himself in a very vulnerable position, I'm afraid."

"It looks like it," she agreed. She felt numb for the moment. She wanted to get rid of him before that numbness turned to pain.

"What a stupid, dangerous thing to do," Humphrey persisted. "He must have been mad to take such a risk."

"If you started rooting round the private transactions of half the heads of corporations in this country, you'd find they had all sailed close to the wind at some point in their career." She got up; it was the only way to dismiss him.

His pale green eyes gleamed at her as he rose to his feet. "It reads to me," he said, "as if he didn't just sail close. He crossed the line. And I hope you'll appreciate what an exposure could mean to your position, if your—er—friendship came out."

Davina took a deep breath. "I appreciate it," she said. "That's why I asked you to look into it. I'd also appreciate it if you treated this as confidential. Officially."

He said angrily, "Of course—you really don't need to mention."

"I'm sure I don't," Davina said. "But what was an unofficial inquiry had better go on file as an official one. We must keep the records straight. On all of us. Thanks for your help." She sat down and took up the telephone. He went out of the office, and she put the receiver back. She opened the file on Tony Walden and read it slowly. Then she put it aside and buzzed her secretary. "Get me Sir James White, will you?"

He listened while she explained briefly what Humphrey had found out.

"It makes sense now," he commented. "Not very nice for you, my dear, but not as nasty as it might have been. Quite simple in fact. What are you going to do about it?"

"There's only one thing I can do," she said flatly. "You're not surprised, are you? When did Humphrey tell you?" She heard the little chuckle on the other end.

"Humphrey is entirely loyal. He never talks about the office when we meet. You mustn't have such a suspicious mind, Davina. I'm not surprised because I never trusted Walden in the first place. But I hope you're not too upset by it."

Upset. . . . She said, "No, more disappointed. If he was going to be a shit, I'd rather he did it with style."

Sir James White went into the garden to find his wife. She looked up from her book expectantly. "James? You've got that cat's-eaten-the-canary look on your face. What's up?"

"Davina phoned," he said. "Humphrey gave her the news about that nasty piece of work, Walden."

Mary said sharply, "Poor girl. She doesn't have much luck with men. Such a pity she gave up that Major Lomax. He was an attractive man, I thought."

"You've got no business to think like that at your age," he reproved her, smiling. "They were too much alike for it to work for long. But she's lucky to have got off lightly with a man like Walden. A really slippery customer. I thought so from the first."

"He was attractive too; in a different way, James. Not a clean-cut Englishman type, but very dynamic, full of sex appeal. You didn't like him because you're prejudiced."

Sir James smiled again. "And rightly, as it happens. I wonder what explanation he'll give Davina? If she lets him explain at all."

"Stop gloating," his wife said; she picked up her book. "I'm sorry for her. I'm sure she was in love with him. It's very bad luck."

"I'm sorry for her too, Mary my dear. You know I'm very soft-hearted underneath."

She didn't look up at him. "You never felt anything but satisfaction when people made mistakes," she said crisply. "And retirement hasn't made you any better. Now let me finish this chapter, and I'll see about the tea."

"I'll do it," he said. "I must congratulate Humphrey. He's a marvelous old truffle hound. He'll sniff out any dirt, however deep it's buried."

He sent for his protégé, the young doctor. A brilliant psychiatrist with an extraordinary understanding of the human mind. He was a strange-looking creature, almost feminine, with tiny bones and a pale, translucent skin. It was hard to imagine him eating, sleeping, defecating, like other men. But he had taught his protector how to enlarge *his* special talent . . . the use and pursuit of power. The doctor had explained the technique as psychological sculpture. From the common clay of humanity, it was possible to form a man or woman into a willing instrument, capable of doing anything on orders. It was a topic that moved the young man to faint excitement; he loved the exercise of his power, and he regarded the human element with as little compunction as a cage of rats in his laboratory.

Watching him come into the room, his protector reflected that there were people who kept tarantulas as pets. It amused him to mock the Christian myth by calling the pitiless little fellow St. Peter, the first of the Apostles, Keeper of the Kingdom's Keys. He called him St. Peter and laughed out loud. The doctor managed a polite giggle.

"Now, I have a problem for you. A real problem this time, not a simple matter like the others. We have a new target. A very important target."

The doctor said, "If you will tell me the name and the circumstances, I will do my best." He listened, his head tilted to one side. After a time he said, "I understand. How long can you give me to find the solution to this problem?"

He liked subjecting the doctor to stress, just to see if anything could open the slightest chink. So far, he hadn't succeeded. Perhaps that was his fascination, he thought. He challenges me by always being right. "I can't give you any time," he answered. The doctor said simply, "Then I will start immediately, I don't think it will be too difficult; I shall look up the relevant records."

"Good. Will you ever disappoint me, do you think?"

"I don't believe I will."

He smiled and wagged his head. "But one day, perhaps ..." The smile disappeared. "This time it is vital that you succeed. Don't underestimate the challenge."

"I work best of all when the situation is impossible."

Suddenly he was irritated by the pallid face and the inhuman confidence. Something will have to be done about you, he thought. When I don't need you anymore. If you were as clever as you think you are, you'd know one crucial thing about human nature. It finds perfection impossible to forgive. He turned away and the doctor was dismissed.

The head of Special Branch was a small wiry Scotsman in his fifties called MacNeil. He had two hates in life, and he confided his feelings about them loudly and clearly that late June evening. "Bloody foreign VIPs and that bloody woman in Anne's Yard! As if I didn't *know* Hauser was going to be a top security risk after what happened in Italy and France! What does she think I am? A bloody bobby just off the beat? Jesus Christ, I don't know why they ever gave women the bloody vote. She hammered on at me about a network of terrorists starting out on a campaign of political murder, lecturing me like a bloody schoolboy!"

His assistant and closest colleague was a taciturn man, an Englishman with the reputation for saying as little as possible. He didn't swear either. At first his superior's constant use of the word bloody irritated him. By this time, after six years, he didn't notice it. There was no better man at the job than Jim MacNeil.

"She's paranoid," he said when he'd calmed down. "Like all bloody women; they get a bit of muscle and they start imagining things. . . . Persecution mania, and now she's stirring up Downing Street about it. That's all we need!"

"You don't think she's right, then?" said his assistant feebly.

MacNeil had been walking round his office; he was a pacer, unable to think on his arse, as he liked to say. He stopped, and perched on the edge of his desk. "About the conspiracy? Looks like it to me. The Eyeties have shoved it under the rug—locked up some bloody kid and put the lid on it. The bloody French won't give anything away. Graham says we'll have it here next, and she could be right. And I've got three bloody VIPs to worry about in the next six months. Hauser, the queen of Sweden, with a state visit for Christ's sake, and the Americans are fixing up for Bush to come in the autumn."

"That's apart from the royals," his assistant remarked. His pipe had gone out.

"Just don't start on that one." MacNeil got up and started walking around again. "There's no way we can protect them. Hauser's arriving at Heathrow; there'll be a bloody guard of honor. The PM's going to meet him, then there's the drive to London and lunch at Downing Street. All closed cars, motorcade escort, that's not so bad. But a gala performance at the opera. That's going to be a bugger. Graham thinks Moscow's behind it."

"She would," was the reply. "Paranoia, sir, like you said."

"Reds under the bloody beds again," MacNeil muttered. "We've got enough of them here already. I told her I thought that was a bit farfetched. She didn't like that. She's not used to being contradicted."

"What's your theory, then?" MacNeil shrugged. "Franklyn was a hard-liner on the right of Reagan. Duvalier was a liberal leftist. I never believed that business about the brother-in-law being the target. Nobody kills bloody arms dealers. They're too busy buying from them. The political motive doesn't add up."

"The next one might give us the clue," the assistant said. MacNeil came to a halt.

"So long as it isn't on our patch," MacNeil said. "I'm going to look over the arrangements tomorrow morning and we'll call a conference for ten o'clock. Maybe we can get them to cancel the bloody opera."

"The Foreign Office?" his assistant queried, heavily sarcastic. "You'll be lucky, sir."

"If they say no," MacNeil stated, "I know just the person to go to. There's no love lost there. Come on, time we shut up shop."

* * *

Davina was in the bath when the telephone rang. She had spent a long tiring day, going from Scotland Yard to the Foreign Office and back to Anne's Yard. Conferences with Humphrey were followed by further meetings with MacNeil and his Special Branch experts; the atmosphere was overtly hostile. She didn't mind the initial bristling of the male; but MacNeil infuriated her. The issues were so serious there was no time for male chauvinism. The afternoon at the Foreign Office had been politer but nonetheless adamant. It was impossible to cancel the gala evening at the opera without alerting the West German president to the threat of assassination. And there was no valid ground for that assumption but one terrorist attack in Venice and a multiple murder in France, which had no proven political connection. The Special Branch could take the necessary precautions and of course if Miss Graham's theory could be substantiated by hard facts, then the matter would be reviewed. It was a typical stonewall response, clothed in maddening courtesy.

Davina left Whitehall, and after an hour in her office going through the latest telexes, she packed up for the night and went home. Some friends had asked her to dinner and the cinema. But she felt too tired and strung up to enjoy anybody's company. She ran her bath and slipped into it. She tried to empty her mind of the day's anxieties. Perhaps she should look for a cottage outside London, somewhere with a garden where she could relax on weekends. When the telephone rang she answered it wrapped in a towel, leaving wet marks on the carpet. It was a voice she hadn't heard for a very long time.

"Davina? It's Mummy. How are you?"

She stammered when she answered. Her family had always had the power to knock the struts from under her, even over the phone. "I'm fine," she said. "Fine. How are you?"

"Well, mixed, not too good I'm afraid. That's why I'm ringing you, Davina. Your father's had a stroke. I thought you'd better be told right away."

"Mummy—he's not dying ..." She felt her throat tighten, making the words difficult to say.

"I rather think so," Betty Graham said quietly. "Please forgive him, darling. Come down, will you?"

"Oh, my God ... of course I'll come. I'll be there as soon as I can!"

She dressed, threw a nightdress into a bag, and then rang the night operator to say where she could be found if she was needed. She drove out through London onto the M3. Her foot flattened on to the accelerator. "Please forgive him," her mother had said. Forgive him for loving her sister Charlie best and letting her know it, even as a tiny child? Forgive the hurt and the lifelong sense of inferiority he had inflicted upon her? She blinked the tears back. He was dying; her father was dying, and there wasn't anything left to forgive with. That was what really made her cry.

Her mother came to meet her; they embraced and Davina could feel the tremor in her body. She looked much thinner than Davina remembered and her pretty, lined face was pinched and very white. "He's upstairs, darling," she said. "He's had a lot of drugs—it was so painful." Her mouth tightened for a moment, but she went on, Davina's arm round her shoulder. "Don't expect him to know you," she said. "He's very dopy. The doctor wanted to move him to hospital. Intensive care, he said. But I made him tell me the truth." She looked at her daughter; her blue eyes were full of tears. "He's paralyzed; he'll never be able to do anything again. So I said no, leave him at home. I did the right thing? Do you think I did the right thing?"

"I know you did," Davina answered, and when she went into the bedroom and saw her father, she repeated it. "Thank God you kept him at home. He'd have hated anything else." She stood at the edge of the bed. It was almost impossible to recognize him.

Her mother stood beside her. "I can't get hold of Charlie," she said. "I've been ringing her flat for hours."

"I thought she was here," Davina said.

"She's been in London for the past month. She comes down on weekends to be with Fergie. I'm so glad you came; I was worried when I couldn't get an answer from Charlie and I thought you mightn't come down ... He didn't mean to be unkind, Davina. He didn't realize he was being unfair. You do believe that, don't you?"

"Of course I do," Davina said gently. Poor mother, trying to excuse him and comfort me. She's been doing it for years.

"Why don't you go and make some tea and sit down, Mum? I'll stay with him. Is the doctor coming again?"

"I said I'd phone if there was any change. He was cross about the hospital. He said I wasn't giving him a chance."

"He wouldn't want a chance like that," Davina answered. "Can you see father living like this? He'd never have forgiven you, I'll deal with the doctor when he comes." She knew her mother had begun to cry. The sounds were pitiful, as if a child had started sobbing. She looked at her father once more. He was sleeping, his breathing loud and harsh. Her mother was in greater need at that moment. "Come along," she whispered, and gathered her in her arms. "We'll both go down; and don't you worry, Mum darling. I'll ring Charlie and I'll run up and down and keep an eye on father. And you've got to believe me; you did absolutely the right thing for him. He's perfectly peaceful in his own bed. That's how it ought to be."

The next two hours seemed to go very quickly. Davina made some sandwiches but didn't insist when her mother said she was so sorry, but she just couldn't manage anything to eat. The doctor came, a brisk man in his forties, who hoped to persuade the elder daughter to be sensible and have her father taken to the hospital.

"There's no point," she dismissed the suggestion. "He's only got a little time to live and it would just prolong the agony for my mother to see him strung up to drips and monitors. He certainly wouldn't want to be dragged back to live like a vegetable!"

"Well, I'm glad it's not my responsibility," the doctor retorted. "You seem quite calm about it, so perhaps you'll keep a watch and let me know if there's a change." He left without saying goodbye. When she came back from the front door Davina found her mother dialing Charlie's number again.

"It's no good," she said gently. "It's nine o'clock, she's gone out for the evening. Stop worrying, I'll try her later."

"It'll be dreadful if he dies without seeing her," Betty Graham said. "She'll be absolutely shattered. Davina, you've been such a help. I don't know how I'd have coped without you."

Davina squeezed her hand. "You coped all right," she answered, thinking of the forceful man who had just left. It was midnight when she got her mother to bed in the spare room. She looked like a wraith, as if all her stamina and energy had dissipated in the course of that evening.

"You promise you'll call me," she whispered. "I want to be with him."

"I know you do," Davina said. "And I'll call you if there's any change. I promise, Mum. Now go to sleep."

She sat in a chair in her father's room. It was very warm, with only the light by his bedside, so she could see him. He lay huddled under the covers, a tall man grown suddenly small and anonymous, and the ugly breathing filled the room. Davina looked at her watch. It was 2:00 A.M. She didn't feel tired; she didn't feel anything, that was the awful part. She tried Charlie's number again. Her father seemed to have slipped down into a deeper unconsciousness. His face was very flushed. The number rang, and then Davina heard her sister's voice. There was noise in the background, and the throb of music. She must be having a party.

Davina didn't waste time. "Charlie," she said. "It's me. I'm at Marchwood. We've been trying to get you since six o'clock." She heard a gasp and then the cry: "Fergie? It's not Fergie."

"No, he's fine. Fast asleep. It's Father, I'm afraid. You'd better come straight down. He's had a stroke and I don't think he'll last till the morning."

"Oh, my God! Are you sure it's that bad?" There was a brief aside, and the background noise stopped.

"Look," Davina heard her voice harshen. "If you want to see him alive, you'd better leave your party or whatever and get down here."

There was a sound from the bed. She put the phone down without waiting to hear any more. Her father's eyes were open; the breathing had altered; she knew what that meant. She ran to the spare room and roused her mother. Together they came to the bed. "You hold his hand," Davina said to her mother. "You're the one he wants now." She stood back, leaving the two people to their final moment in privacy.

Suddenly his breathing stopped. The silence in the room was broken by the ticking of their bedside clock. An old clock with a loud tick. They had used it for years, and never been kept awake. Mrs. Graham bent down and kissed her husband. "Poor darling," was all she said. "Davina, I'm not sure what to do now."

She put her arm round her mother. "Open the window for him," she said gently. "Just as they did for all the Grahams, I'll do it." It was an old Celtic tradition to free the spirit by loosing it into the air. She took her mother out of the room and downstairs. They sat together and waited for Charlie.

She arrived just on the hour. Mrs. Graham's old Labrador, Toby, roused itself and trundled out to bark at the sound of a car.

Davina went out into the hall. Charlie stood there, wearing a long dress and a lot of pearls. There was a man in the background, in evening dress. "I'm afraid he's dead, Charlie," Davina said. "I'm terribly sorry. He's upstairs if you want to see him."

Charlie's face drained of all color; she put her hands to her mouth as if she was a child and broke into a flood of tears. The man came and put his arm round her. Mrs. Graham joined them, and the man stood back, looking both concerned and embarrassed. Mrs. Graham just held on to her daughter and said something too softly to be heard.

Davina didn't move; she had a longing for a cigarette. And a drink. A stiff drink. Nobody was going to comfort her. The penalty for being strong, Ivan Sasanov had told her once when she complained. It was strange that she should remember his words at that moment, when the sense of being alone was so acute. Perhaps he had come on the same wind that took her father's spirit to eternity. It was a superstitious thought, so unlike her, practical cool-headed Davina Graham. She turned away and went back to the drawing room. She found the cigarettes and poured herself a brandy. Charlie had gone upstairs. She knew every creak of every board in the house. Toby waddled back and came to sniff at her hand. He rested his muzzle on her knee, and the soft brown eyes were worried. She patted his head. The dog made it intolerable. There was a noise and she looked up. Charlie's escort was hovering in the doorway. A nice-looking man, obviously upset. "Are you all right?" he asked. "Can I do anything?"

"No thanks, I'm all right." She held up the glass of brandy. "This will put me right. Why don't you have one with me—it's on the table over there."

"Thanks, I will," he said. "I drove Charlie down; she was far too upset to come alone. I hope you and your mother don't mind."

"Of course not, it was very sweet of you. It all happened so quickly. Father wouldn't have known Charlie anyway, so she mustn't worry about not being here."

"She was saying how close they were," he said, "on the way down. She adored him, didn't she?"

Davina wasn't aware that she smiled, "Oh, yes, she did. It was mutual; he worshiped her."

"I'm sorry," he said quickly, "I haven't even said who I am. I'm

Peter Vereker; Charlie works for me. We'd been to the theater to-night and it turned into a bit of a party afterward. What an awful thing for you, having to manage on your own. I'm sure she'll feel dreadful about not getting here in time, but honestly it wasn't anybody's fault."

You remind me of old Toby, Davina said to herself. You've got the same loyal, anxious look, like tonight, when he knows something's wrong and he doesn't know whether he did right by barking. She's got her hooks into you, Peter whoever-you-said-you-are, and you don't even know it. Aloud, Davina answered, "It was just as well. It wouldn't have done Charlie any good to see him like that. Have another drink?"

"No, no thanks, I'll be driving back. Just as soon as she comes down. Can I get another one for you?"

"I don't think so," Davina stood up. Her body ached with tiredness.

"I'll need a clear head for the morning. My mother's been marvelous but she'll have a reaction to what's happened. And Charlie will be too upset to cope. So I can't drown my sorrows, can I?" She saw the puzzled look on his face. Surely she couldn't be sarcastic at such a time.

"Look," he said, "maybe I shouldn't wait to see Charlie. I'll slip back to London. I brought her car down, so the best thing is to phone tomorrow and see what she wants done about it." He came over to Davina. A good-looking man. Not late thirties—forties, she decided. And with money. Funny how you can tell when people are rich. Ivan used to say it was a smell. A smell of expensive soap and clothes that weren't worn twice running. Ivan again. He must have come in on the wind, she thought, and put the glass of brandy down. He shook hands. "Well, goodnight. And I'm terribly sorry. Do please tell your mother . . ."

"I will," she heard herself say, "and thank you for being so kind to my sister."

That Saturday Soviet Foreign Minister Nikolaev made his journey to East Berlin airport for the flight to Warsaw. He had a busy schedule to get through in his brief visit to the Eastern trouble spot. A private meeting with Poland's head of government at his home thirty miles outside the capital. It would be cordial on the surface, but the undertones of threat had to be maintained. Poland's internal counterrevolution was not completely under control. The existence of its leader, Lech Walesa, was a constant reminder of the self-determination Poland had lost. What to do about him? Nikolaev knew that a Russian solution wouldn't solve the Polish problem. Confinement in a KGB mental hospital worked very well with troublemakers at home The Polish military weren't so lucky.

His personal bodyguard, Alexei, was in the seat immediately behind him. Nikolaev preferred his usual escort, but Borisov had been insistent that he needed the protection of his best officer.

The trip in East Germany had been very successful. He had made a speech that would embarrass the West about disarmament and put the West German chancellor in difficulties. Nikolaev didn't enjoy going to East Germany, though he wouldn't have admitted it. He found the people dour and grim, and the atmosphere oppressive. Poland was a political nightmare but it had certain lighter aspects. Good food and vodka and women with pleasing faces. . . . He settled down for the short trip across the border and slept. Behind him, Alexei kept vigilance.

Davina put her mother to bed. Charlie was locked in her room. Mrs. Graham said anxiously, "She's crying and crying, poor girl. She won't let me in, Davina. Do you think she'll be all right?"

"I'm sure she will," Davina said. "It's the people who can't let it out who suffer afterwards. And that means you, Mum. Never mind the stiff upper lip, you've been brave enough already. Try to go to sleep and don't worry about anything. I'm here and I'll look after everything." She bent and kissed her and Betty Graham reached out and held her elder daughter in her arms.

"You're a wonderful girl," she murmured. "Don't think I don't know it. Goodnight, darling."

Davina made the funeral arrangements, and called the doctor, on her mother's insistence. Charlie was prostrate in bed. He gave her a sedative and came down to find Davina.

"How is she?"

He made a slight grimace. "She's had a bad shock; rather surprising for a woman of her age to go to pieces like that."

"They were very close," Davina said.

He gave her a cool look. "So I gathered. She'll pick up now. She's rather a hysterical type, I should say. She'll sleep for a few hours and you'll find she's a lot better. Ring me, but only if you have to. I'm not on duty after five. It's supposed to be my weekend off."

When Davina closed the door behind him, she felt he had left his irritation with them all like an aura. But there was Fergie to be looked after; Davina hadn't seen him since he was a baby. She found him a lovable toddler, who couldn't be left alone for a minute before getting into mischief. He had her sister's glorious blue eyes, little that reminded her of his father. He would be brown-haired, that was the only resemblance. She phoned the girl who looked after him and asked her to come back and take over. When she appeared in the doorway, he held on to his aunt Davina and didn't want to go. It affected her so much that she spent an extra twenty minutes with the little boy. Her own child had never been born. She had miscarried only a few days after the car blew up and Ivan Sasanov died in her arms. She would never have a child now. She had a lover who'd betrayed her and no personal life that was worth a damn anymore. She buried her face in Fergie's little body and held him tight for a moment. Then she took him to find his nanny.

"Needs must when the devil drives." She'd quoted that to James White, and the old tag kept coming back to her during that day. The devil of being the strong one. Nobody expected her to have hysterics or collapse. She'd lost a father, but it was Charlie's grief that dominated the household. Mrs. Graham was frail and incompetent, at a loss in the house where she had been the mainstay of the family for all their lives. Without her husband, she had lost her bearings. She didn't say so but she dreaded being left to cope with Charlie.

Davina got through to her office. Humphrey rang back and was glumly sympathetic. A call from Sir James followed; his offer to come over was brisk and genuine. It surprised her, knowing his incapacity to feel for others. And his majestic selfishness. Undoubtedly his wife was urging him on. Davina hesitated; the Whites were old friends, it might help Betty Graham if they came. She said, yes, that would be very kind, and rang off before he could change his mind.

The Whites arrived in the late afternoon. The captain's body had been taken away, and there was a stillness about the house that even Fergie's muffled shouts couldn't dispel. Davina kept busy. She cleaned and dusted and made cups of tea and coffee. Marchwood had been her only childhood home. She loved the old house because it had always been a friend, when human friendships were not in evidence. And she had brought Ivan Sasanov there for the weekend that changed both their lives. That was another link with Marchwood, and one of the strongest. She took her mother out into the garden that afternoon. It was overcast but very warm. They sat together on the terrace where there had been so many family gatherings. "Your father loved sitting out here," Betty Graham said suddenly. "I did all the gardening, but he loved to look at it. He had a very good life, you know."

"I know he did," Davina said. "Mostly thanks to you."

"It wasn't always easy," her mother said. "We had ups and downs during the war. We were separated such a lot and he was an attractive man." Her gaze was clear as she turned and looked at Davina. "But he always came back to me. And then of course there was Charlie. And Fergie. He adored Fergie."

"I'm not surprised," Davina said. Ups and downs. But he always came back . . . How little she knew of her parents' private lives, or her mother's strength. "He's a love," she said. "Full of life and mischief. Mum, before James and Mary come, I think you should go back with them till the funeral. I'm going to suggest it. You will go, won't you?"

Betty Graham looked bewildered. "But what about Charlie and Fergie? Who's going to look after the house?"

"I'll see to it," Davina said. "But I can't stay on. I've got to go back to the office and I don't want to leave you here on your own. Charlie can stay and the little nanny says she is quite happy to move in and do everything for the next few days. I want you to go away, Mum. Please?"

"I'd like to," her mother admitted. "Just a break for a day or two. I feel very feeble, darling. I couldn't manage here without you, and Charlie won't stand on her own feet while I'm around to lean on." That was a surprising comment, and Davina saw her mother smile. "I'm not a fool," she said gently. "Your father was stone blind to Charlie's faults but I never was. Perhaps it'll help her to grow up now that he's gone. I'll go away with the Whites, if they'll have me. There they are now, old Toby's out there barking." She reached out for Davina's hand and for a moment held it. Her own hand was very thin and had no grip.

"I'll never forget how good you've been," she whispered, and then got up to go and meet her old friends.

Davina was sitting watching the television news. She looked up when the door opened, expecting to see her little nephew coming in to say goodnight. Charlie stood there, dressed in trousers and a cotton shirt. Davina noticed that she had put on makeup and done her hair with her usual skill. She looked extraordinarily beautiful and young. "Where's Mummy?"

"She's gone back with James and Mary White," Davina explained. "I thought it would do her good to get right away until the funeral. I looked in on you before tea but you were fast asleep. How are you feeling?"

"Better," Charlie came in and closed the door. She sat on the sofa on the other side of the fireplace. "But shattered. I just can't believe it. I can't believe that I'll never see him again. You sound as if you've arranged everything."

There was no doubt about the hostility behind the last remark.

"I fixed up the funeral and got Mum away," Davina answered. "You can change it if you like. All the papers are on Father's desk over there."

"Just tell me when it is," Charlie said coldly. "So I can be there." Davina got up and switched off the TV set. She didn't feel angry. It seemed such a waste of time to snipe at each other in the circumstances.

She poured a drink for herself and then said, "Charlie, do you want anything?"

Her sister shook her head. "No, I'm still full of dope. But do help yourself, won't you?"

"I already have," Davina answered. "Can't we try to put the past behind us, Charlie? Father's dead, Mum's going to need a lot of looking after if she's to get over this. I'll say it first, if you like. I'm sorry about everything that's happened to you. I'm sorry for both of us, because we've lost Father."

Charlie reached into her bag and took out a cigarette. She lit it with a slim gold lighter. "You're not sorry, Davy," she said after a pause. "I appreciate what you've said, but I don't believe it. You're not sorry you hounded John out of the country. You're not sorry you helped to break up my marriage and leave Fergie without a father. You didn't see anything wrong or inhuman about what you did. Now you're trying to patch it up because Pa's gone and Mum's all alone, and you've got a bit of a conscience. But deep down you'd do it all again, and still be surprised that I took it so badly."

"There was nothing else I could do," Davina said slowly. "John was a Soviet spy; he'd been in Moscow's pay for years. God knows how many people were killed because of him, apart from Ivan. You never considered that, did you? He tipped off the KGB where we were living. And you know what they did."

"You haven't any proof," protested Charlie. "It sounds good, that's all. But if he did do it, then you got your own back through Fergie and me, didn't you?"

"If you think that," Davina said, "then why the hell didn't you follow him to Moscow? Maybe he wouldn't be killing himself with drink if you'd joined him! But that's not your scene, Charlie. I don't blame you, it's not mine either. But wouldn't it help to be honest? You were right to turn your back on him, but you're not right to blame me for what happened. And to turn Father against me like you did. I haven't been in this house for nearly two years, because of you."

Charlie put out the cigarette; she had hardly smoked any of it. "What's the point of arguing?" she said. "I haven't got the energy. Did Peter Vereker phone?"

The change of subject took Davina by surprise. Under the lamplight Charlie looked gray in spite of her clever makeup. "Yes," she said. "He called twice. I told him you'd get in touch when you felt up to it."

"When are you going back to London?" She had leaned back and closed her eyes. "If you've fixed everything up, there's nothing for you to stay on for now."

Davina said quietly, "You'd rather I went? Don't you mind being alone?"

Charlie opened her eyes. So large and blue, so skillfully emphasized by liner and mascara. The hatred in them beamed at Davina. "I shan't be alone," she said. "Peter will come down tonight and stay with me. So there's nothing to keep you."

Davina finished her drink. "He seems a decent kind of man," she remarked. "He'll look after you. Someone always has. I'll see you at the funeral on Wednesday."

She went out of the house without seeing her sister again. She drove steadily up to London, and imagined that she saw Charlie's car speeding down the expressway toward Marchwood. Peter Vereker hurrying to take over where every man who knew Charlotte Graham had left off. Including her own father. To cherish and protect her. It wasn't because he was exiled and disgraced that John Kidson was committing slow suicide in his lonely Moscow apartment. He still loved his wife. Davina drove into the apartment building garage. Walking up the stairs, she felt it an effort to mount each shallow step. When she unlocked the door of her apartment the lights were on. Tony Walden came toward her. "Oh, my darling," he said and took her in his arms. "My love, I called the office. I'm so sorry."

It would have been easy to let him hold her. Easy to grasp at the comfort he offered. Part of her wanted to cling to him, to put off the confrontation and convince herself that to hell with it, it didn't matter. He loved her, he'd be able to explain it all if only she shut her eyes for just a little while. She didn't have to twist the knife in herself so soon. But she was pushing him away before the temptation won.

"Davina, darling, what's the matter?"

She went into the sitting room, leaving him to follow. The apartment seemed very cold. She noted that symptom in herself. Shock or emotional stress always made her body temperature drop. Walden came up to her. "What is the matter with you? Why won't you let me touch you?"

"Let's sit down, shall we? I've had a pretty grueling couple of days. Give me time to collect myself, please."

He frowned; he was very suntanned, but there was color creeping up under the brown. "If that's what you want," he said. "Can I get you a drink?"

"No thanks," she said quietly. Why did he have to appear at that moment? Why couldn't she have been left alone to sleep and heal. Charlie had inflicted the wound. Charlie with her relentless hatred and her blame.

"Well," she heard Tony Walden say, "I can do with one. I fly halfway round the world to see you, and you behave as if you hate the sight of me."

Davina watched him pour a big splash of whisky and drink it neat. She said, "I'm not grieving because my father's dead, he never loved me, and I couldn't feel anything much when he died.

That's upsetting in a different way, Tony. The lack of grief is worse than grieving. Can you understand that?"

"No," he said. "No, I can't. It's a bit too Anglo-Saxon for me."

"I suppose it was a silly question. You love your family, and you're all very close." She sounded weary, flat.

He came and sat beside her. He put his arm around her and she didn't move. "Yes we are. My poor darling, you look absolutely dead tired. I didn't mean to be difficult." He kissed her tenderly.

"How're your family, Tony?"

He sounded surprised. "I told you. I haven't had any news since I went away."

She looked at him. "I have," she said. "Your sister's fine and your brother-in-law's just been promoted to deputy head of his department." She got up and walked away from him. "Why did you tell me a pack of lies, Tony? Why did you make up that story about the KGB arresting him, and your mother and sister being terrorized? Why didn't you tell me the real reason they were blackmailing you? It wasn't difficult to find out."

He didn't answer for a moment. A long moment, it seemed to Davina, while she watched him decide what to say. He looked up at her, cradling the empty glass.

"I should have known you'd check up," he said. "I didn't want to lose you and I couldn't let them expose me. I tried to have it both ways, because I happen to love you very much."

"How could making up that story help you? What did you expect me to do?"

"I thought you'd give me bits of information that didn't matter. So I could feed the bastards and keep them happy. I thought if you felt sorry for me and thought my family were being persecuted, you'd go along with it. I knew I'd lose you if you found what they were really holding over me."

"I see," Davina said slowly. "You say you love me, Tony. You wanted to keep me, and hold off a Russian blackmail. With my connivance. It's a funny kind of love that would try a trick like that."

"I don't expect you to understand," he said. "That's why I didn't consider telling you the truth for a moment. I knew you wouldn't sympathize with that."

"For a fraud involving half a million? Setting up your own business with clients' money, salting funds away in Switzerland, committing fraud? No, Tony, I don't have much sympathy with that."

"Everyone's smuggled money out," he protested. "The bloody Swiss banks are stuffed with billions of illegal funds from all over the world. I have my family to help out in Poland. That's how the Russians got on to me. They traced the money back. But it was my business that was threatened! And I'm going to remind you, Davina, *why* I got fired from the American company and faced losing everything I'd built up over twenty years of fucking sweat and tears! Your boss James White wrecked my deal with the Saudis—remember that little incident? Because of you. He ruined me, and I had to do something pretty drastic or go broke and start from scratch again. I wasn't going to do it. I wasn't going to lose everything I'd worked for and built up, when all I needed was time and the money was there!" He slapped his hand down on the side of the chair. "There, in the bank! I used it, I set up my own agency and I made the bastards a profit."

She said coldly, "And what would have happened if you'd failed? What lie would you have told the people whose money you had been using for yourself?"

He stood up and said harshly. "You've no right to judge me, Davina. I've taken chances to survive. I don't regret them. I don't regret trying to keep you and keep my business at the same time. If you were a different kind of woman you'd understand. Take a good look at some of the things you've done, before you sit in bloody judgment on me."

"I didn't do them for myself," she said. "That's the difference. I suppose you never gave a thought to what my position might have been if I gave you bits of information that didn't matter. Christ Almighty!"

"I was prepared to gamble," he said. "Everything I wanted was at stake. You, and my business. I've gambled for my life, that's what the world is all about. I did think of the risk for you, darling, but I thought we'd get away with it."

"You said if I resigned, you'd marry me," she reminded him. "What would you have done, Tony, if you'd come back from Australia and I'd taken you at your word?"

He didn't hesitate; "I'd have thanked God," he said. "If you were out of the Secret Service, I wouldn't be any use to them. I could have done some kind of deal over the money going into Poland and they'd have dropped the whole thing. It was my connection with you that set them after me. I would have welcomed it, Davina. I'd have paid off Hilary and settled down with you for the rest of my life. I still will, if you love me enough to put this behind us and start again."

"Tony," Davina said quietly. "Tony, I really think you mean it." She saw the hope flame up in his face. Yes, he does love me. If that's the deal that gets me and keeps his agency at the top of the heap, he'll jump at it, and never look back. He'll take me by the hand and we'll walk off into the sunset and live happily ever after.

"I think you'd better go," she said. "You're right, I am dead on my feet."

"What does that mean?" he demanded. "Is it your crisp little way of telling me to get out for good, or are you going to be a human being and give us both another chance? For Christ's sake, we've been everything to each other. Davina, I'll accept all the blame you like, but don't throw our happiness out of the window like this. You've got your job and your principles, but at the end of the day you're going to need a man to love you. And I love you. You know that's true."

"Yes," she said. "I do know it and I'm grateful. I'm grateful for the lovely times we had and for loving you. I did love you very much. You say you couldn't lose your business. All right, I'll accept that. But I couldn't give up my job to marry any man I didn't respect. That's what makes the job as special to me as your agency is to you. Integrity and trust. Those two things are what matter in the end. And it's better to be alone and keep them. Make your deal with the other side. Get them off your back, and I'll make it easy for you. I'll see the right version about our break-up gets back to them and lets you off the hook. Goodbye, Tony."

He looked at her for a moment. "You're a fool," he said slowly.

She heard him shut the front door. She picked up his glass and took it out to the kitchen to wash. For a few seconds the floor heaved under her as if she was on board ship. Then she heard the telephone ringing in the bedroom. It was the special phone connected to the switchboard in Anne's Yard. She ran to answer it.

"Sorry to disturb you at a time like this," Tim Johnson said. "I've got some top-level telexes in; I think you'll want to see them. I can bring them over to you if you like. Save you coming into the office."

The floor had stopped moving under her feet. She had pulled herself together. For God's sake come over, she nearly said. Give me something else to think about.

"How soon can you get here?"

"Twenty minutes."

"Fine, I'll see you then."

He was right on time; the front door buzzer sounded at exactly twenty minutes after the call. Davina pressed the intercom button and opened the door.

"These came in from West Berlin," he said. "And that's the most important one—it ties up with the others."

She sat down and read through the decoded telexes.

Sources in West Berlin reported rumors of an accident to the Soviet foreign minister in Poland. Davina was frowning. Warsaw airport was closed, and there was a news blackout. She looked up at Johnson. "Are they saying the plane crashed? This reads as if he was killed."

She didn't expect an answer; she read the latest telex, and this came from a source in East Berlin. A wholly reliable British Intelligence cell that operated within the government itself. Nikolaev had reached Warsaw airport safely; the plane had radioed in after landing. On the way out of the airport his car was attacked. "An eighty-four-millimeter anti-tank gun—Good God, Tim."

"An ordinary car would've been snuffed out just like that." He snapped his fingers.

"They must have been mad," Davina said at last. "This is the excuse Moscow's been looking for. This is a disaster. What's the Foreign Office reaction?"

"About the same as yours," he answered. "If this is Solidarity, they've committed suicide."

"Moscow'll keep it quiet till they decide on an official story. But it doesn't read quite right, does it? A rocket attack? That doesn't sound like Solidarity to me."

Johnson chewed his lip. "What *does* it sound like to you?" Davina looked up at him. He had a shrewd, feline face, the face of a predator.

"I wouldn't like to put it into words," she said. "Not till we know a little more. Where's Humphrey?"

Johnson decided to risk it. "Gone up to Norfolk," he said. "With his friend."

"Well ring through for me, will you, Tim?"

Humphrey had been expecting the call. He liked Ronnie's family. When he first met them, they'd been shy and awkward with him. Now he and the situation with their son was accepted. They looked on him as a kindly uncle who took care of their boy in London. He and Ronnie stayed at a pleasant local pub when they went up to see them. The visits were important to Ronnie. He had an affectionate nature and he loved his mother. He didn't want the family to think he'd gone grand and forgotten them.

"Humphrey," Davina said, "I'm sorry to break up your weekend. I've had to come back from Sussex myself. I think we should spend tomorrow on an analysis job. Monday will be hectic and we need the time. Do you mind?"

"Not at all," the pedantic voice sounded worse over the telephone. "Things always happen on weekends, don't they? How's your mother bearing up? Is she with you?"

"No, she's staying with the Chief; she's not too bad, considering. Shall we say nine o'clock tomorrow?"

"Nine o'clock," he repeated, and rang off.

Johnson had lit a cigarette and was looking around. It was a pleasant apartment, nice pieces of furniture, comfortable. Photographs on a table. Father and mother with a house in the background. Very much the manor type. And Davina with a man, taken somewhere on a beach. She looked young and laughing, with her arms round his shoulders. It wasn't Walden or his predecessor Colin Lomax. It must be the husband, Sasanov. He squinted at it, trying to focus better. Yes, definitely Sasanov. A big, square man with a Slav face. What an odd woman she must be, he thought. She certainly picks odd bedfellows.

"I'm afraid that means Sunday for you," Davina interrupted his thoughts. "And for Harris and Goodwin. We'd better ask Poliako to come in too."

"If he's sober," Johnson remarked. Serge Poliako was a retired Russia watcher, a member of the old wartime team at Baker Street. He lived on a modest pension and supplemented it by writing articles for political weeklies. He had lived with the same woman for forty years, and they got drunk regularly together.

"Given a bit of warning, he should be OK. I think that's it, Tim." She stood up.

"I'm very sorry about your father," he said.

"Thank you," she said. "It was quick, and at least he didn't suffer."

Johnson did something that was a surprise to himself. "If you've nothing better to do," he said, "why don't you let me give you dinner? My wife's gone off to some Pony Club thing with the boys; they won't be back till late."

Davina was going to say no, it's very kind of you, but I'm—doing what? Staying alone here for the evening. The boss lady, looking at the four walls and the TV, making a sandwich before she went to bed. And bed reminded her of Tony Walden.

"That's very kind of you, Tim," she said. "I'd like to go out, if you're free. I don't feel like being alone tonight."

"Good," he said, and meant it. "Do you like Chinese?"

"Very much," she said. "I'll give you a drink and then we'll go."

5

"So far," Humphrey Grant announced, "we've established no link between these three incidents. Venice and Paris *could* be connected, but Warsaw knocks the idea of a KGB conspiracy right out."

"It seems to," Davina admitted. "Which leaves us with the possibility that three highly important political figures—certainly Nikolaev heads the list—have all been murdered by coincidence within the last three months. I don't know who's going to buy that!"

The head of the Italian desk spoke up. "I'm still confident that Modena will make a breakthrough."

"I'd share that confidence if I thought he was going to tell us about it," Davina said. "But what makes you say that, Paul?"

"Because there's no move to bring that girl Valdorini to trial. Modena's buried her. The papers have dropped it, nobody cares anymore. I think he's sweating her, and he's had some spectacular success with terrorists before."

"In the meantime we all sit around wondering if there's a link or not and who's going to be the next," Johnson interposed. "The SEDECE haven't broken any ground over the Duvalier killings, and now we have some joker loosing off with an anti-tank missile and blowing up Nikolaev."

"And will we ever know if they got the pepole who did it?" Davina asked Serge Poliakov the question. "Will we ever get the truth?"

Poliakov was as bald as a vulture; he was stooped and sinister as the carrion bird, in his dusty black coat and metal-rimmed spectacles balanced on his hooked nose. He had a hangover, but not a bad one. Forty years ago he had been one of the most brilliant analysts of Soviet activities in the Intelligence world. Now he didn't care; he needed extra money and he was prepared to work on odd occasions.

"We'll get the truth by looking at the lies they tell," he answered. "It's been officially called an accident. A blowout at speed threw the automobile out of control. In the crash that resulted, the minister and two others were killed. The bodies are being flown back to Moscow and there will be a state funeral. If you want to understand that pack of lies, you will see that the East German report is true. Ministers, government and party officials do not get assassinated in Russia. It does not happen. That's understood. They have heart attacks or die after an operation, or like this one, they drive in a car and get killed in an accident. They are *never* murdered. That makes them vulnerable. They *never* commit suicide. That makes them unstable. Again, impossible.

"But who did it? We'll only deduce that by what Keremov doesn't do. If there are no repercussions inside Poland, then the killing was not Polish-inspired. There will be scapegoats, of course, but what we have to look for is a major policy shift in Soviet–Polish relations. Personally, I don't think it will happen. Poland has declared a day of national mourning. There are no reports of arrests or activity against the extremists in Solidarity. That says something."

"What?" Davina demanded.

He loved an audience. "It says to me that they have caught the killers," he said softly. "I'd be surprised if they even expected to escape. That is what you want your East Berlin source to find out," he went on. "Who was captured and were they still alive. At that point it should be possible to see if there is a connection with Franklyn and the Duvaliers. One thing has occurred to me, though . . ." He paused and looked around at them. He managed to convey that he didn't think much of their combined powers of deduction.

"In Venice the only contact was a young woman, a student. In Paris, apart from the servants, the only survivor was a young student, also a woman."

Humphrey couldn't resist the chance to score off the old show-off. "My dear Serge, you're not suggesting that this is *feminist*-inspired?"

Poliakov regarded him briefly through his dirty spectacles.

"It's their age, not their sex, that interests me," he said. "Young, under twenty-five, still at university or college. Middle-class background. The French girl has an alibi that can't be broken. The Italian is in one of their filthy prisons as dead to the outside world as if she were buried. She hasn't got an alibi. One of them is supposed to be guilty. The other is innocent. I think they are both guilty." He looked at Davina. "While we wait for Keremov and Borisov to show us something, why don't you do something yourself, Miss Graham?"

"About what?" she asked him. "And don't start suggesting any cowboy operation. We're not allowed to behave like your lot did during the war." Poliakov laughed. It was a rusty cackle that ended in a fit of coughing. His fingers were brown with nicotine stains. "You don't do it officially, but you can always get it done. Send someone after that lucky young lady in Paris. Put a little pressure on her."

Davina didn't answer. She wasn't putting anything on record for Serge Poliakov. Not while he drank a bottle of vodka a day.

She turned to the man responsible for East Germany. Richard Littman; of German parentage, a brilliant graduate who had worked with James White for nearly fifteen years. He ran the East German network and it was one of the most effective in the Warsaw pact countries.

"Can you get news of Nikolaev's killers?"

"I think so," he said. "But I don't want to pressure our contact He'll come through as soon as he knows any more."

"Then there's nothing we can do till we hear," Humphrey declared. "Except stop Hauser going to the opera. Surely the Foreign Office will see sense about that now."

Davina said, "When you're dealing with people who can

mount an attack on Nikolaev and bring it off, I don't know how the hell we can protect anyone. But I'll make the cancellation of that gala night our first priority. Gentlemen—thanks for coming in. And thank you, Serge. As always, you've been a great help."

He smiled at her. "Think about Paris."

She did think about Paris. She thought about it during that week, when the German president arrived and everyone's nerves were fraying with anxiety. The gala performance at the opera was not canceled. The government, headed by a prime minister who would have personally braved the assassin's bullet before backing down, refused to panic and worry their guest. It was said afterward, when they were all breathing easily again, that there were more Special Branch in the audience than invited dignitaries.

The official visit lasted three days. Davina herself was a guest at the Mansion House dinner given by the lord mayor in honor of President Hauser. It was the night before her father's funeral. She was seated among senior civil servants. Those who knew what her job was watched her with interest. The wife of a senior secretary at the Foreign Office stared at Davina for some minutes, and then whispered to her husband. "Is she really head of SIS? She looks too young. Rather striking, with that coloring."

"Striking isn't a bad description," he whispered back. "She's one of these lethal career women, tough as old boots."

"She doesn't look it," his wife insisted. "She's very attractive, in an austere way."

"Sorry, darling." *He* was becoming bored with the subject. "She's not my type." Colleagues had described her as worse than Sir James White when it came to getting her own way. He had been a devious, unscrupulous old bugger, but Davina Graham went through the opposition like a hot knife in a pack of butter.

The German president, a genial, courteous man, spoke in perfect English for twenty minutes. It was the usual diplomatic content. Peace through strength and negotiation, the close economic and cultural links between their two countries. Davina didn't listen. She didn't want to think about the funeral the next day. Ten in the morning in the little church at Marchwood. She thought about what the old drunkard Serge Poliakov had said about Paris. It was a mischievous challenge, a mocking dare to the newcomers to show the guts and initiative of the old hands.

Tim Johnson offered to drive her home from the Mansion

House. "I've got an official car," she said, "but do come in for a drink; it's not that late."

She'd enjoyed her dinner with Johnson. Socially he was easy and interesting. There was none of the irritating keenness that proclaimed him as a young Turk in the office. They talked about their work, and she was impressed by his insight. He reminded her more and more of a fox; sharp-eyed and stealthy-footed, with very sharp teeth. She had wondered about his wife. She hadn't imagined Tim Johnson in the role of father to children who rode for the Pony Club. His wife was extremely pretty. She had met them on their return from Washington. She chatted to Davina about a few safe subjects, but withdrew into silence when her husband discussed the German president's speech. Not one of the "I'm As Good As You Brigade," determined to assert herself. She was obviously very fond of Tim. And Davina noticed that he was attentive to her in a quiet way. The Fox and the Hen.

Captain Graham was buried in the small churchyard in the village. It was a bright summer day without a breath of the wind that lurked over Salisbury Plain. The church was small and Victorianized by an early Graham with more money than taste; only the stunted Norman tower remained. The inside of the church was full of neighbors and friends and a scattering of naval contemporaries who seemed surprisingly old to Davina. It smelled of must and disuse, like so many places where God wasn't worshiped except every third Sunday. She and Charlie sat on either side of their mother. Charlie wore black and cried; Betty Graham was very pale but kept control, even through the gruesome ritual at the graveside. Afterward everyone was invited back to Marchwood House. It had been very well arranged in Davina's absence. Charlie, belying her ethereal looks, had organized lunch for the fifty-odd mourners and stood shaking hands in the hall as they arrived.

Betty Graham was talking to Mary White and a retired rear admiral who had been at Dartmouth with her husband. Davina saw James White edging his way toward her. "My dear girl," he pecked at her cheek like a cold draft, not touching it with his lips. "What a sad day! Thank God it wasn't raining, I said to Mary this morning, if it rains I'm not going—I shan't be able to stand it. I was very fond of Fergus you know."

"I know," Davina answered. "You did wonders for Mum; she looks far stronger, and she's borne up so well. I don't know why we have to make such an ordeal out of funerals."

She lit a cigarette. There was no Walden at her elbow to nag her anymore.

"To convince ourselves it's not the end," he said. "I am the resurrection and the life. Marvelous words, aren't they? Do you believe they mean anything?"

"I don't know," Davina said quietly. "For Mum's sake I hope so. And for mine."

"Come outside, Davina," he suggested. "Let's get some air, it's stuffy in here." He took her by the elbow. "Now," he said, "Isn't that better?" He took a deep breath. "How is Charlie bearing up? Betty said she was hit very hard. . . . We had lunch, did I tell you?"

"No," Davina said, "You didn't."

"Oh, it was about two months ago. She asked a lot about Kidson. I'm afraid she's very bitter about that still."

"Yes, she's made that very plain since Father died," Davina answered. "She told me to get out of the house as soon as you took Mum back with you. So I did. I only came down this morning. I shan't stay if she's going to be here."

James White looked pained. You bloody hypocrite, Davina thought suddenly, you probably stirred it up when you saw her. You might have warned me anyway. But she shrugged mentally. It didn't matter. Her link with her mother was restored and stronger than ever. Charlie was of no importance; all she had ever brought Davina was unhappiness. Shut the door on your personal life. Shut out everything but work because that's the one thing you've got left and it won't let you down.

He guided her to a garden seat. "Shall we talk shop for a moment?"

"Why not?"

He lit his Sub Rosa cigarette, hesitated, then offered her one. When she took it he remarked, "You're smoking again, I see."

Davina ignored this remark. "You know Nikolaev was murdered." He nodded. Of course he knew; he had informants everywhere.

"We had Poliakov in our meeting on Sunday. He made one of his bloody-minded suggestions. I don't know whether to take it seriously or not."

"Unfortunately, nobody's been able to take Poliakov seriously for the last fifteen years. Was he sober? Or rather, how drunk was he?"

"Not at all," Davina answered. "Very on the ball. He says there's a link between the girl in Venice and the student in Paris. He suggested we send someone over to Paris and check on her ourselves."

White didn't say anything. He could imagine the old Russian putting that forward. Still living in the past when methods were so unorthodox. He waited for her to speak. If she decided as he hoped, he had a suggestion of his own.

"I think it's a good idea," she said after a while. "I don't believe we can hang about waiting for the report from our East German contact; if they've caught Nikolaev's killers, the Germans won't get hold of the details. So we could be up another blind alley there. The Italians are sweating the girl Valdorini, and they've got time on their side. Nobody who hasn't been hit has any time left. I think the old devil was right. We should go after the French girl ourselves in case she isn't genuine. SEDECE have taken the heat off her, and meantime nothing happens. What do you think?"

"I shouldn't give advice," he said smoothly, "but old habits die hard, my dear. I would do what Poliakov suggested. But there is one complication, isn't there?"

"We can't use one of our own operators," Davina said. "I thought of that. SEDECE would bring the roof down if they found we were interfering in their territory."

"You make it sound like a cowboy film," he chuckled. How he loved the possibility of intrigue. His eyes were sparkling with enjoyment.

"You won't like the idea, but you and I know the one man who'd be right for the job. He's been out of the Service for nearly two years, he's in a business that keeps people like him on their toes, and he's completely trustworthy. Colin Lomax."

"I had thought of him," she said calmly. "But I don't think he'd do it. We didn't part on the best of terms. He thought civilian Intelligence was a dirty game."

White laughed. "Nonsense," he said. "He objected to your being mixed up in a male preserve. And he was jealous. By the way, what did you do about Mr. Walden? Or don't you want to discuss it at the moment?"

"There's nothing to discuss," Davina said. "I faced him with the truth. He admitted he'd told me a pack of lies. I shan't be seeing him again. Let's get back to Lomax."

White eyed her carefully. "But you can't just leave Walden in midair," he remarked. "If he's under Soviet pressure ..." He didn't finish the sentence.

She said sharply, "I'll come to that later. Without me he's a busted flush for them anyway. What's happening in Europe is important; he isn't."

"You don't need to snap at me," he said. "I agree entirely. That's been your only fault, Davina; you've allowed yourself a personal life. It simply doesn't work with women. And I'm not being a chauvinist."

"I'll try Colin," she said. "I suppose we'd better go in. And I'd better talk to Charlie about Mum. She ought to go away for a bit."

She found her sister in the kitchen, supervising tea for those who were still there. The little boy, Fergie, was sitting with his nanny in the window seat, making gurgles of delight as she played airplanes with a spoon of jelly. Some things never changed, Davina thought; I can remember our old nurse doing exactly the same thing with me, but it was rice pudding, and I hated the stuff ...

"Charlie," she said. "Can we talk a minute?"

"What about?"

How she hates me; Davina looked away from her sister. "What's Mum going to do?"

Charlie went on laying out biscuits. "Peter and I are taking her to London tonight, when you've all gone," she said. "So you can get on with your marvelous top job, and not feel worried about her. She doesn't expect any help from you."

Davina glanced at the nanny and the little boy. Charlie had never minded making a scene in public. She couldn't bring herself to do the same. She walked out of the kitchen without answering.

Betty Graham looked white and exhausted; when Davina put an arm round her she was trembling. "You're going up to London with Charlie," she said. "Mum darling, I wish I could take you away, but I just can't leave my office at the moment. There's a real crisis blowing up. When it's over, we'll go off and have a nice holiday together. Anywhere you like. And I'll ring you—what's Charlie's number?"

"It's this Peter Vereker's number," her mother said gently. "He lives in Chester Street. She's got everything organized. I felt sure she would when she'd got over the shock of losing Daddy. And don't you worry about me, darling. You were here when I really needed someone. I'll ring you in a day or so. You look tired; you mustn't fret about it. I shall pull myself together and come home after I've had a break. Your father loved the house and the garden. I'm not going to neglect them. Goodbye, Davina. Take care of yourself, won't you?"

Igor Borisov went up in the private elevator to the president's apartment on the top floor of the Kremlin. Keremov was not well enough to come down to the weekly meeting of the Politburo; he was reserving his strength for a public appearance at the state funeral of his foreign minister. He sat upright in a chair, and he had visibly shrunk in the last few weeks. Folds of gray skin hung down from his jaw where the supportive fat had fallen away. He is dying, Borisov thought, and his heart quickened. And at the same time it was sad. The old man pointed to a chair beside him. "Sit down," he said, "and tell me about it."

"It was very carefully planned," Borisov said. "The car was attacked a mile outside the perimeter of the airport. Two rockets hit it; the car exploded like a firework." Keremov cleared his throat. He raised his head slowly and the little eyes fixed upon Borisov under their bushy eyebrows. Dying he might be, but he could stare down any man in Russia.

"Nikolaev was not a supporter of yours," he said. "Did you do this, Igor Igorovitch?"

Borisov held the old man's look.

"No, Little Father, I did not. It was my man Alexei who killed him, but he wasn't carrying out my orders."

"Nobody will believe that," Keremov said. "If you had the man alive he could have proved your innocence in front of the Politburo. Now you have no defense against what your enemies will say. Who turned your man, Alexei?"

"I wish I knew," Borisov answered. "They tried to make him say before he died. But all they got was one word. 'Russia.' "

"You mustn't punish the men who shot him," Keremov said

slowly. He lowered his eyelids, closed them, and waited.

Borisov said, "Punish them? They're the only witnesses I have. I've got them safe in Moscow. Hidden, where they can't be found. They heard him say that word. What it means we don't know. But somebody does. And that's all I have to work on."

Keremov's eyes opened; he smiled a little. No stress, no excitement, the fool doctors kept insisting. How could a man live under those strictures? "The American, the French, and now the Russian. There is a link between them all, isn't there."

"I am waiting," Borisov said, "before I commit myself to that."

"Waiting for what?"

"For the next attack. Two from the West, one from us. Or two from NATO and one from the Warsaw Pact. When the fourth happens, I shall be officially convinced. Unofficially, I am sure already."

He left the President soon afterward. The old man was visibly exhausted after their conversation. Borisov went back to his office. There was no Alexei waiting for him. No bodyguard, no mindless instrument of his superior's will.

"Russia." That was the only word he mumbled before he died from the bullets of the Polish and KGB security men who had hunted him along the road after the car had exploded. Alexei hadn't got far. He must have known his chances of escaping were almost nonexistent. The mission was what the KGB described as closed off. The operative carried out his orders and then committed suicide. Alexei killed without hesitation; he was prepared to die in the same fatalistic way. They had found an uncrushed cyanide capsule embedded in his upper tooth. When he was shot, shock broke the reflex mechanism in his brain. Dying, as they manhandled him he choked out that one word. "Russia." That was reflex too. But Borisov knew Alexei had made a kind of statement with that final word.

It was getting dark. From his office windows Borisov looked out over the panorama of the city, watching the lights spring up like jewels. On the top of Lenin's tomb the Red Star glowed like a drop of blood against the evening sky.

He couldn't have burdened the sick old man in the Kremlin with his fears. Keremov wanted him to succeed. He believed in Borisov's strength and skill. Only a man who possessed both qualities in superhuman degree could hope to rule Russia. There was nobody in the world Igor Borisov could tell that he was afraid, because for the first time in his life, he didn't know who his adversary was. All he could do was look around at his colleagues in the Kremlin and begin a process of elimination. Because nobody outside Russia could have made a traitor of Alexei.

Colin Lomax couldn't believe it. But the message was there on his ansaphone. Miss Graham would like you to call her. After six-thirty. A number he didn't know. She had moved from the apartment they shared together. It was a Belgravia exchange. He switched off the tape. It didn't affect him hearing from her suddenly like that. His love for her had died the night he found her locked in Tony Walden's arms. He had never really possessed her anyway. They had worked together in Mexico, became lovers and partners in the hunt for the traitor hidden inside SIS, but she had never really belonged to him. And in the end she had let herself be taken over by that whiz-bang advertising tycoon.

Lomax didn't hate people anymore. He hated the thugs his company contended with, but bank robbers and gangsters were faceless men. He had a very clear picture of Tony Walden and his hatred for him was purely personal. Why had she called? Why seek him out when there was no meeting point between them. He had resigned from SIS, gone into business with an old army friend, made a life for himself that was satisfying and free from emotional commitment. He had girl friends, but that was all they represented in his life. Women who were friends who slept with him. He had had his bellyful of love. He played back the message. If Davina had made the first move then there must be a damned good reason. Pride was her middle name. He remembered her saying it was his first. He waited until after six-thirty and then dialed.

She knew she would hear his voice. It was exactly six-thirty-five when her telephone rang. He was punctual to the minute, a man who never cut corners. That was what had made him so good at his job. "Colin? How are you?"

The faint Scots burr was emphasized on the telephone. "I'm fine, and yourself?"

"I'm fine too," she said. "Would you meet me? Something's come up and I'd like to talk to you about it."

There was a long pause. "Okay. Where?"

She said, suddenly, exasperated. "Stop being so bloody off-hand, Colin. It isn't easy for me to speak to you like this. If you don't want to meet, then say so!"

"I don't mind," his voice was cool, "so long as I don't see lover-boy."

She kept her temper this time. "Don't worry. You won't. Do you know the Bunch of Grapes in Brompton Road?"

"Lady, I know every pub in London. It'll take me about half an hour."

"I'll see you there, around seven." When Davina put back the receiver, it rattled. Her hand was not quite steady. She looked at herself in the mirror. It was a pale face, with lines on the forehead that hadn't been there when he knew her. A pale face with a tight mouth. Embittered and alone. She turned away quickly.

The Saloon Bar at the Bunch of Grapes was quite full, mostly young people having a drink before going home. Davina pushed her way through to the bar and ordered a whisky and soda. "You can make that two," Colin's voice said behind her.

He hadn't changed. The fair hair was shorter, the gray eyes still keen and colorless in the light. They didn't shake hands or touch. He paid for the drinks and carried them to a corner table. He sat down, put a packet of cigarettes on the table. She looked up in surprise. "You're not smoking, are you?"

The affair in Mexico had left him with only one damaged lung, and a later transplant had saved that.

"I have one now and again," he said. He offered her the packet. "Thanks."

For a while they sat in silence. Then he said, "You're not looking well."

"You haven't lost your tact, I see," Davina retorted. "I'm working very hard. That's why I called you."

"I didn't think it was for Auld Lang Syne," he said. "You looked tired and pissed off. What's the problem, Davina, besides lover-boy? How is he, by the way—still selling Tampax or whatever it is?" He reached out and lit a cigarette.

She couldn't stop herself. "You shouldn't, Colin," she said. "Put it out."

He looked at her and shook his head. "Still the bossiest woman I've ever met," he said. But there was no rancor in his voice. "Drink up; we'll have another and call a truce. How's that?"

"There's no point in my staying unless we do," she answered. "Before we get down to business I'll put one thing straight. There is no lover-boy. It's finished."

He raised his eyebrows, mocking her. "Already? That didn't last long. I did better than that. Did you kick him out?"

She didn't look at him.

"He kicked himself out. And it's none of your business, Colin. Make it a single this time. I've got to get my facts straight."

He laughed for the first time. "Don't give me that bullshit, darling. You have a head like a rock and you never balked up a fact in your life." As he took their empty glasses, she said, "One thing hasn't improved, and that's your language."

"I'm in a rough business," Lomax retorted. "And so are you."

Later he said, "So you're the Chief now? What do they call you, behind your back, I mean?"

Davina said, "The boss lady. I've got a pretty sharp assistant, one of the bright young career men. He started it."

Lomax grinned. "The boss lady. I suppose you'd be annoyed if I said it doesn't suit you?"

"I'd be much more annoyed if you said it did," she came back at him.

He picked up the empty glass. Davina took the opportunity. He had needed careful handling, but then he always did. Proud and quick to take offense. Never an easy man to deal with. "I'm in trouble," she said. "We've got a very nasty situation, and nobody competent to deal with it. Leave the drinking for the moment. Will you listen to me while I tell you about it?"

"I don't hear well on an empty stomach," Lomax said. "There's a steak house down the road. Let's get something to eat." He looked at his watch. "I'm meeting someone at ten-thirty."

Davina got up. "Let's go, then. We can walk, can't we? I found a place to put my car. This is a rotten area for parking."

"Yes," he agreed, opening the door for her into the street. "Marylebone was better." That was where their apartment had been. She walked into Brompton Road and didn't answer.

While she explained the situation, Lomax didn't ask a superfluous question or interrupt. When she finished he took his time before he made a comment. "Why don't you get an independent to check on this girl for you? There are plenty of them around."

It was very calmly said, a friend offering advice. She hadn't asked him to take on the job, but he had just said he wouldn't.

"Colin," she looked him in the eye. "You're the one we want. Don't toss it out of the window like that."

He leaned back in his chair, hands behind his head. He had a broad chest and heavily muscled arms. She knew his body well. Too well. But nothing moved her anymore.

"I tossed the whole thing out of the window when you walked out on me," he said. "Now you and the Service are in a fix, so it's send for Lomax. I'm not amenable to orders anymore, Davina. I'm not in the army and I resigned from your gang. I'm not going back."

"I'm not asking you to come back," she countered. "This is a one-shot assignment. A freelance job, and I'm in a position to pay very well. Colin, this isn't a personal issue between you and me. That's over. You've got your life, and I've got mine. This is to fight something important. Organized assassination. Can't you think of it like that?"

"I've spent the best part of my life thinking of it," he said. "I've got a body full of bomb splinters and a rubber lung to prove it. Don't give me the morality bit, Davina. There is nothing to choose between their lot and yours." For a moment the pale eyes narrowed. She saw it and knew she had made a mistake somewhere. "Tell me about the pay."

"If that's your attitude these days, I wouldn't give you a brass farthing," she snapped at him. "Forget I mentioned it."

Lomax leaned forward and rested his elbows on the table. "Didn't fall into that one, did you? Clever girl. I wouldn't take any bloody money if I did do the job, and you nearly screwed up everything by mentioning it, didn't you? What kind of rubbish are you working with anyway?"

She reached for his cigarettes. "Oh, shut up," she said.

"You smoke too much." He put his hand over the packet. "How are the family?"

"My father died a fortnight ago."

He was genuinely upset. "Oh, hell—I'm sorry. What about your mother?"

"It was an awful shock, but Charlie's looking after her for the moment. I've promised her a holiday when I've got this business under control."

He was watching her intently. "How's Charlie?"

"Much the same. She's got herself a new man, and she hates my guts because I blew the whistle on John." She gave him a quick glance. "She wouldn't be too keen on you either, come to that. We did do a good job of work together."

He laughed. "You don't give up, do you? Flattery will get you everywhere. But not this time, darling."

She picked up her bag. "Do you mind not calling me that? It doesn't sound friendly. If you've got an appointment at ten-thirty, you'd better get the bill." She opened her bag and began to count out money. Lomax said very quietly, "Just put that away, will you?" She shut the bag. "Thanks for dinner, Colin."

He walked with her to her car. "Good luck, darling," he said. "And it is friendly, I promise you . . . I hope you get this business sorted out." He waited while she started the car, then lifted his hand in a slow salute to her and turned away.

His bell rang at ten-forty-five. He opened the door and kissed the girl outside. "Sorry I'm late," she said.

"How did it go?" Lomax asked and kissed her again.

"Not bad," she said after a while; "it'll make a good family series. Dead boring, but it'll run for *ever*."

Lomax didn't ask anymore about the series or her part, or the day spent at the TV studios, until they were undressed and in bed. "Making love to soap opera," he murmured. "It'll be a new experience . . ."

She giggled and held him off long enough to murmur, "It always is with you . . ."

She left early the next morning; they had bacon and eggs together, which she cooked. She was a very sexy girl, who liked making love but didn't have any hangups about playing house.

Lomax's office was a smart address and the office was in an unobtrusive building off the main Tottenham Court Road. But he and his ex-SIS colleague Captain Foster were making money out of protecting the vulnerable. Small businesses with a payroll to bring in used Foster and Lomax, Inc., to guard against robberies; the jeweler carrying diamonds or keys to his safe was protected by one of the company's men. Business flourished, which meant that crime was doing nicely too, as Foster said. He was in the small interior room that they used as their private office when

Lomax arrived. He looked up and grinned. "You look rough," he said. "Have a good time last night?"

Lomax sat at his desk, leafed quickly through the opened mail. "Not very," he said.

Foster looked up. "I thought you were seeing Joan?"

"I was," Lomax was reading his mail. "Trouble is, I didn't get much sleep. Not the way you're thinking, cock. I mean I didn't *get* to sleep. How busy are we?"

"Today?" Foster was also reading, not really paying attention.

"No, not today. Generally. How busy are we?"

"Busy enough, why?"

Lomax shuffled the letters and clipped them together.

"Because I'm going to take some time off," he said. "I'm going to Paris. I can't say how long for, but give it a couple of weeks anyway. You can manage, can't you?"

Foster looked hard at him. "It doesn't sound like pleasure."

"It isn't. More like damned lunacy. Let's get on with it today, then. I'll leave things in good order for you."

Foster and he had been friends and colleagues in places as far apart and as dangerous as Oman and Belfast. "No questions, Colin?"

"No questions, Jim."

The head of the Special Branch had gone through a list of the speakers at the CND rally. It was the climax to the great peace march that had brought Central London to a halt. Supporters had streamed in from all over the country. There had been endless marches converging on London and the finale was the meeting in the Albert Hall for an audience of selected delegates from the CND branches all over the United Kingdom. The speeches would be relayed to a vast gathering outside, confined to Hyde Park. There was almost a festival atmosphere; MacNeil was glad about that. The vast crowd was good-humored, determined to keep its dignity and its public image intact. He wasn't too interested in his colleagues' nightmares about crowd control and possible clashes with fringe mobs of neo-Fascists. That wasn't his worry. The bloody subversives hiding behind the genuine pacifists were what bothered him. The principal speaker was a well-known left-wing politician, openly in contention with his party and its leader on all the major topics, especially the possession of nuclear arms. There was nothing subversive about him, MacNeil grimaced. It just gave Special Branch a pain in the ass trying to protect the damned idiot.

The next-most-influential member of the peace movement was a vociferous Anglican priest. Father Marnie was no ascetic, no spiritual descendant of John Knox, thundering against the evil doers. He was a rotund, kindly Christian soul with a fanatical belief in the principle of Christian meekness preserving the earth instead of trying to inherit it. He had aroused no passions, and he didn't rate a star on MacNeil's list of security risks. He wasn't likely to be assassinated, or to be secretly in Russian pay.

The rally was timed for seven o'clock that night. All day the crowds had been pouring into London. Banners were waved, songs sung, slogans chanted. There were women with children in arms, couples pushing prams, stalwarts who had marched from the Midlands and the North. Members of all political parties, Trade Unionists, nuns and atheists side by side with grandparents and teenage boys and girls. Impressive, he had to admit. But mistaken. How mistaken to think you could buy off the bloody Bear by dropping your fists and showing him a noble example.

MacNeil had his eye on some of those who organized behind the scenes. They didn't call attention to themselves. They didn't get arrested or sent to jail. They were what he called the paper workers. They set up the protests and let the faithful take the consequences. Always last in the street and first on the telephone to the media.

He had decided to go to the Albert Hall himself that evening. A bird's eye view was available to him, high above the stage. His men were positioned up there too, where they could watch for anything unexpected in the crowd.

The crowd opened the rally by singing the anthem to peace. Even MacNeil was impressed by the volume and sincerity of that hymn to human survival. Then the speeches began. Two were comparatively short. They congratulated the ordinary men and women who had gathered in London and whose example had made such an impression outside Britain. They introduced the Anglican priest. There was long and sustained applause for him and some cheering. He was very popular. Down in the crowd, close to the rostrum, a group of boys and girls were leading the clapping. They raised their arms high and beat their hands together above their heads. A young man in jeans and sweatshirt with the emblem of the dove printed on his chest shouted louder and clapped harder than anyone. The good minister smiled and waved his arms, trying to get the crowd to settle. Banners were unfurled. The white dove on a deep blue background, olive branch in its beak, waved and danced in the auditorium. Slogans undulated on their placards as they were waved triumphantly in the air.

"Isn't he marvelous?" the girl next to the young man in the noisiest group shouted to him, and he shouted back. "Yes, look at his face. It's shining!" He leaped up and opened a banner with the letters painted in red. "Blessed are the Peacemakers."

He was less than twelve feet from the smiling priest, who was trying to hush his supporters. He furled his banner loosely and drew the gun out of his cowboy boot. Behind the shelter of the banner he slipped the safety catch, then opened the banner again and took aim behind it through a slit that gave him a clear view of his target. He waited until there was a final roar of affection, then fired four shots in succession. The bullets had a secondary explosive charge, which caused enormous damage upon impact with the human body. The priest fell like someone dropping off a cliff, arms outstretched and mouth agape in shock. He was dead even before anyone on the platform reached him. The man who was called "Ireland" had joined the scrambling, hysterical crowd in a stampede toward the exits. He had vanished before MacNeil and his men got down into the body of the hall.

"It's like a nightmare," Davina said. She was watching the television news. Humphrey, Tim Johnson, other members of the staff were gathered round the set. Everyone had been recalled. Colin Lomax was in the background keeping himself apart from them. He had been called round to Anne's Yard for a private briefing. There was nothing private about it now. Hundreds had been injured in the panic that followed the assassination. Some were seriously hurt. Earnest commentators came and went, giving their views; eyewitnesses reported, some so harrowed that they broke down and cried.

"Well," Humphrey remarked, "at least it's over, that's one thing. We've been biting our nails waiting for it to happen here. And without being callous, it could have been worse."

Davina turned on him angrily. "Worse? Good God, that man

dead and all those poor devils injured! I don't know what you'd call worse!"

"A head of state murdered." Humphrey was unmoved by her reproof. "Supposing they'd picked on the German president instead . . . or the queen's birthday parade? We've got to be realistic. It could have been much worse for us." He hunched up his thin body and stared at the television screen.

"I'm waiting for the first report from MacNeil," Davina said. "But so far whoever did it got clear. Naturally enough in that crowd."

"With close on a quarter of a million in that march and three thousand inside the hall, nobody could stop a professional from getting away with it," Johnson said. From his position in the background, Colin Lomax sized him up. He'd been briefly introduced. Foxy-faced, sharp as a tack. That was the new assistant Davina had mentioned. Lomax recognized the type, and didn't care for it much. He didn't think Davina would either. And then he wondered why that should concern him. It was none of his business what she felt about other men. He'd misjudged her badly once; she had a weakness he had never suspected. There was no other way he could account for Tony Walden. He looked at his watch. He was catching the plane at eight the next morning. He wanted his instructions and background information so he could get back to his apartment. He didn't want to stay with this little group clustered round Davina, watching the same ugly scenes flashed on and off and hearing the same lugubrious commentaries. He came forward and lightly touched her arm. "Any chance we can finish my end of it?"

She had forgotten him for the moment. Venice, Paris, Warsaw, London. A nightmare was an understatement.

"I haven't got all night to hang around," he said curtly.

"I'm sorry," Davina said. "Tim'll come to your flat and bring the relevant stuff with him. He knows the set-up in Paris."

Lomax felt like taking her by the shoulders and shaking her till her teeth rattled. "You asked me to do this," he snapped. "You send in that ginger-headed bugger and the deal's off. I'm at 443 the Barbican, East!" She smiled at him. "You haven't changed a bit, have you?"

"Well you have," he said. "And I don't like it. You come or I don't go tomorrow. I mean it."

"I know you do," she said. "You price yourself very high these days, Colin, but I need you. I'll get over to your flat as soon as I can." She turned away from him and didn't see him leave.

There was nothing new from the Special Branch. No weapon had been found, no eyewitnesses could help. MacNeil and his observers had seen nothing to alert them. They had spent hours sifting through the debris of torn banners and smashed placards that littered the hall. The only thing beyond dispute was that the killer had been close to the rostrum, because the gun that fired that caliber of bullet was a P-32 and they weren't accurate beyond a range of thirty feet.

MacNeil sounded depressed and frustrated; the number of bloodies in his conversation on the phone were almost three to one with every other word. That was a sure sign of deadlock in an SB investigation. Davina packed up; the night staff came on duty and the rest dispersed home. It was nearly eleven o'clock.

She surprised Tim Johnson by asking for the file and briefing material for Lomax. "I'll take it to him," he offered. He was curious about the major. He'd heard rumors that he and the formidable Miss Graham had once been very close.

"No thanks, Tim. I've brought him in on this and he's insisting that I stay with it."

Johnson said, "That's a bit unreasonable, isn't it? You have got other priorities."

"He wouldn't agree otherwise." Davina pulled on her jacket. He wasn't quick enough to help her into it. She didn't wait around for men to pay her little attentions. He felt that she didn't even expect them anymore. "And unreasonable is exactly what he is. However, we need him; more than ever after this! So I'm going to do your job for you, if you don't mind." She smiled slightly at him. "We used to work together. He was always a bit tricky. Goodnight. See you in the morning."

He liked her for that. She had the knack of suddenly showing a human side. It caught him off guard more often than not. He really didn't expect to like her, but it was happening just the same.

Davina drove fast through the city. The streets were empty of traffic; it was quiet, almost eerie, with deserted streets and lightless windows. As if the war all those people were so determined to prevent had stolen up on them and she was a survivor, driving through a dead city to meet the only man left alive.

"You've got a very nice flat," she commented.

"It does," he answered. "I can run to baked beans if you haven't eaten."

"Just coffee, please," Davina sat down and unlocked her brief-case. He went out and she heard a distant clatter from the kitchen. He always made a noise when he did the simplest do-mestic task. And a mess. Making a cup of tea left more debris than when she cooked them dinner. They had lived in Marylebone in a small rented apartment, owned by the Service. Funny to remem-ber how happy they had been for a time. And then not happy. This was a homely place. She wondered if he had a woman living with him. There was a big bowl of roses on the table. That surely answered her question.

"The one thing that strikes me about these killings," Lomax said after he'd read through the reports, "is that there's no con-nection between the victims. Franklyn, okay. American, hard-liner. Some anti-nuclear freak might take a pot at him." He glanced at her briefly. "But he wouldn't have the know-how to blow up that launch and get himself out of the way, with a safe house lined up for him. That sounds like a pro to me. Point one. The next on the list is the exact opposite of Franklyn. Isabelle Duvalier; French Socialist minister, women's rights, gay rights, the whole left-liberal bandwagon.

"A massacre there, taking out the whole family. Again, a cold professional killing. No trace. Only possible witness left besides the staff is a student friend of the daughter, crashed out on sleep-ing pills upstairs.

"Then we have Nikolaev. According to this he's a Soviet hard-liner at heart, not too popular with Keremov, but a career man who's known to trim to the winds. He gets blown to bits by an anti-tank rocket. That, my dear boss lady, is Professional with a capital P. They seem to have got the killer that time, if your in-formation is right. But nobody's passing any details. Next we have, immediately after the Soviet Hawk, the Christian Dove. One victim supports nuclear threat, the next is one of the found-ers of the peace movement. Those bullets are shit; you haven't got a chance if one hits you. A competent marksman gets four of them in and disappears in the panic.

"So what the hell is anyone to make of it? Where's the link be-tween these four people that a very well-organized group have set out to kill them, one by one? Nobody's claimed responsibility.

No political advantage has accrued to anyone by these deaths. It doesn't make sense. It might, except that Nikolaev got it. That's blown the obvious answer to hell and gone."

Davina's coffee was cold. She pushed the cup aside.

"I was sure Borisov was behind it," she said. "Even now I'm not quite prepared to give that up. Nikolaev wasn't an ally; he might just have used the other killings to cover an assassination of his own."

Lomax gave her a mocking grin; he shook his head. "That's not good enough," he said. "Not up to the old Davina standard. If Borisov wanted to get rid of a party enemy, he'd do it nice and quietly. This was a bloody public murder, and they haven't even tried to pretend that the Poles were responsible. You'll have to sharpen up. That's sloppy thinking."

Davina said curtly, "Maybe if you were as tired as I am—" She stopped, angry because she had defended herself. He was right; it was sloppy thinking. Ignoring the obvious. The KGB had disposed of public men in Russia with a pinprick in the arm. They didn't need to fire a rocket at them. And yet . . .

He watched the expressions changing on her face. She'd lost that guarded "I'm here on a professional basis" look. Tired, yes. Unhappy; depressed wasn't a word Lomax liked, but it seemed to fit her as she sat there, frowning, thinking in that incisive and unorthodox way he knew so well. He had needled her, which was unnecessary. But the urge to bring her down a notch was stronger than he reckoned. He hated her coolness and the efficient Head of Department aura that she wasn't even aware of now. He shouldn't have resented it, but he did. He'd goaded her into the sharp exchanges. They were a relief, and a reminder. He lit a cigarette and passed it to her. "If we could get to the girl in Italy," he said.

Davina dismissed the suggestion. "We can't, Colin. Medina has got her sealed up. And she hasn't broken, or this last murder wouldn't have happened. Medina would've given us a lead once he knew it was more than Italian terrorists; that's what they're so cagey about. The Red Brigade and what happened to Moro have left a real scar."

"This student," Lomax said after a minute, looking back over the file, "there's nothing to connect her with what happened. Except being lucky enough to get a sick headache on the night."

"I don't believe in that kind of luck," Davina answered. "I said as much to SEDECE. The colonel disagreed. They've checked and double-checked, but she's absolutely clean."

He went on, "It says she's living with her aunt and attending school. No regular boy friends, normal social contacts. No medical treatment after the first few days on sedatives after the murders. A lot of girls take a Valium if they have a row with the boy friend." He put the file aside. "But not this one. She wakes up in a house where her best friend and the rest of the family have been gunned down and within a fortnight she's back at her studies and going on as if nothing had happened."

"What's your plan of campaign?" Davina asked.

"I'll know more when I've made contact with her."

Davina looked up in surprise. "You're going to try a direct approach?"

"Why not? Investigating her hasn't turned up anything. And SEDECE are damned good. I'll see what the personal approach digs up." He pulled the identifying photograph out of its cellophane slip. "Not bad-looking; but why do girls have that awful butch haircut? She'd be quite pretty if she let it grow. I'm glad you haven't cropped yours."

"I don't have time to worry about hair styles these days."

He leaned back, crossing one leg over the other. He no longer wore the faded jeans that had irritated her when they first met. But then he was out of the Service. He was a respectable director of a security firm. Somehow he looked odd in the dark suit.

"Do you want to tell me about lover-boy?" he said.

"No," Davina replied. "And don't keep calling him that. It sounds childish."

Lomax laughed out loud. "I am childish; I pick up a catch-phrase and I can't stop saying it. What do you suggest I call him? Tony? Mr. Walden? I can think of other names."

"Colin, I don't think this is a good idea. You're just in a bloody-minded mood and having a go. Things were going wrong with us before he came into my life. We would have broken up anyway."

"I'm not denying that," he answered. "What I don't like is the sneaky way the bastard winkled his way in. He had the money and the style."

She felt her face burn. "How dare you say it had anything to do with money!"

"What was it then? Sex?"

Davina stood up. "I'm going," she said. "I know you when you're like this. You want to pick a fight, and I'm not playing. I'll wait to hear from you in Paris. Where's my coat?"

"I hung it up outside," Lomax said. He didn't move to get it for her. "I'll have to work fast," he remarked. "I can't leave my outfit for more than a fortnight."

Davina stopped by the door. "Don't be ridiculous!" she said. "You can't put a time limit on a thing like this!"

"I have," he remarked. "Two weeks, darling. That's all. I'll be in touch. You can see yourself out, unless you want to sit down and be civilized."

"With you," she snapped, "I'm afraid it's just not possible. I haven't started sniping at you over your private life. And whoever arranged those roses should go and take a course!"

"She's not very good at it," Lomax agreed. "But she's a simple girl; not very high-powered. You wouldn't have much in common."

Suddenly Davina's anger drained away. "No," she said. "I don't suppose we would. If you're honest with yourself, Colin, you'll stop blaming Tony Walden. It was my job that really came between us. Not him." She opened the apartment door and let herself out.

Lomax flew into Charles de Gaulle Airport the next morning. He had booked himself into a modest pension on the Left Bank; he carried a minimum of luggage and a draft for a thousand pounds drawn ·on the Crédit Lyonnais. All expenses paid. He spent the afternoon wandering round the city, getting his bearings. He didn't feel comfortable in Paris; it was too artificial, too cold-hearted in its symmetrical beauty to appeal to him. London was shabby and meandering and unplanned. He preferred it. He preferred the Highlands of his native Scotland or the rain-swept bleakness of Northern Ireland to any city.

He located the lycée where Helene Blond studied; walked past it several times, noted the students coming out at the end of the day. He didn't attempt to identify the girl. He had to fix the time-table in his mind first. She could have been among the throng of young men and women who streamed out into the evening sunlight and made their way home. He took the metro to the unfashionable suburb where the girl's aunt lived.

He cruised past the apartment block, and then told the cab to return to the center of Paris. He treated himself to dinner at a restaurant recommended by Foster. Superb food, French prices, and no tourists. He sat on drinking coffee and ordered an Armagnac. The Service was paying.

Davina kept coming into his mind. He sipped at his brandy and let the memories flicker back. The first time he saw her, in the grand Wiltshire manor house, Labradors to order, ancestors on the walls. He had disliked her on sight. An uppity, bossy woman, oversure of herself in a professional role. But not sure of herself as a woman. He had detected that very quickly. And she was easy to needle, quick to rise when goaded. A brave lassie, but oversharp, his father would have described her. God, Lomax thought, finishing his drink, how much I loved her. We started out in the worst way, and ended in the best. Or so it seemed until that last assignment. Davina had set out to find the traitor who was operating within the top level of the SIS. Success had wrecked her sister Charlie's marriage; caused a break with her father that hadn't been mended before he died, and brought another man into Davina's life at the crucial psychological moment.

And Lomax had fallen out of love with her. The disillusionment had been bitter; he had stopped trusting her because his instincts detected a change. She was slipping away from him, borne by the current of dedication to her job. The man who took her away from him didn't present a challenge, he could see that now. He made no demands, offered no competition. He was another hungry tiger, prowling his world in search of money and success. He had offered freedom to Davina, where Lomax wanted strings. Permanent strings, like a home and a wedding ring and all the old-fashioned things like children that went with it. He sighed. Hitting out at her was futile, and even unfair. But human. He didn't love her anymore. He had remade his life, formed his relationships and kept the whole thing under control. Now here he was in Paris, getting involved in the squalid world of SIS, which he had grown to despise. Because she'd asked him. He paid the bill and walked slowly back to his pensione. He fell asleep wondering what kind of girl Helene Blond would turn out to be. The next day he'd make his first move toward finding out.

The wardress made a lot of noise when she unlocked the cell. Elsa Valdorini sat on the edge of the hard chair and waited. She saw the wardress on duty when her breakfast was pushed inside on a metal tray, and again when she was taken for half an hour's exercise round a deserted inner yard, the silent guardian a few paces behind her. She had begun by refusing to walk at the prescribed pace. She didn't defy authority anymore. She exercised as she was told, ate the food, cleaned the spartan cell to their satisfaction, and lay through the endless nights on the iron-hard bed, sometimes sleeping, often awake in her despair. Nothing had happened for so long. She had no watch, no radio, no books, no newspapers. Nobody was cruel; if the rules were broken she didn't get her food and the lights were left on, glaring down on her all night, with constant supervision through the observation hole in the door. Her nerves frayed but nobody took any notice when she screamed abuse and obscenities. If they were listening, there was no reaction. She might as well have been an animal, snarling defiance at captors who didn't understand and didn't care.

The sense of deprivation, of monotony without end was the worst. She was prepared for interrogation, for conflict. But there was nobody to challenge her. Just a system that ordered her life and went on regardless if she chose to disobey. She had lost count of time. She had stopped wondering whether her parents were trying to help her, get a lawyer, or insist on a trial. She had hated the thought of them, despised them for so long; but for a long time now she had hoped they might help her. That hope had withered too. She cried a lot, sniffling and weeping, denied even the comfort of a handkerchief, so that her sleeves were wet and slimed from wiping her running nose. She had no looking glass, no makeup. Only a blunt-edged comb, a cake of harsh soap, and a towel. She had forgotten how she used to look.

When the door to her cell opened she was suddenly shaking with fear. The routine had been broken.

Alfredo Modena stood looking at her. The big uniformed figure of the woman guard loomed behind him, making him look shorter and slighter than he really was. He advanced a few steps inside. "How are you, Elsa?"

She paused for a moment, focusing on him. She had a tiger's heart and it came to her rescue then. "What the fuck do you want?" Suddenly she felt better; energy returned and her sallow face flooded with color.

Modena said mildly, "I've come to take you out of here. We're going to take a trip." He spoke softly to the woman behind him. She came in with Elsa's jacket in her hand. "Put this on," she said.

The girl didn't argue. She struggled into the coat, which hung loosely on her.

"Come on." Obediently, Elsa followed the guard outside. Fear and hope competed. A trip . . . to court? A trial? No. No, an interrogation. She didn't mind that. She didn't mind being asked questions. It would be a relief if they hit her or hurt her.

She thought suddenly, "They've got him! They've got that arrogant shit who did the killing and wouldn't sleep with me."

"Hurry up," the wardress said and gave her a slight push in the small of the back. She increased her steps.

They traveled in a car. She could see out of the windows. Normal life bustling past her, people jaywalking through the Rome traffic, the sun beating down, dust, smells of food and refuse in the air, the glimpse of landmarks that mocked her, reminding her of freedom.

"It's not Venice," Modena remarked. "But Rome is just as beautiful. Have you been here before?"

"Yes," she muttered, not meaning to answer. "Twice."

"With your family?"

She nodded. The word was emotive. She hated her parents. She hated everything they stood for. But the word family made her eyes sting.

They had been driving for almost an hour. She could tell, because she could see the watch on his wrist. They were leaving the city behind them, traveling along the sweep of the Appian Way. No trial. No interrogation either. Out into the countryside. But where? What was at the end of it for her? She said, "Open the window, I feel sick."

The wardress was on the other side of her. She looked at Modena. He said, "You're only sick because you're afraid, we're nearly there."

They had left the main highway. The road was bumpy, the countryside flat and desolate, with a few sparse vineyards that looked untended. And then she saw the place. There was a road leading up to it. It had been built a long time ago, when the thickness of the walls could withstand the siege engines of the Middle Ages.

As the car approached, a massive door opened and they were inside the fortress. Modena got out. Elsa Valdorini stayed huddled tightly into the seat, her body refusing to move.

"You've got to get out here," he said. The powerful woman gripped her and she was lifted out and set down on the ground. The walls rose round her like a cliff. There was no sign of life. Modena said, "You don't know about this place, do you Elsa?"

She didn't answer, but continued to stare around her.

"It was built by the Sforza in 1480. They controlled the countryside round here for hundreds of miles. This was their headquarters when they went campaigning against the Borgias."

"Thanks for the history lesson," she managed to jeer, but it wasn't convincing. "It was the place they held their hostages," Modena continued. "And their important prisoners. Nobody ever came out alive when they were shut up here. And now it's been put to use again. This way."

She followed him with the woman behind her. They went in through a side entrance. It was an amazing transformation. The inside of the shell had been made into a honeycomb of stairs leading to one landing of cells after another. The stairwells were heavily protected by steel mesh; fierce lights played overhead, and uniformed guards patrolled the landings.

Modena paused, spoke gently to her, "We'll go to the women's section. There are only half a dozen women in here."

They climbed down a flight of steps. An official joined them, and gave the girl a searching look. A look so coldly calculating that she shivered. And she heard him say in a quiet voice to Modena, "Is she coming to us, Signore?"

She didn't hear the answer. They were still going down. Down into the bowels of the dreadful place, with its reinforced walls painted a steely gray and the unblinking lights overhead. Alfredo Modena stopped in front of a row of metal doors. The upper part was a square of unbreakable glass. "Prisoners are observed all the time here," he remarked. "The cameras are never switched off. And the guards keep a watch through the glass. They aren't allowed to speak to the prisoners or have any contact. They serve the food through the flap. Open the door, please."

The man in uniform stepped forward, pressed an unseen mechanism and the door swung open. Modena put his hand on her arm. "I want you to take a good look inside," he said. "I want you to see for yourself."

There was a canvas cot and a canvas chair. A small table was bolted to the floor. There was no window, only an extractor fan and ventilator. The light glared overhead in a protective steel cage. The walls were padded.

She couldn't move. Her limbs felt paralyzed, and a scream was welling up and threatening to tear her to pieces. She felt his hand on her arm again, urging her to cross the threshold into the cell. "No! No!" she thought she was shouting but it was a whimpering cry.

Modena drew her away from the open door. "Calm yourself," he said quietly. "You're not going in there."

She needed the woman's support to get her up the stairs and back onto the main floor. Modena showed her into a room that was simply furnished, with a table, several chairs, and a religious print on the wall. "Sit down, Elsa." He stretched a little, and wandered round the room. She sat watching him, hands clenched on her shaking knees. He lit a cigarette, hesitated, and then offered her one. The wardress stood with her back leaning against the door.

Elsa said through lips stiff with terror, "Stuff yourself!"

Modena shrugged. He put the cigarette back in the packet and away in his pocket. "You're a brave woman," he said. "I have to admit that. That's why I brought you here. I knew that telling you about this place wouldn't frighten you. You had to see it with your own eyes."

"I haven't been tried!" She cried out. "You can't hold me forever." "Not forever," he agreed. "But for a year or two. And by the time you do come to a court, you won't be fit to plead. You saw the room, didn't you? You know why it's fitted up like that? Women go mad in this place. You will go mad like the others." He spoke to the impassive woman at the door. "You can wait outside." The warden glanced toward the girl. Modena shook his head. "I can manage. If I need you, I'll call." She went outside and closed the door. Then he sat down. "If you don't talk to me, you will be sent here by the end of the week. Everything is prepared for you. Nobody cares, Valdorini, what happens to you now. Your family have abandoned you. You realize they haven't even tried to help you. You're not news anymore. The world has forgotten you. Your friends, the ones who recruited you and let you take the blame for something you didn't do—they've forgotten you too."

Elsa didn't answer. He sat patiently, smoking his cigarette down to the filter. Her head sank, and her hands came up and covered her face. He listened to her crying. After a while he said, "Are you going to condemn yourself to this, for the rest of your life? You didn't throw the bomb, Elsa. But you sheltered the person who did. Think of yourself now, while you have the chance. And it's the last chance. If you refuse me, I shall forget you. Like all the rest. Then you'll be really lost. Buried alive, in that cell I showed you. Talk to me, Elsa." He waited. Very slowly she lifted her head, wiped her blotched face with her hand and then the hand on her skirt.

"It was a man," she said. "He stayed for two nights."

6

LOMAX spent the next three days following Helene Blond. He followed her from her aunt's apartment to the lycée every morning. He noticed that she frequented a small café two streets away for lunch. He also noticed that she seemed to avoid her fellow students.

Lomax, hiding behind a newspaper and dark glasses, watched her carefully, and judged that she was definitely not part of any group. She didn't talk much or laugh with the others. Her companions were typical of their age; cheerful, disputatious, or conspicuously in love and holding hands. Helene Blond didn't fit in anywhere. Perhaps the ordeal she had gone through had made her withdrawn. Perhaps she didn't feel at ease among her contemporaries anymore, after the death of her friends the Duvaliers. Her best friend had been the daughter. But there was no obvious sign of nerves. She seemed to have a good appetite. She was a very cool young woman, Lomax decided. Aloof and self-sufficient.

After the third day he made himself noticeable. He followed her from the lycée to the café, took a seat quite close, and let her catch him watching her. He did this for two days until the weekend. Then he shadowed her home. He parked on the other side of the road in his hired car with the window down, and made a clumsy job of pretending to read a newspaper when she came out. He followed her on foot when she went shopping with her aunt. She knew he was there; he saw her glance behind her, scowl, and hurry on. She didn't lose him; she wouldn't until he decided to step out of sight. He passed the house three times during the Sunday morning, and glanced up at the windows. He saw the curtains move. On Monday, her aunt drove her to school. He wondered what excuse Helene had given.

By Wednesday she knew he was there and she was rattled. She actually went white when she saw him come through the door into the café and sit down. He didn't look at her. He ordered something to eat, and while he waited, pretended to read a paperback. She didn't finish her lunch. She paid her bill and hurried out. Lomax put his book down and caught her eye. He looked away. He didn't get up and go after her. But he was parked outside the lycée when she came out.

Helene dived down into the metro; she was nearly running by this time. She bought her ticket, jumped in the train and settled back out of breath. Who was the man who was shadowing her? He didn't look French. He wasn't even very skillful about it. She wished her heart would stop jumping up and down. She wasn't afraid; she had faced the professional inquisitors of the SEDECE and the police, and kept her head. Rather enjoyed the challenge.

But then she was prepared. Geared up to the game of wits on which her life depended. She wasn't expecting this. She cursed under her breath. Her language was vile by any standard. Her aunt wouldn't have believed she even knew such words. She never used them out loud. What did he want, this clumsy shadower? Should she report it? No; the publicity had died away. The police weren't interested in her anymore. She was out of the limelight and safe. Perhaps she should challenge him. Maybe he was some kind of crank, picking on her because of her involvement in a mass murder? She didn't like to think that. It made her nervous.

When she left the metro station and came up into the street, she paused, looking this way and that. Lomax saw her, but she didn't see him. He saw the furtive look, and the relief on her face.

By the time she reached her front door, he was well ahead of her, and standing with a map in his hand only a few yards away.

He actually heard her gasp when she saw him. He didn't move. He didn't look up. She opened the door and he heard it bang as she slammed it shut. The way a woman shuts a door when she's afraid, not angry.

The next day he didn't go near the house, the lycée or the café. He spent the day in Paris, enjoying himself, wandering round the Tuileries and the Louvre. He thought how surprised Davina would be if she could see him. Art collections and museums used not to be high on his list of activities. But he had changed since they parted. His life had slowed down from the old hectic momentum. He had set out to enlarge his horizons. After all, he should have been dead on at least two occasions. Once in Ulster and again in Mexico. Medical science and old-fashioned luck had given him a second chance each time. He made up his mind not to waste it. By seven o'clock the next morning he was outside Helene's metro station, and this time he followed her down and onto the train. She jumped out at an early stop, but he didn't attempt to follow. It was an old trick to suspend the harassment and give the victim a brief feeling of security. When it started again, the impact was doubled. He wondered how long she would go before she either faced him or did what he hoped. Made a contact and asked for help. If she went to the police, then she would be quite a way to establishing her innocence. Lomax felt instinctively that she wouldn't.

She didn't leave the lycée that lunchtime. That meant she was getting really jumpy. At the end of the day Helene Blond was not among the crowd that flowed into the street. Lomax drove away, parked his car, and slipped back to watch. She came out an hour after everyone else had gone. She hurried down the road, not looking to right or left; she thought she had given him the slip. He was well satisfied to let her think so. Until she arrived home. He'd decided to take it one stage further, to precipitate a move on her part. There were areaways to each house; he got there ahead of her and went down the basement steps of the house two doors away. From there he could see her approach. She was at the front door, taking out her key, when he came up behind her. She gave a cry and swung round; the keys clattered to the ground. Lomax picked them up. He held them out to her. For a moment her eyes blazed at him, fierce with terror and defiance. It was a look he'd seen before, and it had nothing to do with an innocent girl afraid of being molested. In that second, Lomax knew that Davina's instinct had been right again. The key to the Duvaliers' massacre was standing in front of him. "You dropped your keys, Mademoiselle," he said.

"Get away from me! Stop following me or I'll call the police!"

"I want to warn you," he said carefully, speaking his slow precise French. "The others have been killed. You will be next."

The words meant nothing to Lomax. But they did to her. He could see by the instant contraction of the pupils in her eyes. He'd made a meaningless threat and it had worked. He turned away before she could say anything and hurried off down the street.

From now on, he would be watching but she wouldn't see him.

Brunson of the CIA was as good as his word. His investigator in Venice had turned up some information and followed it through. The results were sent through to SIS. Davina handed them to Humphrey. "We have enough here to put pressure on Modena," she said. "And let him know we haven't just shelved what happened in Venice."

She looked tired, Humphrey thought, and she was visibly irritated by trifles. The strain was telling on her, and he couldn't help feeling pleased. First her love life goes up in flames; he had been given the brief instruction what to leak about Tony Walden and to get it through immediately. So the affair was over. Out, out brief candle, he thought maliciously. He was snug in his own relationship. He didn't sympathize with Davina, and encouraged the ambitions of Tim Johnson by remarking how pressure was affecting the boss lady. To his surprise, Johnson snapped back that it wasn't surprising. Humphrey's mind, jaundiced and incapable of judging a woman's reactions to a man, wondered whether there was something brewing between those two. The idea made him wince. If he was right, he confided to Ronnie that evening, she was nothing better than a tart, like her sister.

Ronnie nodded in agreement. He didn't know what his friend was talking about and he had never met any of the people mentioned. He didn't know exactly what Humphrey did in his official guise. He accepted the Foreign Office in a loose way, and thought no more.

But Humphrey did as Davina instructed. He leaked through

their East German contact that Davina Graham had parted from her lover. While he was absent in Australia, she had taken up with another man. They could make what they liked of that. He had only made one comment. "Isn't this letting Walden off too lightly?"

She hadn't raised her head when she answered, "I think that's my business, don't you? Just see the information gets through."

Tim Johnson suggested that he fly to Rome and put the American evidence in front of Alfredo Modena. Telexes could be acknowledged and responses delayed. A direct contact might force out the vital information.

He caught a morning flight, and was in Modena's office by mid-afternoon. There he was told that the head of Security was at the prison. After consultations in rapid Italian between his subordinates and a telephone call made out of Johnson's hearing, he was driven to the prison.

He found the Italian sitting in a little improvised office, shirt-sleeved and puffy-eyed with tiredness. As soon as they shook hands, Johnson detected that the man was tired, but very excited. He put the CIA report in front of him. "Miss Graham wanted you to see this," he said. "It probably just corroborates your own information."

Modena glanced up at him. "And you have come all this way to bring me something that you think I may already know? Come, my friend, you and the Americans have been trespassing in my country without my agreement. Not for the first time; nor the last. But please don't treat me like a fool. Let me see what they've found out. And please, it's very hot. Take off your jacket, make yourself comfortable."

Johnson sat and waited. Hot wasn't the word. There was no air-conditioning, and the smell of human beings in confined spaces was sweet and sickly. Prisons smelt the same wherever they were; only some, like this one, smelled stronger.

Modena said at last: "I am grateful for this. It ties in with some very important facts I have established myself."

Johnson didn't hesitate. "In view of the assassination of Father Marnie ten days ago, I hope you'll share them with us."

"You believe the two are related?" Modena inquired.

"Yes." Johnson was emphatic. "So was the multiple Duvalier murder, and the so-called accidental death of Soviet Minister

Nikolaev. Four separate incidents with a common denominator."

Modena raised his eyebrows. It gave his saturnine face a rather devilish look.

"What common denominator is there between the killing of a right-wing American, a left-wing Frenchwoman, a Soviet minister, and a leader of the anti-war movement? It seems to me that the only common denominator is the lack of any connection."

Johnson hadn't expected this. "That's exactly our point. Whoever is organizing these murders isn't following a pattern as expected. The victims are quite unrelated, but the method of killing them is not. A single assassin, a public place, guaranteed maximum publicity. And before you counter this with what happened to the Duvaliers, it couldn't have caused a greater sensation if it had been done in the middle of the Place de la Concorde. So the objective was achieved. I hope you will take us into your confidence, Signore Modena, as we have done with you."

Modena wiped his forehead with a handkerchief. "You've put forward a very convincing case." He pushed his chair back and stood up. "Come with me. We'll take this report with us."

"Now Elsa," Modena said. "I want you to look at these. Do any of them look like the man who stayed with you?"

Brunson's agent had been patient and thorough. Every hotel and pensione had been visited, and questions asked about who stayed there during the week of Henry Franklyn's murder. Continuous probing and handouts of money had produced a number of candidates. Out of these the expert had drawn up a list of a dozen. And the drivers of the taxi launches were searching their memories for passengers on the day of the killing. The police had tried to cover up the death of their colleague as a drowning accident, but rumors spread and the truth was soon known.

Two drivers remembered a young man hiring the little *vaporetto* that morning; their descriptions didn't quite tally. But then descriptions never do. To one he was tall, the second said slight. Age varied but both settled for less than forty, and both agreed, without being specific, that he wasn't dark and didn't look Italian. From all these fragments, the CIA had built up an identikit picture with a rough schedule of movements. The picture was among half a dozen others, with less convincing credentials.

Johnson stayed in the background of the cell. He was fascinated by the girl. She was very young, very thin and sallow. She reminded him of a trapped animal. She had glared at him when he came in after Modena and then looked away. But she hung on the Italian's words, staring at him with a helpless dependence. He'd done a good job there, Johnson decided. He'd got her totally subjected. He preferred not to wonder how he'd managed it. That wasn't his business. She took the pictures and leafed through them. Then she stopped. She held one out to Modena. "That's him," she said. "Near enough."

"Good," Modena smiled approvingly at her. He glanced over his shoulder at Johnson and said in Italian so she could understand. "Elsa has been a great help to us. Not without a lot of soul-searching, you understand. And she has suffered considerably. Now she has decided not to suffer for other people's crimes. Which is very brave as well as sensible."

Johnson saw her blush. Christ, he said to himself, I've heard about his technique but I've never seen it working before. It's like getting a bloody tiger to lie down and lick your feet.

Modena stood up. He smiled at the girl again. "Good," he repeated. He took Johnson upstairs.

"They'll send in some lunch," he said. "It's not bad. Let's put this together, then."

Slowly the picture was emerging. The killer had stayed at a pensione; the *padrone* remembered him talking about architecture and saying he was a student. Both men dismissed this. Also the cover that he was going on to Padua. The girl Valdorini said he had a northern accent, which the *padrone* corroborated. He looked like someone who lived in the open, and who walked a lot. Not a city type, more of a village man, but not a laborer. The girl had noticed his hands, as she did his other physical details, when she was thinking about sleeping with him. His hands were well kept. He was clean in his habits. Fair hair, blue-gray eyes, outdoor skin, but not a laborer. The trail had gone on to the airports, which were closed until some days after the man had left Valdorini's house. That left the railways. A close study of the timetables for the day he left Venice established that there were two connections he could have caught to Trieste.

Modena was working on the assumption that the assassin had gone home and into hiding. And home was in the north. "We'll get the trains and buses checked," he said. "And from there we'll send men up to make inquiries at the places where the buses call.

People in that region of Italy use the bus more than the car, and the bicycle isn't suited to the Dolomite area. That is where I think our killer came from, judging by the accent Valdorini described. He used certain expressions that you find in that part of the country. She remembered them because they were comic to a Venetian. So, we will have to follow up our leads and wait." He leaned back, stretched out his arms and sighed. "I see her every day," he said. "I keep the contact going between us. Otherwise she could go back on it and refuse to testify if we catch this man. You can never trust these people."

"How did you get her to make a deal?"

Modena managed a slight smile. He didn't smile or laugh often, Johnson noticed. He was not in the least lighthearted. "I showed her what would happen to her if she didn't," he said. "Fortunately she was too conditioned to look at it too closely. It was a prison for dangerous criminal lunatics and it's been closed for two years. I put on a little window dressing for her benefit, and it worked. Strange, Signore Johnson, the things that break a human spirit—I could have stood that girl against a wall and lined up the firing squad and she'd have spat in my face. But the sight of a padded cell was just too much. Ah, well. Will you take some coffee? I've been drinking too much espresso. It's bad for the nerves."

"What will happen to her?" Johnson asked.

Modena grimaced. "Fifteen years. She'll go to the south. That's where we keep the women. On a small island, off the coast of Calabria. They don't escape from there."

Helene Blond didn't eat her dinner. To her aunt's inquiry she said irritably that she wasn't hungry, and added a clipped plea not to fuss. She had become very short-tempered in the last few days, the bewildered woman thought. Quite unlike her usual self. She'd changed since that dreadful experience. It wasn't a nice thing to think, but she couldn't help being glad that the influence of people like the Duvaliers was gone. Too much money, no moral sense, and a disregard for old-fashioned standards that she found disturbing. She kept an eye on her niece, but was careful not to say any more. There was a difficult, even forbidding side to the girl's character that made her feel uneasy sometimes.

Helene excused herself. "I'm going out for a walk," she said. "I won't be late, so don't worry about me." She bent and gave her aunt a kiss. It was a contact she hated, but it pacified the old bitch. It stopped her asking questions and following her round.

She couldn't have eaten anything that night. Her stomach was in a knot, and she couldn't stop thinking about the man who'd broken his silent watch on her that day.

"The others have been killed. You will be next."

The one who had killed in Venice, the one who had destroyed the Soviet minister in Poland . . . the one who had shot the peace-mongering priest in London. Others. She couldn't think of any others but those who had done what she had done.

Killed by whom? The question was gripping her guts with suspicion. Killed by their own, to stop them being caught and talking? Nobody had approached her since she came back to Paris after the deaths of the Duvaliers. That was the formula, agreed and understood. The preparation for the mission after you had been chosen, the mission itself, and then silence for the rest of your life. A return to normal life with the secret of what you had done locked away forever.

But in her case something had gone wrong. She went up to her room, paced up and down, looked at her watch and then very carefully, with the lights out, drew back the curtains and searched the street below. It was empty. There were no parked cars, no strollers idling past. He wouldn't still be watching, whoever he was. He'd given his warning. She went downstairs, opened the front door and made sure there was nobody in sight. Then she slipped out and began walking very rapidly toward the metro station. She didn't see Lomax. She didn't see him follow her onto the train and get out after her at the station on the Twentieth Arrondissement.

She didn't see him because he was in jeans and denim jacket, dark glasses and sneakers. He blended so skillfully into the evening crowd making its way to the center of Paris that she didn't give him or anyone near him a second glance.

They arrived in a little square, charming and antiquated, with a cobbled surface and eighteenth-century houses and shop fronts. A secret corner of the old Paris. Lomax hung back, sheltering round a corner. The girl's footsteps echoed across the uneven road surface. She stopped at a door and waited. It opened after a few minutes and a beam of light shot out into the semidarkness shrouding a tall figure that stepped aside and let her in. The door closed and the square was dim again, lit only by the two street lamps that had been adapted from gaslight. Lomax didn't go near the house. He turned back and went home to his pensione. From there he made a telephone call to Davina's apartment. It rang and rang and he swore, thinking she's out, where the hell is she? But then someone picked up the receiver. "Davina? It's me."

"I heard the phone as I was opening the door," she said. She sounded out of breath. "Any news?"

Not how are you, or any civility of that sort, he thought, and felt angry. "I think I've stirred it up," he said. "I'll let you know more tomorrow." He could be brisk too. He was going to hang up when she said, "Colin? Don't take any risks, will you ..."

He paused. "Don't worry! How's it going at your end?"

"Well," she answered. "We've got a breakthrough too. Italy at least. If you can establish something there we could be closing in. When will you call tomorrow?"

"After I've sussed out a house," he said. "Our friend went scuttling round there tonight, after I'd had a word with her. I want to see who lives there."

"You spoke to her?" Davina sounded anxious.

"Just a few well-chosen words," he said. "My French isn't exactly fluent. But good enough to put the fear of God into her. We'll know more by tomorrow. I'll call you tomorrow evening. Will you be there?"

There was no hesitation. "Of course. But if you run into trouble, don't wait; call the red number."

"Yes, Ma'am," he mocked.

"Goodnight, Colin. And thanks for doing this."

He grinned. About time she said that. Not that he cared.

"Don't mention it." He hung up.

"I've been followed," Helene Blond insisted. "A man's been following me for the last four days. And this afternoon he came up and said something. I had to contact you!"

The man looked at her; a cold impassive face, with a glint of anger in the hooded eyes. "You've broken the rule," he said. "You were told never to come back again, whatever happened. You are the only member who has lost her head."

Helene could feel her panic growing. They weren't going to help.

They were sheltering behind the very rules that had once made her feel so safe. And how did she know what the others had done?

"He said I was going to be killed!"

The expression on her listener's face didn't change. "You must go away," he said. "I don't want to hear any more. You know the rules and you swore to follow them. You don't exist and we don't either. If you are being threatened, then do what an innocent person would do. Go to the police." He crossed and opened the door into the hall. "Leave at once."

Helene didn't move. "Suppose he knows something about all of us? Don't you care about that?"

The answer was uninterested.

"Nobody knows about us. If you think you have been discovered, you know the rule."

She glared at him, and the fury in her overcame the fear. They all possessed that inner core of seething violence, the man knew. He knew it could erupt at any moment. They wanted to kill, these people, and to die themselves. But not this one. He could see the defiance flaming in her, the refusal to carry out her oath. So he said, "You go home. I will see what we can do. But don't come here again. Trust us to take care of you."

"You'd better," Helene said. "I want to know one thing. How are the others? How are 'Italy' and 'Russia' and 'Ireland'? Are they safe?"

He didn't lie to her. "Only 'Russia' is dead. They caught him and he was killed. He didn't speak. The rest have gone their ways and we know nothing about them. You should leave now." There was an insistent note in his voice.

"All right, I'll go." She went with him to the front door. "If I see him again, what do I do?"

"Go to the police. And leave the rest to us."

There was nobody in the little square when she came out. A peaceful, pleasant summer's night. She hunched a little as if there was a wind, and walked all the way home to her aunt's house. She was not going to obey their rule. She was not going to be a good girl and commit suicide if anything went wrong.

The man watched from a darkened room as Helene crossed the cobbled square and vanished round the corner. Nobody had followed her. But somehow the strongest link in the chain was showing weakness. She had made a slip without anyone realizing, and the man who followed her had threatened because he knew she would react as she did. And done the one thing that was forbidden to all of them. Returned after the misson. He went into the back of the house and down the stairs into what had been the servant's quarters in the old days. The big gloomy kitchen didn't exist. It was entered by a reinforced door, and inside it was brightly lit and equipped with a highly sophisticated communications system. Three people were on duty. Two women and a young man. They stood up when he came in. They spoke in a language that was clipped and tonal. He checked the time, paused and then announced his decision.

Lomax saw her leave for school the next morning. He didn't follow her. That side of it was over for the moment. He ordered a cab and gave the name of the square. "What number?"

Lomax shrugged, "I'm not sure, but I'll recognize the place." The driver said something to himself, which Lomax didn't catch, but he was fairly sure it wasn't complimentary about foreigners who didn't know where they were going.

When they turned into the square he leaned forward and said, "That house, second on the right. No, don't stop, just drive past, will you." He ignored more Gallic mutterings and they drove up to the entrance; he saw the brass plate and read the inscription. The House of Ma-Nang. "Okay, drive back on the main street. Do you know that place? Ma-Nang—what does it mean?"

The driver looked round, raised his eyebrows and said, "I don't know, Monsieur. I'm not Chinese."

Lomax got out and gave him something to complain about by not adding a tip to the fare. He went to the Bibliothèque Française. The woman at the inquiry desk was helpful. She suggested that Lomax try the Oriental section. He did, and the librarian was eager to assist him. Ma-Nang. They consulted the *Dictionary of Cantonese* but without any success. There were many hundreds of versions of the Chinese language and thousands of derivatives. Lomax said yes, he appreciated that, but what did she suggest? They looked through the religious and philosophical reference books, and the hours were running away. The House of Ma-Nang. The librarian was at the end of her suggestions. Why not look in the telephone directory? It might explain the meaning. Lomax thanked her, wondered why he hadn't done that first, and went into her office. And there it was. The

House of Ma-Nang. School of Meditation. They looked at each other and laughed with relief.

"What a lot of trouble we took," the lady said. "And it was here all the time. Well, Monsieur, at least you've found out what it means."

"I have," Lomax agreed. "And I feel very stupid to have taken up all your afternoon looking for something that was right under my nose. I do apologize."

She had a cheering smile. She wasn't young by any means but there was a sweetness about her that made him want to ask her out for a drink just to make up for it. But he didn't. As he was leaving she put her head a little on one side, like a thoughtful sparrow, and said, "Monsieur, there is one thing. Perhaps we didn't find Ma-Nang because it isn't Chinese. If it had been a recognized philosophy it would have been listed in our reference books."

"That had occurred to me, Mademoiselle." Lomax said quietly. "Maybe we couldn't find it because it doesn't mean anything at all." He left her staring, rather puzzled, after him.

" 'France' has broken cover." He read the decoded message slowly. "She reports threats and surveillance from outside. Request instructions for immediate solution to possible breakdown in our security." There was always one, he thought angrily; one who slipped through the psychological screening, however thorough. And she had seemed to be the best; the one with the coolest nerve and the psychopathic hatred of her fellow human beings. A pity, and a nuisance. He didn't make up his mind in a hurry. He thought it out in relation to what had still to be accomplished. He brushed aside the question of who had approached "France"; it could be any one of the intelligence services involved. It didn't matter. What mattered was to stop them getting any closer to her. Or to anyone else. He wrote down a sentence on his pad, pressed the bell by his chair, and handed it to the aide who came into the room. "Have this coded and sent at once," he said.

It was a beautiful morning; the sun rose high above the cool pine forest. He would go down to the river. Watching the gentle flow of the water eased the soul's discomfort. It was an old saying, which, like so many things belonging to the past, turned out to be true.

* * *

151

Davina said, "We've put it through the computers and come up with nothing. There's no such institute listed and Ma-Nang simply doesn't make sense. It's gibberish."

Humphrey looked gloomy. "A meditation center with a phony name; it's hardly important whether it's made up or not. Surely all we want to know is why Helene Blond should go there, after Lomax had made contact."

"We won't know that till someone gets inside and sees the setup," Tim Johnson insisted. "And it can't be Lomax in case the girl's described him. It would be too much of a coincidence. He's sure she's a prime suspect . . ."

He left it as a part question, and Davina said firmly, "Definitely, and he's got a lot of experience. He says she's wrong, and that's good enough for me. God, if only we could hear from Modena!"

"It'll take time," Johnson said. "They've got to check out a large area in the Dolomites and the place is honeycombed with villages and ski resorts. When will Lomax call in again?"

"He says he's going to check out the center," Davina answered.

"Wouldn't it be better to turn the whole thing over to SE-DECE? We are getting a bit hot, going it alone from now on," Humphrey suggested.

Davina shrugged. "I can't call Colin off now," she said. "He wants to follow it up and he's very experienced. If he finds out anything when he goes there, I'll tell him to pull out and we'll give what we've got to the delightful colonel. I doubt he'll be grateful."

"And Helene Blond?" That was Tim Johnson.

"They're welcome to her," Davina said shortly. "I don't know how you both feel, but I think we're going to crack this one quite soon. And before any more damage is done."

Humphrey stood up. He didn't look optimistic, but then he never did.

"Let's hope you're right," was all he said before he went out.

Johnson looked across at her. "I know he's senior to me," he said, "but he's the gloomiest bugger I've ever met in my life. I don't know how you stand it."

"Quite easily," Davina answered. "Because he's also one of the cleverest men *I've* ever met in my life. Gloomy or not, Tim, don't underestimate him. Do you want some coffee—I'm going to have some."

"I won't, thanks," he said. "I've got a deskful of stuff waiting."

Davina sipped the coffee that her secretary Phyllis brought her. She was James White's long-time assistant, and she hadn't committed herself to working for his successor without a trial period. She was middle-aged, highly competent, and knew more about what went on inside the house in Anne's Yard than anybody else.

Davina hadn't been in touch with White since her father's funeral. She hadn't phoned Charlie at her boy friend's apartment to inquire how their mother was; she'd been completely absorbed in her work. And she realized with surprise that she hadn't thought of Tony Walden since she sent Colin Lomax out to Paris. He hadn't approached her. She was relieved, but surprised too. It wasn't like Walden to give up when he wanted something. Perhaps he was busy too. Buying off his Soviet blackmailers. The thought was as painful as it was nauseating. How could he have done it? Even to save his business. How could he have so lacked any moral standard as to try and juggle with her on one hand and Borisov on the other? And imagine he would succeed . . .

She put the coffee down. It tasted bitter. If he had been a fool then so had she. With as little judgment as Walden. She had been deluded by the dash and fizzle of his personality, attracted by a sexual magnetism. He was dynamic, unusual, intensely male, but he belonged at heart to the world of the hard sell. He traded in illusions and the exploitation of human gullibility and greed. He hadn't escaped untainted himself. There were many happy, tender aspects to their time together, and she couldn't yet dismiss them. Remembering them hurt. And would for a very long time. She turned back with relief to her day's itinerary.

Lomax telephoned the number given in the telephone directory. It didn't ring for long. He stammered in deliberately halting French. There was no help from the woman who answered. He was looking for a place to study meditation, he explained, making a lot of mistakes on purpose. Were they Transcendental or Zen?

"We teach the method of Ma-Nang," a female voice replied. It didn't sound French. Too high-pitched, too careful to speak clearly.

Lomax went on. "I suffer from tension," he explained. "I get very strung up."

"You should see your doctor," she tinkled back at him.

"I have," he said. "I've tried Western methods. They don't work. Can I come and see you? Maybe you can help me?"

There was a pause. "We are not medical," she said. "We deal in spiritual peace and inward knowledge. Wait a moment please." She had gone away to ask. Lomax waited, counted the minutes. "I am sorry." The tone was shrill. "We cannot help you. We are closing for the summer." The line went dead.

Lomax put back the receiver. "Like hell you are," he said. He had phoned from a public booth. He came out into the sunshine and lit a cigarette. No genuine school of philosophy turned strangers away, particularly when they asked for help. Vast fortunes had been made by institutions catering to the kind of neurotic he had made himself out to be. From India to the Far East, the cult of healing through meditation attracted thousands who couldn't come to terms with the tensions of modern life. But Ma-Nang didn't encourage the seeker after truth and inner light. Lomax wondered exactly what it did welcome.

He started walking, taking his time, playing with the ideas as he idled along the sunny streets on the way to the lycée. It was later than Lomax realized. The students were coming out. He held back, waiting to see if she was ahead of him. Suddenly he spotted her brisk walk, the head held rather low; she wore the Robin Hood ankle boots that he thought ruined even the sexiest girl's legs. Striding along, not lingering with the others to gossip and pair off on the way home. A loner. Full of inner knowledge and spiritual peace! And then he saw the car. He knew by the speed at which it was being driven, close to the pavement, that it wasn't part of the early evening traffic. Too fast, too close to the pedestrians. And without a second's further thought, he started to run toward the girl.

It was the day before his wedding. "Italy" was getting ready for the family celebration dinner. His mother had been cooking, and every relative in the village had contributed. They would all sit down to a huge meal with unlimited local wine, and every uncle, aunt, cousin, and child would wish him happiness. He was in love, which made the marriage good. She was a girl he had grown up with; a redhead with extensive freckles and a bright smile. There was Austrian blood in her, as with many families in the area. Her father owned a big vineyard and ran the grocery shop. Everybody was happy about the wedding. The village was turning out for them, and they would have a procession to the church, headed by the local band. It would be a great day.

He whistled as he helped bring in the big flasks of wine. It was hot. He wore only a sweatshirt above his denims and his feet slapped on the stone floor in espadrilles. He knew he was a well-set-up man, capable of making his bride happy and giving her children. They'd be comfortable, with a secure future when her father died. Luckily, she was the only child. The business and the vineyard would go to her. Life was good. He'd settle down and follow the pattern of his family and their forebears for the last five hundred years. He'd die and be buried in the village churchyard with a headstone listing his name and age. A respectable bourgeois living his life out in the mountain village. Except for a trip to Venice and a moment of hidden glory that must stay hidden.

They wouldn't carve that on his tombstone, but he would die knowing he wasn't just an ordinary man. He had his moment of immortality, of super power, when he killed. It had cleansed him of his hate and frustrations. He could live normally now, a bomb that had exploded and was harmless.

His sister came to the door and called him. "Someone's asking for you—no, he didn't say. I've never seen him before."

He set down the last of the heavy flasks, wiped his hands on his trousers, and went outside. It was a man in motorcycle leathers, wearing a heavy helmet with a black shield. He pushed it up and "Italy" saw a face he didn't recognize. He heard his name and said, "Yes?" The man came towards him. "Italy" waited, wondering what he wanted, why he knew him. The blow struck him once, then twice between the ribs. The knife was thin and sharp, shaped like the deadly stiletto used by assassins in Italy four hundred years before. It pierced his heart and killed him before he could do more than grunt. Inside the house his sister heard the sound of a motorcycle stutter into life, then roar away. There was a long pause while she went on with her work. After a time she called out her brother's name. There was no answer. She didn't worry, and finished making the pasta.

The report of the murder reached Modena's team of investigators. They were working through the district forty miles west of the incident. One of them decided to drive up to the place and make some inquiries. By the end of the next day he was back, with a photograph. It showed a boy still in his teens, smiling against the sunshine, his arms round a laughing girl. Taken three years ago, when he and his family were at a local wedding. The girl was to be his wife that day. So sad, everyone said. His parents were desolate, his mother under a doctor's care, lying in a darkened room. The whole village was in mourning, and full of police making inquiries. But it was a motiveless killing. There had been urban gangs of motorcyclists attacking women in the larger towns, and two robberies had been reported. Modena's man wired the photograph back to Rome. He did so because one of the people he questioned said that the murdered man had been on holiday on the Adriatic at the time when Henry Franklyn was assassinated. They had only mentioned this in case he had somehow met his attacker when he was away from home.

When the report and photograph arrived in Modena's office he took it to the Regina Ceoli prison. Elsa Valdorini was brought to see him. The moment he saw her face when she looked at the picture, he knew they had lost their only lead. "That's him," she said. "Have you arrested him?"

"No," he said. "He was stabbed to death yesterday morning."

"Oh." Her eyes didn't stay on his face. They darted away. "Elsa," Modena said. "Do you know who did it?"

She shook her head. "No," she said. "But I'm glad I'm safe in here."

"Don't be too glad. Without this man there can't be a deal. Unless you tell me the other things you're holding back," Modena said slowly.

Lomax launched himself at her as the car swerved viciously to the right and mounted the pavement. His body collided with hers, knocking them several feet to the ground. There was a shattering crash and terrible screams. Lomax lay for a moment on top of the girl. She was partly knocked out and he was badly winded. The car had struck into a group of people waiting by a pedestrian crossing.

Grimacing, Lomax picked himself up, and got his breath back. A few yards away it looked like a battlefield. There were more screams, hysterical and meaningless, and the sound of the car revving, reversing away from the sprawl of bodies.

Lomax lifted Helene Blond to her feet. She was dazed and

stumbling. Then she started to scream too as she saw what had happened. The car had got clear and was speeding away, tires screeching as it cornered and vanished. Lomax didn't waste any time. He didn't go to the injured; enough people were already crowding round, and he could see that at least two were dead. He grabbed hold of the girl. His French had deserted him.

"You speak English? Do you?" He shook her. She nodded in a daze.

"We've got to get out of here," he said. "Come on, walk. You're not hurt, are you?"

"I don't know."

His arm went like a vise round her shoulders and he hustled her quickly away from the crowds that were gathering. A siren sounded, getting closer, followed by another. Ambulances, police. Blood was beginning to puddle in the street. He hurried her down into the metro. At the bottom of the stairs she stiffened and started to resist. He debated whether to hit her and pretend she'd fainted.

"Who are you?" she said in French. "What are you doing?"

"I've just saved your life," Lomax said. "That car was aiming for you. You must come back with me. You'll be safe there."

"I'm going home," she muttered. "I'm not going anywhere."

It was a chance he had to take. "Okay," he said. "We'll go to your home. Then you can choose."

She didn't ask what he meant. She was gray with shock, but there was a tough resilience about her that was hardly usual in a girl who'd just witnessed violent death. When they came to her door she turned to him. "My aunt will be home. Who are you? What do I say?"

"You tell the truth," he said quietly. "You were in a street accident. I brought you home. Then get rid of her so we can talk."

"We haven't got time to argue," Lomax said. He was standing by the window of the sitting room, watching the street. Behind him, Helene Blond sat hunched on the sofa. He was right and she knew it. She had gone to Ma-Nang for help and they had sentenced her to death. That car was a weapon, as deadly as the gun she had used on the Duvaliers. She knew this because she had learned how to hit and run as part of her training. She had felt physically sick at first. Fear and the boiling hatred for her betrayers made her sit and listen while the Englishman talked. Now there were two lots of enemies; her own organization and what this man represented.

"By now," Lomax said curtly, "they'll know you got away. You heard the news flash; two dead. It won't take them long to find out you're not one of them. Or the injured. And then, Mademoiselle, they'll come calling round here. Which is it to be? You come with me and save your life or you wait here for them?"

Helene stood up. "I wouldn't be any safer with you. We have people everywhere."

"I'm sure you do," Lomax answered. One of them was at the Albert Hall not long ago, but he didn't say it. "But I am in a position to hide you where nobody will be able to get at you. And to arrange a deal for you, if you cooperate." He looked at his watch. "I'll give you five minutes."

She turned her back on him. The release was upstairs. All she had to do was pretend to agree and go and get it. Take the way out that she had promised when she first joined Ma-Nang.

"I don't need five minutes," she said in English. "I will come with you."

Lomax didn't sound surprised. "Get your passport," he said. "And don't bother to pack anything. We're not going to have time for luggage."

The blood-stained car with its shattered lights and damaged radiator was hidden in a garage. Within a few hours it would be dismantled and taken out in sections to be scattered on the metal dumps outside the city. In the operations room at the Ma-Nang meditation center, the principal received the list of casualties from the accident. He spoke in their curious tonal language. It sounded staccato and angry. "France" had escaped. They must retrieve the error that night. Before their failure was reported to Moscow.

Helene's aunt watched them go. She stood by the window where Lomax had kept watch only a few minutes earlier. She was shaking and she found it hard to breathe.

She had met them in the hall, her niece carrying a shoulder bag, making for the front door. And when she intervened to ask them where they were going, the girl rounded on her. The effect was so horrific that the woman literally shrank away from her until she felt the wall at her back. The language was a hail of filthy epithets, the vilest insults couched in the crudest possible terms. And the girl's face close to hers, contorted with hatred.

The Englishman put an end to it. He said, "I don't know what you're calling her, but you stop it! Stop it! He gave Helene a rough push toward the front door. Then he said to her aunt in slow French, "We have to go, Madame. She is in danger. Don't talk to anyone. Don't answer the door till I telephone you." And then, seeing the stricken look on her face, he added, "Whatever she said, she didn't mean it."

Then they were gone. The door opened and shut after them, and she didn't even say anything. She ran to the window in the sitting room and saw them hurry down the street. The man was holding Helene's arm, urging her forward. She closed her eyes for a moment; she felt sick and dizzy. The names she'd called her, the naked loathing on her face ... She didn't know what to do. She sat down, still trembling, and tried to understand what the man had meant. In danger? In danger from whom or what? She recovered herself after a few minutes. Anger and disgust were driving out shock. She reached for the telephone, and dialed the police.

Lomax hailed a taxi. "Charles de Gaulle Airport," he said.

"Where are we going?" The girl said sullenly.

Lomax didn't look at her. "England." He heard the gasp of surprise beside him. "You'll be safe there from your friends."

She'd said it all in her aunt's sitting room, made the confession that would have taken months of trained interrogation to extract. "We have people everywhere."

"You don't mind if they hurt your aunt?"

She sniggered. "Why should I? Do her good."

Lomax didn't say any more. "We." She was a member of the group who had just mowed down innocent people on the pavement in their effort to get to her. No, she wouldn't mind what happened to her aunt. As they sat in the speeding taxi, threading their way through the traffic toward the airport, he thought, what a pity I have to take her back. My instinct tells me to push her out onto the street. Let them get rid of her. But he tapped on the driver's glass and asked him to make up speed if he could. He had already calculated on getting the six o'clock plane to London.

The police arrived very quickly. She congratulated them on their efficiency when she opened the door. There were two of them, polite young men. One took down everything she said, while the other made notes. Her niece had vanished with a man she thought was English. By his accent, of course. Saying she was in danger. That was very disturbing. They didn't say where they were going—no indication at all? No luggage? No. Where did she keep a passport? Upstairs. Perhaps Madame would take them up and they could check. If she had taken her passport that would prove she was leaving the country. Seeing her expression, the policeman who'd been asking questions added, "Outside the EEC of course." She went up the stairs with them. There was no passport in Helene's desk drawer. They were sympathetic, but seemed in a hurry. They'd put out a general call for her. They stood back to let her go downstairs ahead of them. The one taking notes had put his pad away. He hit her hard on the back of the neck and she was dead even before they threw her down the stairs. They stepped carefully over her body and let themselves out. The car with the local gendarmes inside pulled up at the house ten minutes after they'd gone.

They reported back to the room in the rear of the house on the square. An Englishman. The same who had dived on her and rolled her to safety when the car drove at her. The driver had lost concentration and hit the crowd. An Englishman who had followed her and tricked her into revealing her connection with Ma-Nang. By now she would be on her way to London. To the interrogators of the SIS. There was nothing to do, it was decided, but admit what had happened and pass the initiative to Moscow. It was no longer their responsibility.

Helene sat slumped in her seat. They had caught the flight with only minutes to spare. It was British Airways and her companion had waved a card under the nose of a harassed young man at the ticket office. It worked so quickly that she knew immediately that her first impression of him was right. The enemy. The official enemy, with the power to commandeer seats on an over-booked plane. The power to hide her away from her colleagues. She sighed, looking out of the window at the gray clouds that flew past them. Her head ached, and her pulse was uneven. She didn't like flying. It made her tense and uneasy.

The man beside her didn't speak. She could feel his hostility. That didn't worry her. She knew how to harness hatred better than he did. She was afraid, yes. For the first time, except for the blinding moment of panic when that car screeched after her like an avenging angel. Now she was afraid of what was at the end of the flight. Afraid of the cool, impersonal forces of the enemy who would come forward like a Greek phalanx and surround her as soon as she left the plane. Hate and courage wouldn't avail her now. Now she had to rely on nerve and cunning. Just as she did after the Duvaliers were killed and the cold-eyed bloodhounds of SEDECE were asking questions. If she could fool them she had a chance with her new adversaries. What had the man said that alerted her? Something that had made her stomach lurch long before the plane took off. In the taxi on their way to the airport. "Your friends." That was it. She'd made a slip somewhere, or was it just a guess? Never mind. She took several deep breaths, calming herself, slowing her pulse, silencing the jangling bells in her nervous system. He might know that she belonged to the organization, but he didn't know she'd murdered the Duvaliers. That was what she had to conceal, at all costs. And she could buy her way out by betraying the comrades at Ma-Nang, by explaining how it worked, how they were chosen from the other students. The killers, that is. Not simple converts to the idea of nuclear disarmament and world peace like herself. She was setting up the answers to imagined questions, her mind darting back and forth like a rat in a puzzle cage, looking for exits.

She wouldn't give in. No, she'd made up her mind to live and escape if she could. But the hate burned in her like a coal. Killing the Duvaliers hadn't extinguished it. Probably, she thought as they came in to land, nothing would, but death. Only in darkness was it possible to find real peace. They had taught her that at Ma-Nang.

Lomax nudged her. He hadn't spoken once during the flight. "Put on your seat belt." Helene fastened it. She wanted to say something provocative, but there was something about him that didn't invite challenge. It was an odd sensation, being hated. New to her, who thrived on hatred for other people. She said nothing. She followed him out of the plane and onto the airport bus. Nobody was waiting for them, nobody came forward when they passed through customs on the production of his card. He gripped her tightly by the arm while they pushed their way through into the main hall. He stopped at a telephone cubicle, pushed her in front of him so that she was wedged in the upper half, found change and dialed a number. The conversation was too quick for her to follow any of it. "Good," said Lomax. "Let's go."

It was just getting dark as they turned into the little cul-de-sac in Anne's Yard.

7

"**H**OW did they find you?" Modena asked. Two days and two nights, with brief snatches of sleep for both of them. Food on trays, endless cups of coffee, air stale with cigarette smoke, some wine for him, to keep his energy from flagging. He had forgotten how much older he was and how the tension would exhaust him. He could understand how some men would have dispensed with patience and started using other means. Sometimes he felt sorry for her. Sometimes he saw the haggard face and hollow eyes as belonging to a frightened child. A child condemned to a living death in the notorious prison on the island. All chance of life and love forfeited. For what?

But now she was breaking up; the façade was peeling away, and this gave him the energy to go on, chipping and probing her. And it made him pity her, which he knew was a mistake. But if he lost that capacity then what difference was there between them? What right had he to judge if he wasn't any better? "How did they pick you?" he said again.

She sighed, brushed the lank hair back from her forehead. "They gave me tests," she said. "Everyone who went to the institute filled up forms, answered a lot of questions. They said it would help to decide what sort of meditation and relaxing exercises we needed."

"And you did this," he prompted. Getting her to describe the way the institute categorized its students had been like drawing teeth. She'd resisted so strongly that he detected some kind of mental block. From defiance at first she changed to evasions, twisting and turning in her efforts to avoid answering.

And then at last she gave way, and the answers started coming, hesitantly, almost furtively. "I filled in the form," she said.

"What sort of questions were they? Intimate?"

She looked away from him. "Some of them. They said it was to find the sources of tension."

"And were you tense? Frustrated, repressed perhaps? Is that what made you look for a place like this?"

"I felt I was going to explode. I hated everything; my college, my parents, my life. I didn't know where to turn. There'd been a man."

"Ah," said Modena. So must the priest feel in the confessional. But compassionate: determined to be compassionate. Not like him, a man committed to hunt down and punish. "Tell me about the man."

"No." The voice was sharp, the spot too tender to be touched. "I was ten," she said after a pause. "Nobody knew."

"You don't have to talk about it."

There was a long pause.

"After the questionnaire?" he prompted.

"I was given a helper," she muttered. "A woman. They said I needed a woman to guide me." Of course, Modena thought.

But just to satisfy the curiosity of his own mind he asked, "Did you have lovers?"

"No." The dark eyes were glazed with tears. "I couldn't bear it. That made it worse for me. But afterward, I did."

"Tell me what they did to help you." He spoke gently.

It sounded simple, innocent enough. Deep breathing, relaxation in small groups, therapy through music. And hypnotism. And drugs to help the process? Sometimes. They made it easy to concentrate, to listen. He could imagine how easy. And so the ideas had been implanted. Very gradually and subtly, and always as part of a group. A small gathering of specially selected pupils. First the myths were dispensed with. Religion in general. She repeated the old Marxist maxim, "Religion is the opium of the people." In the case of the young Italians, Christianity was the special target—legends developed to repress the natural human instincts. All Christianity offered was a bitter tyranny. And they turned all its tenets upside down. Pride was a virtue. Sexual expression a right, in any form. Anger was energy and should be developed. Hatred was strength. Indifference was necessary to survive. And death was an end in itself, to be embraced at will. They were told society had crippled them. To free themselves they had to strike back. And mingled with the deeper psychological suggestions, were a few clichés about disarmament and peace to soothe the remnants of conscience.

Modena listened, seldom interrupting. They had taken a sick girl and used her problems to pervert her mind until the sickness was nearer madness. She found the liberty, the peace they promised her. Drug-induced, filled with suggestions, influenced by group indoctrination, Elsa Valdorini had been recruited into the select band of students who were pledged to attack the enemy. Wherever Ma-Nang said it was to be found. Among that group had been the young northerner. The chemist's son from the sleepy village in the Dolomites. God knew what inner turmoil motivated him. Now Modena would never know. The girl had stopped talking; she leaned forward, her head hanging in exhaustion. "I can't tell you any more," she mumbled.

Modena got up, stretched his stiff body, and yawned. "You've been very helpful." She looked up at him. He felt very sorry for her.

"You can still save me from that place?"

He understood now why the cell with the padded walls had held a greater terror for her than death.

"Yes," he said. "I can save you from going there." He pressed the buzzer and a wardress opened the door and came in. "Take her back to her cell," he said. He went out without turning round to look at her. He was feeling too sorry for her. It would be better not to see her again.

The staff at Anne's Yard were used to crises, but there was an electric atmosphere that evening. The night staff had come on duty only to find that their daytime colleagues were still there. And the boss lady and her assistants were in the upper office on the first floor waiting for what? The rumors were inexact; they centered round an ex-agent, Colin Lomax. He was bringing someone in.

Humphrey didn't join in the excitement. He didn't believe in dramatic successes. Long experience had taught him to proceed carefully, and always to err on the side of pessimism. Davina sensed his reserve, but shrugged off the irritation. He was jealous of Lomax; jealous of her and of Johnson. It was a pity, because it denied him the satisfaction of his immense skill at the job. "Tim," she said, "you've made all the arrangements?"

"They've got a room ready at Welton," he said. "Everything's fixed up, including a car and the escort." MacNeil at Special Branch had alerted the staff at the SIS training center in Gloucestershire. A room was prepared for Helene Blond there, with absolute security—to keep her inside, and any unwanted visitors out. Welton was a large Victorian mansion, enclosed in a three-hundred-acre estate. It was a deceptively informal place, where a suspect would easily lower his or her guard. The atmosphere was geared to a stay in a friendly country house. There was no sign of the elaborate system of alarms and TV surveillance. Helene Blond would remain there while she unraveled the mysteries of Ma-Nang and its killers for Davina Graham.

"Humphrey," she said suddenly, "I think we should telephone the Chief."

He couldn't help showing his surprise. He thought he was the only one who called Sir James that. "He suggested Colin," she explained. "He'd like to know what's happened. Why don't you speak to him?"

"Shouldn't it be you?" She seldom bothered to score. But he had gone behind her back over Tony Walden; and James White knew the result of his investigation before Davina told him.

"I don't talk to him as often as you do," she said, and noticed a tinge of color creep into Humphrey's gray cheeks. He picked up the phone.

Davina didn't listen; she looked at her watch. Lomax had called at just after six. They should be arriving any minute.

"He wants to speak to you." She turned, and took the phone from Humphrey. The brigadier's voice was briskly cheerful.

"Good news, I hear. He's an able chap, your friend Colin. Well done to both of you."

"I don't deserve the credit," Davina answered. "He did it."

166

"Nonsense," came the reply. "You persuaded him back. Don't let him slip away again."

When Lomax came in with the girl, there was a moment of silence while they all stared at one another. She was an ordinary-looking girl, maybe less than twenty years old. Brown hair hanging straight to her shoulders. A pleasant face that could be pretty if it had a different expression. And eyes like flat brown stones.

Davina moved toward her. "Mademoiselle Blond. It is good to see you here." Her French was better than the man's, Helene thought. She had that air of authority that Helene hated. She remembered the supercilious Irena Duvalier, with her condescending manner to her niece's unimportant friend. This woman had a different kind of self-assurance. Not because she was rich, but because she was powerful.

"Thank you." She made it sound like an insult.

Lomax had lit a cigarette, withdrawn to an armchair, where he perched on an arm. Out of the corner of her eye Davina could see his foot swinging backward and forward. She knew it was a danger signal. "You came to England of your own free will?"

"Yes." The answer was curt. "He said I'd be safe here."

"That's right. Do you place yourself willingly under our protection, Mademoiselle Blond? I have to establish this before I can authorize your stay in this country."

Helene looked round. "What would you do if I said no?"

Davina didn't hesitate. "Put you on the nine o'clock to Paris."

The girl stuffed her hands into her skirt pockets; she shrugged slightly. "I want to stay in England," she said. "Will that do you?"

"I think so." Davina sounded casual. "My colleagues are witnesses, and what you've said has been recorded. A car is on its way for you."

"Where am I going?" There was a note of anxiety in her voice. The first sign of anything but dour hostility, Davina noted.

"To a house in the country," Johnson answered in his very confident French. "It's a comfortable place, like a good hotel. You'll be free to do what you like so long as you stay on the grounds. And it's absolutely secure. Nobody can do you any harm. I'm sure you'll like it."

She didn't answer. She gave him an unpleasant smile. "I have no clothes," she remarked after a pause. "And no money. No cigarettes."

"Everything will be provided for you," Johnson assured her. There was a buzz on the intercom. "I think that's MacNeil's people now," he said to Davina. "Shall I take the young lady downstairs?" There was a tinge of sarcasm in his description.

Davina nodded. "Yes, Tim. Thanks." She walked over to Helene.

"Goodbye," she said. "I'll come down and talk to you tomorrow. Go with Monsieur Johnson, the car and driver are waiting downstairs. And when you get to the house, ask for whatever you need."

Helene Blond turned to the door. "I will," she said. "You can be sure."

When the door closed behind her, Davina went over to Lomax. "Colin," she said. "You're a marvel. How did you do it?"

"You want an official report?"

"No, of course not," she said quickly. "Tomorrow will do. Just tell me how you did it. Tell me what happened."

"As I think I said the other day," Lomax remarked. "I talk better when I've eaten."

She answered immediately, "Then that's what we'll do. It's my turn this time."

"I'll go home now," said Humphrey. "When are you setting off in the morning, Davina?"

"Nine-thirty," she said. "And I want you to come with me, Humphrey. And Tim. He's bilingual, he can translate for us without missing anything."

"Congratulations," Humphrey said to Lomax. "Before I hear the official version, I'd like to make one comment."

"About the girl?" Lomax asked him.

"Yes." He hunched his shoulders for a moment. It was a funny movement, expressing contained repugnance.

"I think we should be very careful. I kept thinking of a word that described her while she was in this room. It's not a very fashionable one nowadays. She's evil."

"I wouldn't argue with that, Humphrey," Lomax said quietly.

Within half an hour the office was in darkness; the day staff had dispersed and the house was quiet except for the night telex operator, a security guard, and the duty officer.

Humphrey went home to Ronnie and relaxed, thankful to be cozy and to lose himself listening to the cheerful trivia of Ronnie's day. Johnson drove down to his wife and sons and spent a happy evening watching television, and thinking as he did so of the interrogation that would begin next day. His family believed they had his full attention. He had a gift for thinking of several things at once without losing concentration on any of them.

Davina and Lomax went back to the steak house in Brompton Road.

And in her luxurious bedroom in Welton Manor, Helene Blond lay wide awake, staring at the ceiling with the bedside light on. She was safe. For the moment. But tomorrow another contest began. And again, as with her mother and Isabelle Duvalier, who'd befriended her, her opponent was a woman.

Davina didn't ask any questions until they ordered coffee. Colin had lost the look of strain around the eyes. They narrowed when he was tense, as if searching for an enemy.

"I've been very patient," she said quietly. "But I can't sit through the coffee *and* the brandy. Now, Colin, please tell me about it."

He didn't waste words. She liked the economy of his style. It was more like an official report than a description. But when he told her how he'd jumped ahead of the car and knocked Helene Blond out of its path, she said, almost involuntarily, "Oh, my God! What a risk to take!"

He raised his eyebrows mockingly. "I'm not in a wheelchair yet," he said. "I can still move. But it was a shambles afterward. The bastards plowed right through the group on the pavement. Even she was shocked for a minute."

"Which took some doing, you mean? I was amazed when Humphrey said that. Evil. And you ageed with him. Why?"

"Let me tell you about her aunt," Lomax said slowly. When he'd finished, Davina lit a cigarette. "We haven't had brandy," he reminded her. "Why don't we go back and drink it in my flat? I've got a decent Armagnac. Waiter?"

"I'm paying for this," she reminded him.

"I'm still on the payroll. So I'll pay."

Davina said lightly, "It's always the woman that pays, or didn't you know?"

169

"Not you, darling," Lomax answered. "You've got all the credit cards."

When they went into the street he took her arm. "That was a dirty crack," he said. "I'm sorry. Come back and have that drink, will you?"

"On one condition," she answered.

"I don't like conditions," Lomax said. "But tell it to me anyway."

"That you come down to Welton tomorrow and sit in," she said coolly. "Here's the car. And since you're in such a macho mood, you can drive!"

He opened the door and slid in behind the wheel. They didn't talk on the way to the Barbican. Except for that one flash of friction, it had been comfortable, no, she thought in surprise, companionable, between them. And that was very different from their old relationship.

He drank a lot of Armagnac. She had only one glass. They talked, and the picture of Helene Blond began to take shape. But the House of Ma-Nang didn't tie in with the iron-headed girl who'd stood in her office. "There's nothing meditative that I could see in her," Davina said. "The last thing in the world she seemed was any kind of spiritual freak."

"You're thinking of the flower people," replied Lomax. "With bare feet handing out flowers to red-necked policemen. That's a long time ago. I think our little blossom has been meditating on something very different from peace and brotherly love." Lomax tipped some more brandy into his glass, offered it to her, and put the bottle down when she refused. "It seems to me," he said, "that whoever is behind this Ma-Nang lot, whoever they turn out to be, must have a pretty good base in Russia itself."

Davina had forgotten how late it was. Debate always sparked her off and Lomax had the knack of provoking thought. "Which brings it back to Borisov," she said. "I've said he was behind it from the start. I still say so."

Lomax grinned. "You're going to find that bloody difficult to prove. But I've got a suggestion to make. Why don't you stay the night?"

Davina got up. "You're drunk," she said. "Why don't you get a good night's sleep and meet me outside my flat at eight-thirty tomorrow. We can drive down to Welton together."

"I haven't said I'd come yet," Lomax said. "I've got a business to run. And that wasn't a proposition, darling. No funny stuff intended. I can't play the gentleman and take you home, because I *have* had a drink or two . . ."

"You came in *my* car," she reminded him quickly. "I'll see you tomorrow morning. And by the way, you've done a marvelous job. I'm not very good at saying thank you, but I mean it. Simply marvelous." They looked at each other for a moment. Then she turned and went quickly before he moved toward her.

"This is a serious mistake." The doctor shifted from one foot to the other. Not so confident now, my friend, his protector thought, angry and yet satisfied. The crack was shown at last. You are human after all. Too human, because your calculations haven't worked out, and my elaborate system is in danger. Anger was predominant now. You'll pay a high price for that self-confidence of yours, he thought, watching the impassive face and the unwavering look. But the feet betrayed the man. "You assured me that once subjects were programed, they couldn't escape control. But this one has. And she holds the key to everything. I accepted your assurances about the one they have in Italy. But not 'France.' She can tell them everything!"

"I have been looking for a reason," the young man said.

He was interrupted. "I want a solution, not an excuse. What are you going to do about it?"

"I shall apply the final test," the doctor answered. His heart was beating too fast. He was annoyed at his own lack of control. He shouldn't have reacted to pressure. He had programed himself as efficiently as any of his subjects. He prided himself on his mastery of the sympathetic nervous system. "I have worked it out in a way that can turn this to our advantage. It's my fail-safe for a situation like this." His feet were still now. "I promise you, 'France' will obey this signal. She won't be able to resist it."

He didn't answer for some moments. He was still very angry, and his irritation with his protégé was growing. He forgot about the amazing successes he had already achieved. "You perfected a technique," he said suddenly. "I gave you all the facilities you needed, whatever resources you asked for, I accepted what you told me." He banged the top of his desk. "But you didn't warn me it could fail! How do I know this final test will work?"

"Because you saw the experiments," the doctor said quietly. "You were there. In each case, the subject responded. And they were all different. 'France' will respond too."

The other man leaned forward, scowling at him. "You stand by your theories. But how do you propose to do it with someone who is held by SIS? Solve that problem, my friend, and you'll regain some credibility."

"I can solve part of the problem," he said. "But I can't provide the means. That's not my department. I will guarantee that in response to my signal 'France' will be motivated to kill. Because of her captivity I can't guarantee success. Getting the signal to her is up to you."

He smiled at the doctor. "My department will do their part," he said. The smile was full of threat. "You will do yours. How long will it take to prove you are right?"

The doctor didn't hesitate. "It will be immediate. 'France' will find it unbearable until she acts."

He was at his dacha that weekend. Close to the riverside, where he could sit and fish, if he chose, or simply watch the steady flow of water and contemplate. He liked the hot summer days. His colleagues went to the Black Sea at this time of year, disporting themselves in villas as luxurious as those owned by the aristocracy in the old days. The climate was idyllic, the scenery beautiful; there were clinics and private establishments where the powerful elite could go and recover from the rigors of ruling the Union of Soviet Socialist Republics. Sometimes he thought of the holidays he'd spent there and regretted not being able to go this summer. Instead he stayed in the heat of Moscow, close to the center of the power he loved.

He sent for two people that weekend. Two trusted aides. And he explained what he wanted. They listened and he could sense their uneasiness. "It's difficult," he said, "but not impossible. It must be done, comrades. And I am confident that you can do it. You have the means."

"It will break a precedent," the elder man remarked. He wore the insignia of a full colonel of the KGB when he was in uniform. That afternoon he was dressed in a sweatshirt and shorts. His legs and arms were muscled and hairy. His companion was in a track suit. Both were keen on athletics. Neither wanted the other inhabitants of that exclusive area to think they were on official business.

"It's never been done before. It's an unwritten rule," the colonel pointed out.

"Then it'll set a new precedent," he countered. "A new rule. That nobody in the Western world is safe."

There was a moment's silence. The younger officer showed himself to be a brave man. He said, "And nobody in the East either."

"That we've already proved," was the answer. "It will make our task easier, comrades. And Russia safer. Colonel, report back as soon as possible."

They stood up, made a half-salute, and then he was alone again. He would break the precedent that said no head of Security was invulnerable. It had gone on for too long to be tolerable. No more immunity for Brunson of the CIA, the sardonic Frenchman of SEDECE or Davina Graham in London. His self-proclaimed genius of a doctor had better be right this time, or he'd end up as a patient in one of his own psychiatric clinics.

It was seven o'clock in the evening when Davina finally decided to leave Welton. She and Humphrey went into the small lounge reserved for senior officials and accepted a drink. The officer in charge of Welton was a retired brigadier, with an impressive war record. He was sympathetic.

"Of course it's disappointing; but then it's not unexpected. The girl's suffering a reaction. She's not sure she did the right thing, so she's holding out."

"She's lying," Davina said angrily. "She's lying through her teeth and I know it. Don't you think, Humphrey?"

"I'd say so," he replied. "She has made up her mind to cooperate as little as possible. I rather expected this. I've seldom come across anyone so intensely hostile." He sipped his glass of sherry. "Particularly to you, Davina."

"Then perhaps I shouldn't participate at this stage," she said. "Maybe I'd better stay out of it until Tim has made some kind of breakthrough. She seemed to respond better to him. Anyway he speaks perfect French and that establishes some kind of relationship."

Humphrey said, "Her English is better than she makes out.

She understands everything, provided we don't talk too quickly. I think you're right, Davina. You seem to serve as some kind of irritant. I'd like to talk to her alternately with Tim, for the next few days anyway. See if her attitude changes."

"You made no progress at all?" the brigadier inquired. He had been fully briefed on the background of his visitor.

"None," Davina said irritably. "Where is Tim?"

"He said he was going for a quick walk," the brigadier answered. "Wanted to stretch his legs. It's certainly a lovely evening. Have you any special instruction, Miss Graham?"

"I don't think so," she said wearily. "I tell you one thing. If she goes on like this I'm going to call her bluff."

"How?" Humphrey asked. He disliked Davina in this mood. She was snappy and on edge.

"I'm going to hand her back to SEDECE with a recommendation that they give her the full treatment," she said. "She knows who killed the Duvaliers. I'm not putting up with this little-girl act for long. Thanks for the drink, Brigadier. Keep a very close eye on her, won't you?"

"Don't worry," he reassured her. "She can't make a move without our knowing. The whole room is a bag of electronic tricks. I'll see you both to your car." Outside he turned to Humphrey. "Will you be back tomorrow, Mr. Grant?"

"I think we'll leave Tim to it," Davina said. "Humphrey, you take over in a couple of days and give him a break. Goodnight." She hurried down the steps and got into the back of the car. Humphrey followed. He was furious at the way she had answered for him. And then, typically, she made amends.

"I'm sorry I'm so on edge, Humphrey. Of course you must say whether you want to go back, or leave it to Tim. It's entirely up to you."

He didn't want to be mollified. "I think I'd rather leave it as you arranged," he said stiffly.

Davina didn't notice the sulk. She lit a cigarette, inhaled, and sighed. "God, I'm tired. It's the frustration of sitting there, hour after hour, listening to her lie. All that stuff about being shy and feeling inferior, I could have boxed her ears at one moment! And she knew it. She was deliberately mocking me. She knew I didn't believe a word of it." She stared out of the window. "We've got to break through," she said. "After the news from Modena, this is the only hope we've got. Valdorini was only small fry. She's told him everything she knows, and it's not enough. They didn't leave Franklyn's killer around to answer questions. And they tried to murder this one; that *proves* how important she is!"

"We'll never find Father Marnie's murderer," Humphrey said gloomily. "MacNeil's people are combing through all the meditation centers, or whatever they're called. It'll take months to find out which are genuine and which are just making money out of gullible idiots. Let alone if one of them is a British version of Ma-Nang."

"You can bet it is," Davina said. "You can bet they've used the same technique as they did in France and Italy. But that's not our pigeon, Humphrey. We can't do everything. It's up to MacNeil and CID to get together and sort out the freaks. The traffic's heavy for this time of night."

He grunted. He felt tired too. He hadn't enjoyed the session either. He found Helene Blond a most disturbing personality. He didn't envy Tim Johnson her company for the next few days. But Davina was right when she said that the girl reacted violently against her. It was unmistakable; Helene Blond hated Davina Graham with the animosity that some women felt for others of their sex. He wondered why, and then gave up thinking about it. Davina dropped him off at his apartment and the drive took her directly home.

She had waited until nearly a quarter to nine for Colin Lomax to turn up that morning, but he didn't come. She turned on the television, watched impatiently for a few minutes and then switched it off. It had been a hellish day. Frustrating, but worse, she had the feeling of being deliberately baited. Davina got herself a cup of coffee. She couldn't be bothered to eat. Cigarettes. She was nearly out of them. Suddenly she thought of Tony Walden. How he had nagged about smoking. It was bad for your health—a filthy, dangerous habit. I love you, he used to insist, so stop doing it and damaging yourself . . . "Oh, Christ." She said it out loud. Then she picked up the packet, and smoked the last cigarette.

She decided to ring Lomax. The telephone rang for ages before he answered.

"Why didn't you come this morning? I waited for you."

"I overslept. I'm sorry."

"Like hell you did." She could feel her temper rising. "You could at least have called me and said you weren't coming."

"Had a bad day, have you?"

"Yes, bloody awful. Anyway why should you care?"

"You always try to pick a row when you're uptight. Listen, Davina, my part of the deal is over. There's nothing for me to see through, as you put it. So don't be difficult. What went wrong then, that it was so bloody?"

"If you were the slightest bit interested," Davina said, "you'd have come to Welton and found out." She hung up, and turned on the television again. If Helene Blond continued to be obstructive, they'd have to give the information on the house of Ma-Nang to the French. And return the girl. Leaving a vacuum, with the murder of Father Marnie, the CND vice president, unsolved, and everybody depending upon the goodwill of SEDECE, who were unlikely to appreciate the British poaching on their preserves. Especially since Lomax had made them look fools by finding out more in a week than their investigators had done in months . . . She hadn't been concentrating on the new program. And it was a minute or two before she realized that her front door bell was ringing. She picked up the entry phone and said, "Who is it?"

"It's me, Davina. Let me in." She put back the phone, hesitated and then pressed the release knob that opened the front door. He always came up stairs at a run. Two at a time. Unlike the other one, who took the elevator even to the first floor. He wouldn't leave her mind that night; but when she opened her door she almost said "Tony" instead of "Colin." "Well, this is a surprise," she said.

He looked at her. "It shouldn't be," he said. "When you wanted to fight, it always used to end one way, remember?"

"Colin," she started, but he stopped her. "Let's just pretend we've had the row," he said, and took her in his arms.

That night Helene Blond had a nightmare. She hadn't dreamed that kind of dream for nearly a year. She woke, her body cold with sweat, and panting with anxiety. For some seconds she couldn't remember where she was; then she reached out and turned on the light. As she did so the hidden camera operating in the ceiling light above the bed recorded every movement. She pulled herself upright and sat, forcing herself to relax, to be calm. Her mother. She hugged herself tightly, adopting the pose of a child without realizing it. A frightened child, using body language to protect itself. She had dreamed that her mother was in the bedroom, carrying the stick in her right hand, walking toward her. She had tried to scream, but she had no voice. She felt paralyzed, unable to run from the approach of that awful punishment, and her mother's enjoyment in inflicting it. Her father wasn't in the dream. He had no part in Helene's nightmare, because he hadn't been there when it was reality. Away on his endless trips abroad, leaving his wife and the child that she hated in the house alone.

Her earliest recollection was fear. Fear of the woman who had total power over her. And it was a power that only expressed itself in punishment. The crying child was slapped and pinched in its cradle. The toddler was locked in the dark. There was a particular cupboard that reduced her to whimpering hysterics. Her mother shut her in it for the slightest mistake. A dirty mark on her dress, a poor appetite, and, horror of horrors, a fit of bedwetting. That produced the cane. Helene Blond was beaten into seeming submission. And through the anguish of her childhood, her father came and went unknowing, while her mother loomed, the smiling sadist in the background, daring her to complain.

By the time she was sixteen her mother had developed terminal cancer. While the illness progressed she stayed quiet, daydreaming of the moment when she would find the woman helpless, and leaning over the deathbed, put her hands round her throat and squeeze and squeeze. The moment never came. Marguerite Blond went to the hospital and died there. Helene stood by the bed with her father and said nothing. Did nothing. The intolerable hate festered inside her, unrelieved. She carried it out into the world with her, an ordinary young girl, an average student, a walking time bomb who was about to go off and blow herself to pieces.

That was when she decided to try meditation. It helped insomnia, apparently; another lycée student told her about it, and mentioned the institute. They were Chinese, and their methods weren't as other-worldly as the Indian. She had been and found it very helpful. At this time she was living with her aunt. Her father was away so much it was decided that she couldn't stay at home. The nights were spent reading until dawn, her nerves screaming for the sleep that wouldn't come. There was no one she could tell about the nightmare. Certainly not her aunt. She hated her. She hated her because she was kind, and all Helene knew was cruelty. She was weak and easy to dominate. The girl despised her. She wanted strength and punishment, like before. To inflict on others what she had suffered herself. But not to sleep, in case she dreamed.

So she went to the house of Ma-Nang and found there the answer to all her problems. The nightmare stopped. The threatened mental breakdown receded, and a different madness took its place. The desire to kill and destroy.

She kept the light on for some time. She had been taught to rationalize when she felt afraid or disoriented. Her mother's reemergence was the result of her confinement, and the fact that she was at the mercy of another woman. But she had no need to fear. She was strong, invincible in her strength now. She had proved it once. She was "France." Nobody would ever get the better of her now. She turned out the light and went to sleep. Her last conscious thought was about Davina Graham. What would she say if she knew that she had killed all those people? That would make her look at Helene Blond with very different eyes . . .

"It won't work," Davina said. He pulled the pillow behind his head. "I thought it worked pretty well," he said. "You're a lovely woman, but I wish you'd shut up. You've lost a bit too much weight, sweetheart."

Davina looked at him. "Colin, please. Be serious, can't you?"

"No," he said firmly. "Not at the moment. I've made love and I'm happy. And I'm not going to let you spoil it. I didn't ask to come back, but back I am, and this time, it's going to work, whether you think so or not. Let's clear one point first. You're not in love with Walden?"

She reached her arm across his chest and leaned against him. "No. If I was, I wouldn't be in bed with you."

Lomax stroked her hand and twined the fingers in his. "Then that's good enough," he said. "Why don't we start from there? Give it a real chance this time? Or are you waiting for me to say I love you?"

"Do you?"

He pulled her close to him. "I wouldn't be in bed with you if I didn't. So let's call it quits."

He didn't ask her the question. She waited but it didn't come. If it had, she would have been afraid to answer. Did she love him? Yes. As a man, as a comrade, as a lover. But not to the exclusion of that other side of her life. And that was why she had said it wouldn't work. Because she was afraid of a second commitment and a second failure. He didn't deserve to be hurt again. That night she told him why she had broken with Walden.

They talked until it was early morning. "Tony thought I'd solve it all by giving up my job," Davina said. "He really expected me to opt for marriage and forget all about it."

"He didn't know you very well," Lomax said. "In fact he must have been blind as a bat if he thought you wouldn't look into that story about his family. I thought he was clever; one of the bright sparks of private enterprise. But I didn't think he'd sell his country out either."

"It's not *his* country," she retorted. "He doesn't have one. I've realized that since. All he had was his business and me. He doesn't even like his sons much. He was a sitting duck for Borisov's agents. And I was a sitting duck too, in a way. I trusted him."

"But not enough," Lomax said.

"Which was lucky, as it happened."

"So how do things stand now?"

"I arranged for a leak," she explained. "It must have been convincing or they'd have exposed him."

"Which you didn't want," Lomax said casually.

"No, I didn't. Believe it or not, Colin, he suffered enough through losing me. And I'm not being conceited."

"I'm sure," he said. "What was the story?"

"That I'd left him for somebody else."

"And it worked?"

"I don't know. I haven't heard from him since that night. Which is surprising, I must say, I didn't think he'd give up so easily."

Lomax lit a cigarette and passed it to her. "He's still a risk," he said. "You'll have to do something about him, darling. Once on the hook, they never let go. You know that as well as I do."

Davina hesitated. "He's on file," she said at last. "Humphrey will have passed it on to MacNeil. They'll keep an eye on him."

He laughed.

She looked at him in surprise. "What's funny?"

"You are," he said. "You're getting to sound like your friend James White."

She moved away from him. "Don't say that. It isn't true."

He drew her back to him. "No it isn't," he admitted. "Not yet, anyway. Give me a kiss or make me breakfast?"

She looked at her watch. "Breakfast," she said. "My God! Look at the time; I've got to be in the office in an hour."

He showered and dressed, and had coffee and eggs while she checked her briefcase and made two telephone calls. He watched her and didn't say anything.

Tony Walden wouldn't have had a chance. She'd got out of bed and slipped into her second personality the moment her foot touched the floor. Bloody fool, thinking he could gamble with her career and then offer marriage as an alternative. He'd taken her away from Lomax, but he hadn't really known her at all. Any more than she had known him.

He cleared the dirty dishes and looked forward to his day. He was no longer jealous. Now that it was over, he recognized how it had eaten into him, giving a subtle bitterness to everything he did. He wasn't jealous of Tony Walden anymore. And he was going into the first round of what would be a long, hard battle. To get Davina Graham back into his life. It wouldn't be easy, but he was determined that this time he was going to win.

They left the apartment together. In the entrance hall he kissed her lightly. "Dinner tonight?"

"Am I cooking?"

Not yet, my love, he thought to himself. But you will be. "I am," he said. "Come to the Barbican. Make it eight; give me time to get my apron on."

"You idiot," she said, and kissed him hard on the lips.

The arrangement to meet in Brussels had been made at short notice. Tony Walden's secretary booked him into the Amigo as usual, and penciled in the name of his client in the engagement schedule. He was busier than ever these days. He seemed to immerse himself in work and trips abroad, and there was a noticeable change in him that his staff discussed among themselves. He was withdrawn, irritable; he seemed loath to spend a weekend out of the office or not in an airplane. Everyone knew he had been having an affair for the past two years with the woman who had been his assistant for a short period. It was soon obvious that this was over, and it accounted for his changed manner.

There had been other women in his life. His devoted secretary, Freda Young, had known about the weekends spent at hotels in Paris or Madrid, the checks that went to furriers and jewelers; the permanent suite at the Ritz Hotel where he entertained clients, and women friends. Freda had been in love with Walden for years, and suffered miserably when he became seriously involved. She didn't mind the casual mistresses, beautiful blondes didn't worry her. A clever, independent woman like Davina Graham was a rival she couldn't cope with. Better that stupid, glossy wife . . . She was sorry for him, because he was obviously unhappy.

The Belgian client was important; whenever they contacted him, Walden set aside other engagements. She said goodbye to him as he left the office for the airport that Wednesday morning. He looked tired and heavy-eyed; she noticed he had developed a nervous habit of picking at his thumbnail with his index finger. The cuticle was so sore that there was a rim of blood round the nail. She wanted to say something, but she didn't dare.

Walden arrived after a smooth flight. He was met by a hired car and driven to the Amigo. A beautiful city, Brussels. Warm in the summer sun, busy with tourists. But he didn't really notice anything surrounding him, until he was in his hotel room. As always there was fresh fruit and a complimentary bottle of champagne. They knew how to welcome a rich customer. He looked at his watch. An hour to wait. He lay on the bed and hooked his arms under his head. There was no painted ceiling here as there had been at the Gritti in Venice. Davina wouldn't walk out of the bathroom and come to lie beside him. He hadn't slept with a woman since he had left her apartment that night. He had avoided his wife, who seemed poised to ask or tell him something. He didn't know which, and he didn't care. The house in the country bored him as much as she did. He could feel her impatience when he was at home. She had to keep her boy friends out of the way until he went back to London. He found escape in the office. Work was a refuge, and his success was escalating. More accounts were coming, bigger and richer than before. There had been an article on him in the *Financial Times,* describing him as the most dynamic force in advertising. There was a photograph, taken five years earlier, showing a sleek, smiling man, exuding confidence. So much was still at risk, and the danger hadn't disappeared. He had lost the woman he loved. The emptiness was unbearable if he gave himself time to feel it.

At five minutes past midday, the phone rang. He answered it and said, "Yes, let the gentleman come up."

He was a prosperous Belgian in his mid-fifties; overpolite, finicky in manner.

"I hope you had a good flight over, Monsieur Walden?"

"Yes, very good. I was surprised to get your message. I thought we had resolved the matter."

The Belgian shook his head. "Unfortunately not. Your proposal to make over the bulk of the Swiss money to a designated account was well received. I personally recommended it. But there has been a change of mind. My friends are not interested in the money."

Walden felt the sweat breaking out. Not interested in the money. What was this—the carrot-and-the-stick technique? Yes, we'll settle for that and you can sleep easy, but no, we've decided we want something else instead.

"What are they interested in? And don't ask for the impossible. I have no access to information anymore. They know that."

"Yes, yes they do. We have our own sources of information, and everything has checked out. Your former friend has a new man. Well," he shrugged a little. "Not a new one. The one she had before you." Seeing Walden's face he said, "You didn't know this?"

"No." There was a moment's silence. The Belgian seemed content to wait. "This man," Walden began slowly. "The one before me . . . is it a Major Lomax?"

"Yes, that is the name. He worked for the Secret Service." She had given him an alibi as she promised. With Lomax. "If they don't want to take over the Swiss account, what do they want?"

The man's face was bland. "You must make contact with Miss Graham again."

"Don't be a fool! If they think I'd get anything out of her if we did meet, they're crazy! She probably wouldn't even see me."

"Please," he lifted a smooth, rather plump hand. "Please listen to me first. Nobody is expecting you to get information. All you have to do is persuade her to meet you, and give her a present. That's all. Surely," he went on, "surely you didn't part on such bad terms . . . after all, she left you—didn't she?"

Walden saw the trap. The bastard, he thought. If they suspect I admitted the truth to her, they'll smash me . . . "She left me," he said angrily. "I'd been away in Australia and she got bored. I didn't know quite how bored. I didn't know she'd taken her old lover back." He tensed, his suspicion rising. "But get one thing absolutely clear. I won't do anything to harm her."

"Monsieur Walden," the Belgian said patiently, "please don't think we are fools. Nobody would suggest that you do anything that could cause Miss Graham any personal harm. Our friends know that nothing would persuade you to do that. Every man has a price, but he also has a threshold, which can't be crossed. No one is suggesting that you hurt a woman you have loved, however much she has hurt you." He smiled. "You must think our friends are very poor psychologists. Now, let us be reasonable and put this in perspective. You are in an extremely vulnerable position. You have committed a currency fraud that could send you to prison for a minimum of two years. You have used clients' money illegally. Your business is dependent upon you; *you* are the business, Monsieur Walden. The result of an investigation would ruin you financially and professionally. It would disgrace your wife and sons to have you serve a prison sentence. I am sorry to remind you of all this, but these are the facts. Now, all you have to do to avoid this happening is to persuade Miss Graham to see you, and get her to wear this." He took a box out of his pocket and handed it to Walden. "Examine it, please. Satisfy yourself that it is genuine. For myself," he added gently, "I've never heard of any woman being harmed by a present from Cartier's."

Tim Johnson decided that he had been patient long enough. He looked at the girl sitting opposite to him; smoking the cigarettes provided, asking for special food, stalling his questions with a supposed migraine. He decided the time had come to attack. "You've got a headache?"

"Yes," she said, sulkily. "I can't answer you with a pain like this."

"Same sort of headache as the night the Duvalier family were murdered?"

She hadn't expected that. Her anger showed. "That was worse. I was blind with the pain."

"You get headaches at the most convenient moments, don't you? Did you get the headache before, or after?"

"Before or after what? I don't understand you."

"Before your friends killed them," Johnson sprang it on her. "You let them in, didn't you? You opened the door for them and then you slipped upstairs and drugged yourself. Did you know they were going to shoot them all? Even the girl who was your friend? No wonder you get headaches."

He didn't get the reaction he expected, there was something like contempt in her eyes when she looked at him.

"I didn't let anybody in," she said. "I was upstairs with a migraine and I took sleeping pills."

"If you didn't have any part in it," he persisted, "why are your friends trying to kill you? They killed the man who murdered the American secretary of state—you know that, don't you?"

"I know what you've told me," she said. "Maybe they didn't try to kill me. Maybe the car was an accident."

He turned away from her. "I think you're wasting my time," he said. "I'm going back to London. Somebody else can talk to you. But I am going to put in a report about you, Helene. I shall say that you're being deliberately obstructive and that we should send you back to France."

The threat didn't shake her. She made a grimace. "Maybe I will cooperate with the new person." Her eyes lowered and then examined him, still with the gleam of contempt lurking in them. "Will it be that woman?"

"No," Johnson snapped. "You're not important enough to interest her."

The mockery was suddenly gone. A red flush burned in her cheeks. "I'm more important than you think!"

"I don't agree," Johnson was in the ascendant. He pressed the advantage. "I think you're a pathetic nobody, giving yourself airs. My boss has better things to do than waste her time with you. I'll make sure she knows it."

"I won't speak to this other person," Helene shouted. "Tell them that! Tell them not to come!"

He didn't answer. He left the room and walked away down the passage. The cameras would be watching her reaction when she was alone. Before he drove back to London, he had a screening of the film. What he saw made him and the brigadier exchange looks. "Meditating?" he queried. "Autohypnosis," Johnson explained. "She put herself out. Otherwise I think she'd have smashed up the room. I'd better get back. I think we'll let her cool off tomorrow. Maybe for a few days. I'll let you know."

"What nags at me is this so called meditation institute. Ma-Nang sounds authentic but actually means nothing at all." Davina turned to Tim Johnson. "Why pick a phony Oriental name?"

"And why not use it here in England? Unless of course they sent in a foreign operative to kill poor old Marnie."

"You're right. Of course you're right. We couldn't get anything on Ma-Nang on our computers because they didn't set up a place over here. And the question is, why not? Why France and Italy and Russia, for God's sake, and not here? Whoever murdered Nikolaev was a Russian, we know that. So this brainwashing business has a base in Russia too. Tim, listen, it's probably a crackpot idea, but why don't we bring Poliakov in on this?"

"I don't see that it's crackpot," he answered. "As we're leaving Blond to stew for a bit, it can't do any harm. He might have an idea. He's forgotten more about the way the Russians think than we'll ever know." He grinned, "Sorry, I'm talking about myself."

"Don't undersell yourself," she said. "You're as bright as any of us. See if you can find Poliakov. He may be at home; the pubs are shut!"

But Poliakov had taken his vodka with him. He was belligerent and muddled when Tim spoke to him. "I'll have to go to his flat," he told Davina. "Sober the old bugger up. There's no use having him round here like he is."

It was nearly five before Johnson reappeared. The old man was very pale, watery-eyed and distinctly unsteady. But it was sobriety that made his hands shake. He said to Davina, "Miss Graham—this bully has been making my life a misery since three this afternoon. I was sitting at home perfectly peaceful, reading, when in he comes—"

Johnson interrupted. "You were pissed as a newt. And the only thing you'd been reading, old chap, was the label on the bottle. However, black coffee does do the trick in the end."

"I was sick," Poliakov announced with dignity. "What are you paying for this? I expect a bonus, otherwise I refuse to help you. Did you take my advice and send someone over to Paris, Miss Graham?"

"I did," Davina answered. "And you were quite right. She's a guest at Welton this very moment."

"Ah," the Pole managed a painful smile. "Good. I remember what a comfortable hotel that was. Some of our best traitors stayed there, didn't they? Now, if I could have a small drink, just to steady myself after what I've been through." He paused. He was sober, and his eyes were knowing.

Davina decided not to argue. He was notoriously temperamental. Tim must have exceeded his brief to get him to Anne's Yard in lucid condition. "I can get you some brandy from Personnel," she said. "Will that do?"

"Medicinal." He laughed. "Thank you." He flashed a look of triumph at Johnson. A few minutes later, with the drink cuddled in his hands, he said to Davina, "What do you want me to tell you?"

And when she told him, he laughed again. "Oh, I see. You tried the computer. And your friend wasted his time on Chinese reference books. He could have been there till now, you realize that? Ma-Nang. No, my dear Miss Graham, you won't find that listed anywhere." She leaned forward, hiding her impatience. She could see that he had an answer and was holding back. Teasing them both.

"Poliakov," she said, "what does it mean?"

"It means the Company of Saints. In Mongolian dialect." He leaned back and chuckled. "Your therapists aren't *Chinese*— they're Mongolians. Ma-Nang. Didn't you learn about the Last Judgment, either of you? How the damned are dragged to hell by demons, and the Company of Saints surround the throne of God?"

"Good God," Johnson exclaimed.

"Not in this case," Poliakov retorted. "A God surrounded by assassins. The wicked triumphant. Not the Christian concept at all." He sipped his brandy and looked smug.

Davina said, "Who would think up a thing like this? It is Soviet-directed, isn't it?"

"Of course it is." He showed impatience at the question. "It has a smell of the old anti-religious campaign of the twenties. Old

Bolshevik stuff. Jewish-inspired in the beginning. They had little reason to love the Christian church with its persecutions. And there's nothing as savage as atheists with a deep religious consciousness behind them. Ma-Nang. Yes, Miss Graham, Russian-inspired and controlled. But by a curious kind of Russian." He finished his brandy.

"Borisov?" Davina asked.

He shook his head. "I don't think so. He's a modern tyrant. This harks back to the old days. I don't think the Company of Saints is run by the KGB."

"Then you mean there's someone powerful enough to get an organization like this together and set it working independently of Borisov?"

He nodded at Davina. "I would think so. But I'll need to think more. In my own time. At your expense."

"You can write your own bill. How long will it take?"

"To do what? Tell you who I think is the most likely man in the hierarchy?" He shrugged, and put down the empty glass. "I'll need access to your files. I'll make up a plan, like a family tree—going back before the war. I don't know how long I'll need to reach a definite conclusion. I can put up ideas quickly enough, but they won't be backed by research. And that's what you must have. What will you do if I have an answer for you?"

"I'll decide about that when the time comes," Davina said. "You'll have every facility you need, and I hope you'll start here tomorrow."

"I shall be here," he announced. "And sober."

When he had gone, Davina phoned through to Humphrey. He came to the office and listened with his usual lack of excitement. "I think it's the break we needed," Davina said. "Picking up that girl and tying this in will give us the facts, and I hope the means to smash this organization."

"He is a drunk," he reminded her. "Do you believe he'll spend days on end here without throwing the whole thing up and slipping round to the nearest pub? I'm afraid I don't. Poliakov can cope with an odd problem. He hasn't the stamina for anything as deep as this."

Davina mastered her irritation. Quite soon it would turn into real anger at his negative approach. "Then what else do you suggest, Humphrey?"

"Step up the interrogation of Helene Blond. Put heavy

187

pressure on her and don't give her any let-up at all. With respect to you, Tim," he glanced morosely at Johnson. "I don't think your tactics are the right ones. I should like to go down tomorrow and set about her."

Davina hesitated. Then she said. "Right, Humphrey, you do that. You give her hell and you can use any threats you like, I'll back you up. And Poliakov can at least make a start. You know, I think he needs somebody to help him, somebody to keep an eye on him in case he starts slipping. I'll ask Colin if he'll do it."

Humphrey pursed his lips. "You talk as if he'd come back on a regular basis."

"I hope he will," Davina answered. "But it's on a favor basis at the moment."

It had been a long day, but she felt satisfied. There was always a crucial moment when a solution was near, and only the experience of years could identify it. That had been Sir James White's special gift. He had the capacity to sit through disappointments, frustrations, and blind leads without losing his confidence. When the moment came, he recognized it and acted.

Poliakov was the catalyst in this business, and Davina knew it. She had deflected Humphrey's pessimism and relied on her own instinct. Perhaps Colin was right; perhaps she was becoming like the Chief. But not heartless or ready to sacrifice anything or anybody as he had done with her husband, Ivan Sasanov. She sat in a traffic jam outside Sloane Square, and thought about Ivan and James White's responsibility for his murder in Australia. She had blamed him and hated him for it for years.

The traffic began to move. It was raining and congestion increased. There was nothing James White could have done to prevent Sasanov from being killed. She had never imagined she could admit that to herself.

She drove up Sloane Street and branched left, heading toward her apartment. The wipers whirred across the windscreen, and the rain spattered like tears outside.

She had accused James White of using her husband and then neglecting to protect him when he had nothing more to give. It wasn't true. Nobody could have shielded Sasanov against the assassins of the KGB when her own brother-in-law was pointing him out to them.

She had done her old boss a great injustice. She had accused him and blamed him to his face, sweeping aside his explanations. She parked her car, locked it and went to her front door. It was a strange feeling, this acknowledgment that she was in the wrong. Almost as if a weight had been lifted. But it was already moving away. Subconsciously she had recognized that James White had done his best within the circumstances. Taking on his responsibilities had changed her view. That was why she had gone to him for advice about Tony Walden.

It was different, as everyone knew, when the opposition became the government. Now she was the government. She went upstairs, had a bath and thought about Helene Blond and Poliakov. Humphrey could be very daunting. But he wouldn't find it easy to frighten that girl. She was not seeing Colin that night. He had work to catch up on, and she accepted his commitment. He hadn't been pleased that she was so understanding about it, she could tell that, and it made her smile. He would never change. He would always be the macho man, expecting her to be the weaker partner. So long as they stayed as they were, it wouldn't really come between them. He'd accept her commitments as she accepted his. But not without a fight. And this time, she was going to let him think he'd won. She'd learned that much from past mistakes. And perhaps seeing and recognizing the truth about Sasanov's death had liberated her, and made her more mature as a person. Hatred and blame were stunting factors. They crippled the personality. Now at last she was free of them. The bell rang. She thought, "He's finished early and come round . . . I'm glad."

She said into the ansaphone, "Come up, love." And pushed the button. When she opened her own front door she saw Tony Walden standing there.

"I thought you weren't going to let me in," he said.

"I was just surprised," Davina answered. "Why didn't you telephone?"

"You wouldn't have seen me, would you?"

"No," she said quietly. "I don't think I would."

He looked around the room, and said, "I've missed you so much. I never thought I could miss someone as much as I miss you."

"I'm sorry," she said. "I don't want you to be unhappy, Tony. Can't you try and get it in perspective?"

He looked searchingly at her. She remembered how sad his eyes were at times. The sadness of the most persecuted race in human history.

"No," he answered. "That's why I've got to talk to you. I've thought about ringing you so many times." He paused. "I hoped I'd see my way clear if I gave it time. Davina, I know what I did before. I know saying I'm sorry isn't going to change anything, but can't I start with that?"

"Of course you can," she said quickly. "But it isn't necessary now. I don't want you to apologize, Tony, and I don't want you to regret anything. It's over and done with, and we've got a lot of good things to remember."

"I keep thinking," he went on. "Did I really explain it to her? Did I make her understand my motives? Davina—will you listen to me once more, and then make up your mind?"

She felt herself stiffen. I don't want to listen, she thought. I've managed to forgive you and even feel sorry for you, but I don't want to hear it again. In case it hurts as much as it did.

"Tony please," she said quietly, "you did explain. And I did understand. I've thought about it too, believe me. I know you loved me and you tried to play both ends against the middle. But in my work it isn't possible. It isn't possible to have your cake and eat it. I don't think it's a good idea in general, anyway. But for someone in my position it's unthinkable. So why don't we just let it go at that?"

He looked at her and said slowly, "Davina, if you will come back to me, I'll take the consequences. I'll let them go ahead and I'll take my chance. I built my business up once and I can do it again. I'll probably go to jail, but I can face that too, if I've got you to come back to. Will you take me back?"

"I can't," Davina answered. "I can't be involved with anybody in your position, and you know that perfectly well."

"I'm ready to give up everything for you," he said. "All you have to do is resign from your job. Don't you have any love left for me at all?"

It was the question she had been dreading. Easy to be hard-hearted and to hurt him, easy to remind him of how he had cheated and risked ruining her in order to keep what he valued himself. But she didn't want to hurt him. She didn't want to answer, but there was no other way. "No, Tony, I'm afraid I haven't. I did love you very much. But I don't anymore."

"Lomax has moved back in, I hear?"

She felt suddenly angry. "Yes, he has. I suppose you heard from your friends in the KGB? They keep tabs on that kind of thing, don't they? But it won't do them any good to know about Colin."

He didn't look at her. He didn't want her to see his eyes. "Is he the reason you can't forgive me, Davina?"

"No," she said. "If he hadn't come into my life again, I still wouldn't leave my job for you, Tony. I wouldn't be in love with you. That died before I ever saw him again. Don't let's upset each other any more. I don't want to ask you to go, but I think it's the best thing."

He didn't move for a minute, but sat quite still with his head averted.

"Would you like a drink?" Davina said.

"No thanks." He was back in the hotel in Brussels. The smooth face of his Soviet contact swam before his eyes and the words rang in his head. "One of our agents is being interrogated. That bracelet contains an electronic signal that will tell us where they are. It is only effective for a few days. Miss Graham will see the agent and after that it is just a beautiful ornament. All you have to do is put it on her wrist. Nobody will ever know."

He had offered her everything, even to go to prison, if she would take him back and give him another chance. Even so, he might have resisted, if she hadn't replaced him with Colin Lomax. He got up, slipped the little red box out of his pocket. "Davina," he said. "I bought you this. Please try it on before you say anything."

"I won't take anything from you, Tony," she said. "I can't."

He took her left hand in his. "You could look at it," he said. "It's not much to ask." He opened the bracelet and clipped it onto her wrist. It was a series of white and yellow gold links with gold bolts fastening them. A red enamel heart with an arrow piercing it hung like a charm from the middle of it. Davina said, "It's beautiful, Tony, but I can't accept it."

He turned away from her. He wanted to get out of the apartment. He wanted to convince himself that he was right to do what he had done.

"You can't get it off," he said. "That's the whole point. It's locked on. So every time you look at it, you'll think of me. Goodbye, Davina."

He hurried out before she could stop him. The front door banged and she stayed still, listening for the street door to shut behind him.

She pulled at the bracelet. Of course, she remembered reading advertisements for the love-lock bracelet, as it was called. The chicquest thing to give the woman you love. Walden could have thought up the advertisement himself. It could be removed, but only by Cartier's craftsmen. What a stupid, awkward thing for him to do. She turned it round on her wrist and the little red heart gleamed in the electric light. She wondered what Colin Lomax would say when he saw it.

The man code-named "Ireland" turned his television set over to the BBC news. His mother looked up and said, "Why do you want to watch that stuff, Kieran? Your daddy goes mad when he finds you watching them over there!"

"Mammy," he said, "I like the world news. RTE doesn't tell us anything about what's going on. Who gives a fuck if they're having a strike in Cork? They're always having strikes!"

She said the same thing that she did every day. "Don't use that language, Kieran, not round the house. Your daddy'd go mad if he heard you."

Her son didn't answer. His daddy had been going mad at him and his brothers and sisters ever since he could remember. Should have been a priest, with a pot belly and the collection money in his pocket. Always going mad, he was, about doing this or not doing that, putting the fear of God into them all. Mass and confession, family rosary, holy pictures and oil lamps in front of them in every child's room. "Don't do anything to make Our Lady blush," the crabbed old nun used to warn them at school. He'd made them all blush not long ago, when he pumped bullets into that old humbug of a Christ look-a-like, bawling about peace and loving the Russians. Kieran didn't love anyone. He hated the English as much as he hated his canting bully of a father. The poor witless woman nodding at the fireside, mouthing about Daddy this and Daddy that, while she let him make a child a year till she was too old to go on—she didn't count. He didn't hate her. He despised her. He hadn't felt sorry for her, because she wasn't sorry for him, or the other children when they got the belt and the Bible.

There had been a memorial service in London for Father Marnie. The TV showed churchmen and politicians shuffling into a cathedral, eyeing the cameras in case they'd get noticed. And the announcer added that investigations were continuing into the murder. Kieran grinned. They didn't know where to look and they wouldn't ever find him. Daddy wouldn't be going mad about that. He leaned forward and switched back to the Irish channel.

8

"COLIN, I promise you, it won't take long."

"Why can't you get someone else to do it? Jim Fraser's going round the bend. And when are you going to go and get that bloody bracelet sawn off?"

Davina sighed. He had made such a fuss when he saw it. She had to repeat the scene with Walden word for word before he was satisfied. He had even tried to pry the links apart himself. But it was impossible.

"Darling," she said, "I can't trust anyone to look after Poliakov except someone he'll accept as a colleague. He's a temperamental devil, and ten times worse when he's on the wagon. I can build you up as a military expert, and he won't mind having you there working with him. If I send in someone junior he's quite likely to walk out!"

Lomax put his arm round her. "All right, stop getting yourself worked up. I'll nanny the old boy for a few days. And what kind of military expert am I supposed to be? Just so I know."

"Thank you," she said and kissed him. "You're an expert on guerrilla warfare. He's going to dig right back to the beginning: 1919 onward. He's really excited about it. I think he's got an idea but he won't put it forward till he can back it up. But Humphrey doesn't believe he'll last the pace, and if he starts on a binge we've

had it. So you have to keep him in line, Colin, just keep him happy and interested and head him off if he wants to go out."

"Sweetheart," he said softly, "I know my job, you don't have to spell it out."

"I didn't mean to," she apologized. "It's just that I've got a lot on at the moment and we're not making any progress at all with the blasted girl. Humphrey's tried everything, and he's pretty good. She won't budge. She's actually getting him down, I think. I'll have to take it up myself, I can see that, but I don't want to tread on his toes unless I have to. Oh, Lord—when it's over, why don't we take a holiday? Together?"

He smiled. "I have a business of my own, and what I'm doing now is on holiday time. But—we might slip away for a long weekend somewhere. You look tired."

"I'll drive you to the office then," Davina said. "Poliakov's going to start this morning. I think I should drive down to Marchwood on Saturday. I haven't seen my mother for ages. I don't want to run into Charlie if she's there."

"Am I allowed to come along?" The car turned down Birdcage Walk.

"You know you are; they always adored you. Why don't you marry that nice major of yours? They went on and on about you, Colin. I could have screamed at times." She laughed at him. "Just the right type, my father used to say. Splendid chap. Marvelous decoration."

"Shut up," Lomax said. "Pay attention to the road. Your father was dead right, as it happens. You should marry me, and I am a splendid chap. So we'll go down on Saturday. And if Charlie's there, too bad. Why should you care?"

"Because she blames me," Davina said. "I told you. She blames me for ruining her life. It upsets me, and I can't afford that at the moment."

"It's strange," he said after a moment. "She's a worthless, self-ish female, without a tenth of your intelligence, but she's always been able to put you down. It's time you grew out of it, Davina. I'll come with you, and if she starts being difficult, you stand up to her."

"And upset Mother? No, Colin. If Charlie's down there, I'll go another time." She turned the car into the cul-de-sac. He looked at her without saying anything.

"Oh, all right," she burst out. "All right, I am a coward about it. I'll go to Marchwood on Saturday whether she's there or not!"

Lomax leaned over and opened the car door for her. "I'll go and babysit your Pole," he said. "And on Friday we'll both go to Cartier's and get lover-boy's memento taken off. I don't want your family thinking I'd give you a vulgar thing like that."

Borisov went up in the private elevator to the top floor. He was met by Keremov's wife. She looked as if she had been crying. "Come in, Igor Igorovitch," she said, and took him by the hand. He saw the three doctors who attended the ruler of Russia standing like white-coated phantoms in the background. He didn't speak to them. Madame Keremova led him by the hand into the bedroom. Side by side they approached the bed. Borisov stood looking down at his friend and protector.

He had shrunk, the flesh falling away from the skull, leaving the eyes hollowed and leaden. "Go close," she said. "He finds it hard to speak."

Borisov leaned down. He caught the sour whiff of a sick man's breath. Sick and soon to die. "My son," the voice cracked. "I'm finished. You must ... make your move ... your enemies ... your enemy."

Borisov clasped the chilly hand that lay on the cover. It was slack and lifeless. "I know my enemies," he said. "And I won't let them destroy what you have built for Russia." He felt a touch on his shoulder. It was Keremov's wife. The tears were running down her cheeks.

"That's what he wanted," she said. "Now he'll die in peace. Sit with me."

Three hours later Borisov came out of the bedroom. The senior doctor came toward him. "It's time we examined Comrade Keremov before his next medication."

Borisov stared at him and the man stepped back. "No medication is needed," he said. "The president is sleeping peacefully and is not to be disturbed. You will stay here until he wakes." He walked out and the elevator took him to Keremov's office. The staff on duty didn't dare refuse him its facilities. Within the hour the special military arm of the KGB were in control of the president's private apartments and the communications leading out of it. The doctors and nurse in attendance were not allowed to leave or to telephone. They were to wait, they were told in Borisov's words, for the president to wake from his sleep before they went into his room. For the next thirty-six hours, it was vital to Igor Borisov that no one in Russia outside his own organization should know that Keremov was dead.

Helene Blond hadn't slept. Every night for the past week she had been tortured by the nightmare. The monitors showed her waking, switching the light on, sitting up, obviously distressed, and calming herself by deep breathing. But she didn't talk in her sleep or give a clue to what woke her night after night. In the day she battled with the gaunt interrogator, with his greenish skin and skull-like face, going on and on in a voice as maddening as a dripping tap.

"Who were the other students you became friends with at the institute?"

"There weren't any I liked."

"Why didn't you tell your best friend, Louise Duvalier, about the place?"

"Why should I? She didn't need help."

"But she was your best friend?"

"Yes."

"You didn't hate her, did you?"

"No. I told you, she was my best friend."

"How did you feel when you heard she was dead?"

"Very upset."

"Her mother was very kind to you, wasn't she?"

A shrug. It annoyed him when she did that.

"How did you feel when you heard she was dead too?"

"Upset."

"You didn't know the people who killed them, did you?" Without waiting for an answer, "You didn't slip down and let them in, Helene, and then run upstairs, while they went into the room and shot them?"

The scream was in her mouth when he repeated that question, over and over again.

No, I didn't let them in. There wasn't a "them." It was me! I went in and fired and fired until they were dead! She hadn't let the scream out and she wasn't going to say those words. He wasn't winning, but the stress was making her dream that terrible dream again, until she was torn between the longing to sleep and the dread of what would come when she did. And through it all she kept thinking of the Englishwoman who hadn't come to see her. The one who was too important to be bothered by Helene Blond. Why do I care? she asked herself. Why do I chafe and fume because she isn't here? Because I feel her in the background; like knowing my mother was downstairs even when she wasn't coming up to punish me. She's there, and that's part of the fear and the rage that fills me. Like my mother, she can come whenever she feels like it and make me cringe with fear. But she can't. You've forgotten what they taught you, Helene. You are the one who can make other people afraid. You saw the terror in their faces that night when you came into the salon and pointed your gun?

And she decided what to do. She wanted to engage in conflict with this woman who had brought her mother back into her dreams. She wanted to defy her and mock her as she had done with the two men. Then she would feel in command of herself once more. Then she would think of making a deal for her safety by telling them a little more about Ma-Nang, about the people who had sent the car out to kill her when she went to them for help. And the beauty of it would be when she refused to talk to the Engishwoman and sent her away humiliated. She would talk to the first man, the younger one who tried to win her confidence. Helene thought about it, planned how the interviews would go, and became excited. She had a peaceful sleep and the next morning she told Humphrey Grant that she wanted to see Davina Graham. She refused to trust anyone else.

Borisov made a series of visits. He made them unoñicially. The minister for Communications. The minister for Agriculture. The new foreign minister who had replaced his opponent Nikolaev. And the head of the Soviet navy. He took each one into his confidence. The president was desperately ill. He had given orders that nobody was to be told until Borisov had time to alert the men whom Keremov trusted. Borisov was not only his messenger but his preferred candidate for the chairmanship of the party, and the presidency. He didn't pretend modesty. He stated a fact and in each case he showed a letter. The letter came from Keremov and was addressed to each of them. He let them read it but he didn't leave it with them.

He asked for their support in the Politburo when the time came. And he named the likely contenders who would try to take power for themselves. The most dangerous, he said, was Marshal Yemetovsky. This found favor with the minister for Communications, who hated the marshal, and also with the head of the Soviet navy, who was a bitter rival. Second to the marshal was the minister for Internal Affairs. Mishkoyan, the Armenian. An old man with red hands; a ferocious oppressor of dissidents and Jews, who had maintained his position by destroying younger men who might have replaced him. A ruthless survivor from a past that should be set aside for the history books. The future of the great Soviet Union would be dark indeed if it were to be entrusted to him. Without exception, the others agreed with that. They had reason to dislike Mishkoyan. Each had a different reason, but the result was the same. They hardened in opposition against him and were in favor of the man strong enough to shunt him aside. Igor Borisov presented himself as that man. It wasn't high politics or patriotic duty that moved the negotiations in his favor. There was serious bargaining on all sides. Promises were exchanged and undertakings of support given. By the end of the first thirty hours, Igor Borisov felt himself strong enough to go forward as an official candidate as soon as Keremov's death was announced.

The first rumors began inside the Kremlin. They spread to the departments and to the foreign embassies whose spies were operating in the city. Keremov was dying. At any moment, Russia would be without a leader. The reports went through to the Western capitals, and Borisov reckoned that he would have to lift the embargo sooner than he intended. His work was mostly done, the ground as well-prepared as he could make it.

Marshal Yemetovsky called a conference of his senior officers. Mishkoyan gathered his supporters for a meeting and outlined his plans. By consent, the candidates remained in Moscow, waiting for what most of them believed had already happened. Like crows perched on the railings, they poised themselves for the gunshot that would announce Keremov's death and set them wheeling and swooping in their pursuit of his power. The rumors that he was dying were followed by rumors that he was dead and that the death had been concealed.

The Intelligence services of the world also waited for confirmation. Diplomats and correspondents everywhere were drawing up their lists of candidates.

The Soviet marshal was favored by most, and his hard-line attitude produced despondency among the peace lobby. They had little hope of persuading their own governments to disarm unilaterally if a man who declared his belief in war came to power in Russia. Mishkoyan, the Stalinist, was next; a brutal clampdown on the intellectuals and arts was forecast. His dark Armenian face appeared in newspapers and on television screens. He provoked alarm and echoes of the Cold War. There were the moderates, and they had their supporters. Two members of the Politburo who were known to favor detente and had no reputation for suppressing liberties at home. Their faces appeared too. Nobody mentioned the name of Igor Borisov.

Poliakov had set himself up in the filing section. He had been given a computer, a trained operative, and Colin Lomax. For the first two days he unfolded a series of meaningless historical data, stretching back to the early days of the Bolshevik triumph. The counterrevolutionary war of 1919, its commanders on the Red side, the subsequent actions and counteractions of the two armies, the suppression of all religion throughout Russia and the architects of Soviet atheism . . . Poliakov dug deep and conjured old atrocities and tyrants out of the past, poring over them, making his notes, muttering away in Polish.

The computer was fed with questions that seemed to Lomax completely unrelated. So did the answers it gave. But there was an enthusiasm and a suppressed excitement in the old man that was infectious. Lomax and the operator felt they were nearing a discovery, although neither had the least idea what it could be. Poliakov was sleeping in the building. He hadn't asked for a drink or suggested going home. He seemed absorbed.

Lomax reported to Davina every evening, and was back in Anne's Yard as soon as Poliakov had his breakfast the next day. She was still wearing Walden's bracelet. Lomax had arranged for her to go to Cartier's on Friday afternoon and have it opened. When he told her she said, "Oh, good. I'd forgotten about it." And she called her mother at Marchwood and arranged to go down on Saturday afternoon and spend the night there with Colin Lomax. As she told him afterward her mother sounded very pleased indeed that he was coming. "And Charlie isn't there," she added. "She's in Malta, with her new boy friend. Mum thinks they'll get married."

"And the best of British luck," Lomax retorted. He caught hold of Davina and kissed her very hard. It was a plus to have someone like Mrs. Graham on his side.

On Thursday morning Humphrey was waiting for her when she came into the office. She looked at him expectantly. "Humphrey? Any news?"

He pulled a face. "So far as I'm concerned she's refused to answer any more questions. She's being totally obstructive and I believe there's nothing more that I can do. I told her yesterday that I would recommend her deportation to France before the end of the week."

"And how did she take that?" Davina demanded.

"She didn't seem to care," he answered. "She's impossible to shake, Davina. She sat there and glowered at me and said she wouldn't talk because I wasn't the top person. She wants to see you, and nobody else will get a word out of her. That's the ultimatum she gave me. Personally, I would get rid of her as quickly as you can."

He looked pinched and angry, Davina noticed. The girl had known how to get under his skin. "I can't do that, Humphrey," she said. "I can't throw away what Colin achieved without trying everything. If she says she'll talk to me, then I'll have to go and see her. I don't want to, because I know you're the best person for the job. But if she won't cooperate with you, what can I do?"

He surprised her then. "I wouldn't advise you to go near her, if you want the truth. I don't think she'll tell you anything, or has any intention of doing so. She's playing a game with us, and this is a delaying tactic. I think she's a thoroughly nasty piece of work, and I'd be much happier to give her to SEDECE." He got up and stretched a little. He was painfully thin, she thought. "And I'm not saying this because I mind being replaced. Please don't think that."

"I wouldn't dream of it," Davina said. "Why don't you have one more try. Tell her to get ready, have a car waiting for the airport. That might do it."

He shook his head. "That's wasting time," he said. "And it puts us in a hopeless position if she calls the bluff."

"In that case, I'd better go down tomorrow and see her myself. Just once, I won't let her fool around, Humphrey, and I want you there with me." She stopped, frowning. "I wonder why she sleeps so badly? Isn't she showing any signs of strain at all?"

"She looks ill," Humphrey said. "Certainly it's taking its toll, but not enough. Not nearly enough considering how much pressure she's been under."

"Well," Davina said, "I'll give it one more chance. Why don't I go today? What's the point in waiting till tomorrow?"

"Isn't that pandering to her self-importance? I must say, she has the most enormous vanity. Everything's geared to getting attention. The way she said it. I'm not talking to anyone like you. I'm too important to deal with anyone but the top! It was incredible for a young girl like that!"

"I haven't got time to worry about whether she thinks she's scored a point or not," Davina decided. "Tactically you're right, Humphrey, but we can't take the chance. We've got to break through before we have another murder. It's about time, you know. They've been damned quiet for nearly a month. I'll go down this afternoon."

"What I'm looking for," Poliakov announced, "is an ancestor."

"A what?" Lomax stopped studying the last computer printout.

"An ancestor," he repeated. "Ma-Nang. The Company of Saints, in a Mongolian dialect, of all things. Now what kind of man would think of calling a group of trained assassins a name like that?"

"Someone with a bloody funny sense of humor."

Poliakov shook his head. "A sense of irony. A sense of blasphemy. Are you a Catholic, Major?"

Lomax shook his head. "I was brought up Presbyterian."

"Then you wouldn't understand what I mean," the Pole said. "This is a subtle blasphemy, not the hell and brimstone kind. An insult. You have to be a Jew or Orthodox or Roman Catholic to hate the God of your forefathers in that way. It's a sort of compliment, if you think of it. Remember Chesterton's detective, Father Brown? He proved that the atheist was really a believer because he wouldn't spit out a consecrated host. The man who thought of Ma-Nang would spit *on* it. You don't hate what doesn't exist, as Father Brown said. Do you like Chesterton, Major?"

"I haven't read him since I was a boy," Colin Lomax admitted. He wondered if he dared remind Poliakov of his original point. "But why an ancestor?"

"Because the attitude is pure 1920s," the Pole retorted. "The malice toward Christianity is so old-fashioned. First they suppressed religion. Prison, confiscation, even death. Then they derided it. They blasphemed, if you like, to make people laugh at it and feel fools if they believe anything. But that was sixty years ago. So whoever our man is, he has inherited this feeling. That's what I mean by an ancestor. If I can find someone with this attitude who has left a mark on the history of the times in Russia, then I can trace forward, through his family, even the families of his associates. I have several people already. Not Arkaniev. He was an idealist as well as a persecutor. He wanted to tear out organized religion the way doctors want to exterminate plague. He'd have said they were the same thing. Arkaniev was a fanatic and a butcher. His methods were abandoned because Stalin realized that all they were doing by shooting priests was making martyrs. So they mocked and derided and for a long time they were successful. The Church died. And then, like its founder, it rose again. Religion is alive in Russia, and I don't mean the Baptists, who are so brave and are suffering so much. I mean in the secret souls of the Russian people. Only children and old women go to church, they say. The man we are looking for has a background somewhere in religion. He mocks it for his own benefit. He doesn't believe in God, Major, but he certainly believes in evil. Now—let me think again. There was an incident in the Ukraine in '24. Here—here it is. Look at it and see what you make of it."

Lomax read the closely printed page. He found the printouts difficult to read. "Christ," he thought suddenly, "don't tell me I need glasses."

There had been a farming community that was suspected of continuing Easter observances and of harboring a priest. The commissar for the district decided to make an example of them. He had drafted a dozen members of the secret police, known then as the Cheka, into the nearest town. On what was known as Holy Thursday they filtered into the suspect village. Each was wearing a medal round his neck. The medal had particular significance in the district, because it was associated with a local pope, or monk in tsarist times, who claimed to have seen the Virgin Mary with her heart exposed and pierced by an arrow, symbolizing the sins of the world. Lomax was focusing carefully now as he read. The story was brief and horrible. The false Christians had been accepted into the community and invited to the secret ceremonies in a barn. Inside they had produced guns and opened fire on the little congregation and the priest, killing and wounding children and adults. The barn had been bolted shut and set on fire. That was the end of Christianity in the district, and the commissar responsible had been commended and given a more responsible posting.

"Well," Poliakov demanded. "What would you look for, Major? I know it's not your province, but out of curiosity."

Lomax put down the sheet of paper. "This heart with the arrow through it," he said. "Is it common? I thought it was something connected with love—Cupid . . ."

"Not in Russia," the Pole said. "In the Ukraine it was a very holy symbol. I've found the name of the commissar. Do you know what it is?"

Lomax didn't hear the excitement in his voice. He wasn't aware that Poliakov, with his love of drama, had stage-managed the moment of revelation for him. Walden had given Davina a heart pierced by an arrow. A Western symbol of unrequited love. Yes, of course it was. He could think of poems, love songs, Valentines . . . the medal worn by the butchers of the Cheka.

"Major Lomax?" Poliakov sounded piqued. "Didn't you hear what I said? Don't you want to know the name of the commissar?"

"Yes, in a minute. Tell me something. If you gave that to a Russian—that medal with the heart and the arrow—what would it mean to him?"

"To most Russians, nothing. To a Ukrainian—the massacre of the people of Lukina. That has gone into folklore, you know. Major, I have made a very important discovery. Don't you want to know what it is?"

"There's a book I read, a book of short stories . . ." Lomax was talking to himself, only half to Poliakov. "Years ago, when I was a boy. It frightened the hell out of me. It was an Edgar Allan Poe story. 'The Murders in the Rue Morgue.' Just a minute." He sprang up and buzzed Davina's office on the intercom. "Get me Miss Graham." Her secretary's voice replied, "I'm sorry, Major

Lomax, she's out of the office. She won't be back today. Shall I take a message in case she phones in?"

"Where has she gone?" Lomax demanded. "Phyllis, this is urgent, where is she?"

"She went down to Welton with Mr. Grant."

He hung up, and turned to Poliakov. "A bracelet," Lomax exploded. "A bloody bracelet that she can't get off! Like the victims in that story—Jesus Christ. She's gone down to Welton—where that girl is."

Before Poliakov could ask what he was talking about, Lomax had rushed out of the room. The old man turned to the computer operator. "Did you understand any of that?" he asked. "What was the matter with him?"

"I don't know, sir, I wasn't really listening."

"Well what were the murders in the Rue Morgue then?" Poliakov shouted.

"Never heard of them, sir. I've got some more printouts for you."

Poliakov snatched them. He was very angry, he felt cheated. He hated not knowing what was going on. One moment he had a brilliant revelation to make, the possible answer to the question set for him by Davina Graham, and the next he was brushed aside by that lunatic yelling about Edgar Allan Poe. He took a deep breath and said, "I'll look at these later. I have to go out for a while."

"I understand you requested to see me," Davina stated. In spite of what Humphrey had said, she was shocked by the girl's ghastly pallor and hollow eyes. She was standing by the window in the private office, with the bright summer sunshine forming a nimbus round her. She held herself like a caged animal getting ready to spring.

"Yes. I won't be bullied by him anymore."

Davina glanced sideways at Humphrey. "I don't believe he bullied you," she said quietly. "I know that he and Monsieur Johnson have been very patient indeed. I must warn you that I am not a patient person."

The challenge was thrown down so quickly that it took Helene completely by surprise. She had expected the soft approach, the preliminary tact that the two men had shown. The woman didn't give her that respect. She declared herself an adversary in the first few minutes. She was hateful, Helene thought, glaring at her.

Hateful. The dominant female with the cane held behind her back.

"I am going to ask you some questions, Helene," Davina said. "If you don't answer them to my satisfaction, I shan't repeat them, and I shall leave. You will be taken to the airport after we have alerted the French authorities and told them to pick you up. Do you understand that?"

"I understand that you are a worse bully than he is," she said calmly, and made a contemptuous little gesture toward Humphrey. There was a box on the table; she opened it and took a cigarette.

"Then you *have* understood," Davina remarked. "And you can put that away. There will be no cigarettes. This is not a social call. I am here to ask you questions and you are going to answer them."

Helene didn't hesitate. She put the cigarette in her mouth.

Davina stepped forward and knocked the cigarette to the ground. Helene began to tremble. "I told you, no cigarettes."

Helene didn't move. She was staring at the gleaming circle of colored gold on the woman's wrist. And at the bright red heart with the arrow. "I don't feel well," she said suddenly. The room was beginning to recede and she felt icy cold. "Sit down then," she heard the voice, and it sounded muffled and far away. There was a chair and Helene groped for it. She sat down heavily and dropped her head to bring back the blood supply. Her pulse rate was galloping and there was a thudding in her ears. With her eyes shut she could see that crimson symbol of all that she hated most in the world.

"Humphrey," Davina murmured, "get her a glass of water." And lower still, "I think she's cracked . . ."

Helene felt the woman touch her on the shoulder. She went stiff all over her body. As stiff as the little girl who flinched before the blows to come. "Drink some of this. You'll feel better." She took the glass, sipped at it. It was good; her mouth and throat were dust-dry. She saw the heart swinging backward and forward like a little metronome on the woman's wrist. Her pulse and breathing steadied. A deadly calm came over her, very different from the horrible panic of a few moments before. She looked up at Davina Graham. Strength was coming back, coming on a tide. She had been prepared for this moment. She needn't feel helpless. She wasn't a child any longer. Everything was clear to her now.

"I will answer anything you want," she said. She saw the triumph on the woman's face, saw the hard mouth soften into a smile. Oh, yes, you always smiled like that after you'd done it. You'd look at me and smile and say, that will teach you . . . you won't be naughty again . . .

"That's very sensible of you," Davina said. "Tell me about this institute. You were part of a special group, weren't you?"

"Yes."

"And who were the other members?"

She wasn't going to tell her that. But she wanted to see her relax; she wanted to lull her so that she wouldn't be expecting anything but obedience. Obedience and fear. Take off your dress, Helene. I'm going to punish you. She made up four names. Not made up, because they were the names of two teachers who came to mind, her aunt's dentist, and his partner.

"And what did they teach you in this special group?"

Helene had begun to feel strange again. Not faint and weak, but filling up inside, as if the tension was building to explosion point. She knew the time was getting nearer. The blood-red heart gleamed as the woman moved her hand when she talked. "I want to see you alone," Helene said. "I don't want anyone else here if I'm going to tell you about it." And then she added, because she used to say it so often until in the end it was a scream. "Please."

Davina nodded. "Humphrey, do you mind?"

He hesitated. The scene disturbed him. There was a mixture of servility and antagonism in the girl. "Davina—there's a small inner office; you could go in there and leave the door open." He spoke rapidly in English. "I don't like the look of her. I don't think you should be alone with her."

Davina said, "She's just coming apart, that's all. And that's what we wanted. Nothing else was going to work. Don't worry about me, Humphrey. I'll go very gently."

"All right," he said. "I'll look in after a few minutes."

"No," Davina said quickly. "No, don't; I'll give you a buzz in the colonel's office when I'm ready. I don't want to interrupt anything at this stage."

He went out reluctantly. As he closed the door he glanced back. Davina was sitting near Helene Blond. He heard her say in a gentle voice, "Monsieur Grant has gone. Now we are alone and you can talk to me. What did they teach you, Helene?"

Humphrey went to the colonel's office. "I think we're home and dry," he said. "She suddenly went to pieces. Miss Graham is with her now. Could I have some coffee?"

The colonel said, "Of course." He was curious about Helene Blond. He said, "That's great news. There's something pretty odd about her, isn't there? She's so full of aggression; that's the feeling she gave me. And it's so controlled. You feel it ought to burst out but it never does. Your chap Johnson said the same thing. We watched her once on the monitor, after he'd spent a morning with her, and she was in a terrible temper. She put herself into some kind of trance to calm down. Quite extraordinary. Johnson said he felt she'd have broken up the room otherwise."

Humphrey looked up, frowning. "That's what I felt," he said. "I really didn't want to leave Miss Graham alone with her."

"Don't worry, you can keep tabs on her with the monitor. You can always go in if you're not happy with the way it's progressing."

"She doesn't want to be interrupted," Humphrey said. "And of course she's right. When the crisis comes you've got to take the fullest advantage of it and not let them have time to recover themselves. I'll keep a watch—but I'd better leave it till she rings through. I don't know." He hunched his thin shoulders, looking rather like a grasshopper, the colonel thought. "I don't know, maybe I'm getting old. I don't like this sort of thing anymore."

"None of us does," the soldier answered. "Especially when a woman is involved. But they're as deadly as the men these days. In fact, some of them are worse. Have some more coffee. And excuse me, will you? Make yourself comfortable. Ring for my orderly if you want anything."

"What did they teach you, Helene?" Davina asked again. The girl was so white that she wondered if she was going to faint.

"To kill." The answer was given in a flat tone of voice. There was a tiny gleam in the girl's eye, and her mouth was slightly open.

Davina did not react. "I see," she said. To kill. My God, she said to herself . . . what have we got here . . . "Why did they teach you that?"

Helene Blond smiled. She sat straighter, clasping her hands in her lap. "Why don't you ask me who I killed?" she said.

Davina felt it then. She felt the hatred coming to her, like waves of heat. And she began to feel afraid. She couldn't get up and call for Humphrey until she'd got that question answered. He would be watching and listening. She rested her hands on the arm of the chair. The red heart with its cruel little arrow lay on the polished wood like a drop of blood. Helene could not take her eyes away from it.

"All right," Davina said. Whatever happened she mustn't show that she was alarmed or shaken. She had to seem totally calm and unmoved. "All right, who did you kill?"

Helene inched forward on her chair. "The Duvaliers," she said. Her pulse was starting to race again. But don't hurry. Don't hurry this moment when you've waited for it so long. Last time you were cheated. She got cancer but she died in the hospital. Now she's here and you can spin it out, "France," you can watch her face and see her learn to be afraid of you.

"It was funny," she went on. "Those stupid fools asking me if I let them in to do the shooting? I nearly burst out laughing. I'll tell you what happened. You'd like to know all the details, wouldn't you?"

"Yes," Davina answered quietly. "Tell me how you killed them, Helene." It isn't true, she said to herself. She's lying, it's all a hysterical fantasy. She looks quite unhinged. But I'll know in a minute, as soon as she starts telling how she did it.

"I pretended to have a headache," Helene said. "They were all playing bridge. Louise was watching. I left my bag in the salon, so I could get the maid to come up to my room and find me asleep. I wasn't asleep. I waited, and then I went down to the salon and opened the door. There they were, sitting there, playing cards." She gave a throaty laugh. "They were so surprised to see me standing there in my dressing gown. And with the gun in my hand. I shot Isabelle Duvalier in the chest. Then the two men, and Irena Duvalier got hers in the gullet. I did it so quickly. Louise was dead in a second; it was easy, they were all sitting so close."

Davina held herself together. The truth, she's telling the truth. One more question to make sure. "What gun did you use?"

"A Walther XP 45, with a six-inch silencer. Then I went up to bed and took my sleeping pills. What do you think of that?"

Slowly Davina got up. "I think we should take a break," she said.

Helene rose to her feet. "You didn't think I'd have the courage, did you? You thought I was frightened of you, like I always was. Remember how I used to cry and beg? Now it's your turn."

And with a low cry she leaped.

The telephone was ringing in the colonel's office. It shrilled and shrilled, getting on Humphrey's nerves. The monitor showed Davina and Helene talking. "What gun did you use?" Davina asked her. Humphrey wondered why the orderly hadn't come in and taken the call. Never there when they should be. In the end he couldn't stand it. He turned away from the little TV screen and picked up the phone. The operator on the internal exchange said, "This is an urgent call for Miss Graham. Major Lomax on the line."

"Miss Graham can't be disturbed. Put Major Lomax through." He heard the click and said, "Humphrey Grant here—I'm afraid Davina's busy at the moment, can I help?"

"Where is she?" Lomax was almost shouting.

"She's interrogating Helene Blond. What's wrong?" He could hear the panic at the other end.

"She's not alone with her, is she?" Lomax didn't wait for an answer. "For Christ's sake get her out of there! I'm on my way down now . . ."

Humphrey swung round. What he saw on the monitor made him drop the receiver. Tall and awkward as he was, he moved with amazing speed out of the office and raced down the passage toward the little room.

"Mama," Helene was saying over and over, saliva dripping from her mouth. "Mama. Mama."

She didn't hear the door crash open, she didn't hear the thud of Humphrey's feet across the floor behind her. She was aware of nothing but the face of the woman she was choking to death. He tore at her hair; she didn't feel it. He rabbit-punched her to break that merciless grip, and she fell heavily on top of Davina.

Humphrey knelt down and pulled Davina clear. The colonel's orderly had joined him, having heard him shout as he ran out of the colonel's office. They lifted her up.

Humphrey felt for a pulse in her neck. "She's alive," he said. "But only just."

* * *

"My dear Davina, you really shouldn't have come out of hospital so soon." Sir James White shook his head reprovingly at her.

"I didn't want to stay there in the first place," she said. Her voice was very hoarse. It still hurt her to speak. "I'm quite all right, I just can't shout, that's all."

She was in her apartment, her throat wrapped in bandages, and Colin had moved in to take care of her. James White looked at both of them and smiled.

Like to like; first Sasanov, then Lomax. That other unpleasant episode was best forgotten. But plans were in hand for dealing with Mr. Anthony Walden. The bearer of expensive gifts. A very expensive gift it had nearly proved to be for Davina Graham. A minute more, the doctors said, and she would have died. The girl Helene Blond was hopelessly insane. She had lapsed into a catatonic state and was lying in a secure mental hospital under Home Office order, little better than a vegetable. She had never said anything but that one word, Mama, in the voice of a child, before she sank to permanent silence.

"Davina's being very difficult," Colin Lomax said. "Wants to go into the office, won't stay off the phone. I've told her, she could lose her voice completely unless she rests that throat, but she won't listen."

"Well you must rest," James White insisted. "You've not only had a serious shock and near-fatal strangulation, but you have also suffered a nasty injury to the esophagus. So be sensible and take it easy until you're quite fit again. Why don't you take her down to Marchwood, Colin? And cut off the phone so she can't get into mischief?"

"It's an idea," he agreed. "What about that, Davina? Just a week, that's all. It'd do you a lot of good to get away from the flat and just relax and sit around. I ought to know; I was nursed back to life at Marchwood."

She didn't want to argue. She didn't want to give in either, but she felt unsteady and weak. She could cope with the pain and the bruising of her throat, even the difficulty in talking at a normal pitch. But the shaking inside hadn't gone away yet.

Everyone had been kind and concerned. Humphrey had saved her life. He had appeared at her bedside in the hospital at Tetbury, with flowers and an expression of pained discomfort.

It had been a shock for him too, she could see that. Tim Johnson visited too, bringing magazines and a novel. The selection amused her. Glossy, slick publications, geared to the so-called career woman. Most of the contents were concerned with sex and how to find and keep your man. So little had changed under the surface from the gentle pages of her mother's *Woman's Journal* of twenty years ago. The approach was different but the problems were the same. And there was Colin taking over, seeing the doctor and the specialist sent from London. Driving her back home when she dismissed herself ahead of time. And filling the apartment with flowers to welcome her.

She hadn't been in any condition to ask questions for the first few days, even to whisper them. When she woke in the side ward, she noticed that they had removed the bracelet; she felt so dizzy she thought, how funny, they got Cartier's to send someone all this way down, and then she drifted back into a drugged sleep. It was Colin who told her when she got home.

"Walden didn't know," he said. "I paid him a visit. Well, a couple of us did. MacNeil sent a man along with me. He didn't try to hide anything; when we told him you'd nearly been killed he wasn't playacting. They'd given him the bracelet and told him it had a little homing device that would tell them where you were holding one of their agents. Not a word of truth in it. You can guess the alternative if he said no. So that's cleared up."

Go down to Marchwood. She couldn't think of anything more calming than to let Colin and Sir James persuade her. Except for one thing. Poliakov had gone out to the nearest pub to Anne's Yard and drunk himself into a stupor. The next morning he had disappeared from his apartment, leaving his woman friend with a hangover and no idea where he had gone. They'd looked for him with the few Polish friends he had, but nobody had seen him. And his work was unfinished. The name of the commissar responsible for the massacre at Lukina was not on the computer. It was in his befuddled brain. Davina said, "I will go away, I promise. But not until we've found Poliakov. Colin, he was going to break the thing to you that day. We must find him and get him back to finish it off." She put her hand to her throat. It hurt abominably after the long speech.

"My dear," James White said after a pause. "I think you're strong enough now to hear. Poliakov has been found. He's dead."

She reached for Colin and he took her hand. "When?" she whispered. "What happened to him?"

212

"Nothing dramatic," he said in his bland way. "He just poisoned himself with alcohol. Literally. He was discovered sitting on a bench in a public park—Battersea, wasn't it, Colin? With two empty vodka bottles in a bag beside him."

"Oh, God," she croaked out. "Oh, God, what a disaster ... Poor old thing."

"Yes, it is a pity," James White agreed. "However, Humphrey hasn't been idle. He's following up that Lukina clue and he'll come up with the answer. An extraordinary thing, that tie-up with the Cheka killing all those years ago. And the conditioning of that girl to kill whoever wore the bracelet. What a lucky thing you read Poe, Colin! It was a gorilla, wasn't it, in the story?"

"Yes," Lomax said. "The poor brute was beaten and tortured to the sound of a tinkling bell. Then these women were given bracelets that they couldn't get off, with a bell on the end. And the brute was set on them. Anyway, don't let's talk about it. I'm going to get you something to eat, Davina, and make you put your feet up." He got out of his chair and Sir James took the hint.

He shook hands with her, and said, "Mary and I were worried to death about you, Davina, my dear. So no more scares like that, if you don't mind. Bless you, and see you soon."

When he had gone she caught hold of Colin. "My throat hurts like mad," she whispered. "But I've got to talk to you. Sit down a minute, darling, please."

He did so, holding her hand and lightly stroking it. She looked very pale and thin. Whatever she said he wasn't going to upset her by arguing.

"We've got to find out who used that device at Lukina," she said. "We can't wait for Humphrey."

"No, darling," he agreed. "We can't. So what shall we do? You tell me and I'll do it, so you can stop worrying."

"They'll kill again," she murmured. "It must be time for another attempt."

"No it isn't," he said gently. "Don't you see why? You were the next on the list."

"I've been thinking. It isn't Borisov. I was wrong about that. He wouldn't set a precedent by killing me. Or any of us in the West. It's a Russian but it isn't him."

"Why don't you put the mind to bed?" he asked her. "And the voice. Come on, I'm switching the box on in the bedroom and you're going to lie and have supper on a tray." And that was how they heard the news flash that Alexander Keremov had died of heart failure at two o'clock the previous morning.

"Your method failed," he said. "Your fail-safe didn't work. What have you to say to me?" He spoke quite softly.

The doctor dreaded that softness in his voice. "The girl attacked," he protested. "She obeyed the signal she was given. My method didn't fail."

The man behind the desk looked at him and said, "I am not concerned with theories. I asked for a result. You haven't given it to me. The head of the British Secret Intelligence Service is not dead. That's all that interests me." He bent his head and studied a document in front of him.

The doctor didn't know whether he was dismissed or not. But he knew that he was sentenced. He was not a coward and in his heart he knew the charge of failure was unfair. "I cannot guarantee that they will be successful every time," he ventured. "The others didn't fail. This was asking more of the girl than any of them. And she had already proved herself."

Slowly the head raised and the angry eyes considered him. He was sorry he had tried to excuse himself one more time. Now the sentence was confirmed.

"Keremov is dead. Everything that went before was only a preparation for what we cannot do now. Get out of my sight."

Get out and go on your way, but you won't get far. The charges have already been drawn up against you. You will need your own special brand of treatment, my dear doctor. And then you will be as harmless as your patients . . .

"I will do it."

He looked up in surprise. "You will do what?"

"I will kill him for you."

The laugh was bitterly contemptuous. "You? You wouldn't know how to step on an ant. You're a man of chemicals and drugs and mental tricks. Not a man of action. Put a gun in your hand and you'd shoot off your own foot!"

The doctor's face had flushed a dark red. He was a slight man, built like a small bird, with sticklike bones and frail hands like a woman's. Only his brain was strong. He had reduced the physical specimens to slobbering wrecks by means of his brain. "I will kill him," he repeated. "In my way. Not with a gun. Give me this last chance to succeed for you."

"To succeed for yourself." The voice was low and menacing again. "Very well then. Use your own weapons. I will give you until the state funeral."

The doctor's color faded. "But that's so soon. How can I find an opportunity?"

"I don't know," his tormentor said. "But that is your problem."

When the doctor had gone, he lifted the telephone. "Leave him alone," he said. "No, it's canceled. We'll wait." Then he went back to his desk and his work.

"The commissar's name was Rudkin," Humphrey said. She shouldn't have come back to the office; she looked quite shaken still, and he could see the bandages under a colored scarf. He would never have believed he could feel sympathetic toward her, but he did. He didn't try to analyze it.

"That's marvelous, Humphrey," her voice was stronger. "But how does it relate to these people. There's no connection with any of the suspects that Poliakov mentioned within the Soviet hierarchy. It's a common name in the Ukraine, isn't that right? Where do we go from here?"

"There were twenty men involved in the shooting and burning of the barn," Humphrey said. "There must be a record of their names. But it could take months to track them down, and we'd need to use sources inside Russia itself."

She put a hand to her neck. He noticed that she did it often and without realizing. "Then we're completely stuck. There's a massive power struggle going on there at this moment. We could be facing a new leader like Yemetovsky or that brute Mishkoyan, or someone we don't even know about. It's wide open, according to our sources. And there's another factor." She glanced at him. "You've heard it. What do you think?"

"That Borisov is a possibility? I don't believe it. They've never elected a leader from the KGB and they won't now. My money is on Yemetovsky."

"They've never allowed the army to hold power either," Davina argued. "Yemetovsky will be stopped by the civilians. And he's too committed to war as the ultimate solution. It's Mishkoyan that worries me."

"They all worry me," Humphrey admitted. "I suggest we pass

this request to our C Section in Moscow and see what they come up with."

Davina frowned, "What request, Humphrey?"

"The names of the Cheka squad at Lukina." He was surprised that she had lost the thread of their conversation. It was quite unlike her.

"Oh, of course. I wasn't concentrating. Sorry." She touched her scarf again. "It's time I had a holiday," she admitted. "Even if it's a weekend. Yes, do that, Humphrey, but I can imagine the response, can't you? Dig up information about an isolated atrocity that took place in some backwoods village in the 1920s—Good God, what will these Intelligence people think of next!"

He smiled. She would always think of the cruel description of an Irish politician of sacred memory.

When Humphrey smiled it was like moonlight striking a gravestone. Poor Humphrey; nature had been unkind to him in the womb. A misfit among misfits. Where had she heard that before? And didn't it apply to her too, in some measure, and to all people in the secret world?

The state funeral was scheduled for the eleventh of July. Moscow was already full of visitors. Now the hotels and houses were packed with people who had converged on the city. Heads of governments and their representatives from the East European bloc, a delegation from China itself, and the wary emissaries from the West, who felt no grief at seeing the last of Keremov, but considerable anxiety about who would take his place on the Kremlin walls. Whoever stood central was the likely successor. Whoever approached the open coffin first to pay his tribute was the man to watch. It was as rigid as the protocol surrounding any tsarist funeral.

Behind the preparations, the political lobbying went on at a furious rate. One contender was already sliding out of view. Yemetovsky, the famous marshal, the hard military man with his thunderbolt reputation. He was stepping aside. The cynics argued that he realized he wouldn't win, and that an open rejection would mean a loss of face. And a subsequent loss of power. The army wouldn't be allowed to take control. They never had, and the memory of Stalin's suspicions of his generals, even after the Great Patriotic War, was still alive in many influential party members' minds.

The Armenian was fighting hard. He made no pretense about his ambitions. He was gathering support, making promises, rally-ing factions.

Borisov stayed calm. Too calm, in his friends' view. He seemed to think his succession was assured, that Keremov's wishes were some kind of kingly will, to be obeyed. Dead men had no influ-ence upon the living. Only the determination to take power guaranteed it. His friends began to worry about their support for Igor Borisov. He had only begun to worry about it himself that day before the procession left the Kremlin with the body of Keremov on a flower-decked open bier. He was so preoccupied that he refused to see the doctor from Moscow Institute of Psy-chiatric Medicine. He snapped at his aide when he came and told him that the young scientist was waiting in his outer office and would not leave. "He hasn't an appointment and why should I make time for him?"

Borisov had met him several times, attending conferences con-cerning the suppression of dissidents. A flimsy figure of a man, convinced of his own genius. Effective, but uncongenial. Then Borisov restrained himself. His nerves were taut, and that was af-fecting his judgment. The doctor was a senior member of that no-torious institute and its attendant prison hospitals. He must have an urgent reason for making a nuisance of himself at such a time. "Send him in," he said wearily.

The doctor came in like a bird, with his precise little steps, and even when Borisov invited him to sit down, he remained perched, his feet shuffling nervously.

He regarded Igor Borisov with his disconcerting stare. He wasn't aware of how he set people against him with that unwink-ing look. His life and freedom were at stake. If he failed now, he knew his fate would be the same as that he had devised for many others. Imprisonment in one of his own dreaded mental hospitals. There, like the men and women of conscience, he would be tor-tured with hallucinatory drugs and electric shock treatments with the minimum of anesthetic. If he proved too resistant they would operate and make him into a vegetable who lay in his own filth until he died.

"Comrade Borisov," he said. "I came here to kill you. With this." He held out his hand, palm uppermost. There was nothing in it that Borisov could see. He had already pressed a button under the desk with his knee. Before the doctor had finished speaking, the doors had opened and there were armed men in the room. He looked over his shoulder, and then said, "Let me tell you about it first. Then they can arrest me if you like. I have a ring on my finger. A wedding ring."

Borisov leaned toward him. One move and his bodyguards would blow the doctor's head off. "I see it," he said.

The doctor gave a little smile, weak and wintry. "But you don't see the tiny pinhead that comes out when I apply pressure. There is a poison that enters the bloodstream from a scratch so small you wouldn't even feel it. Within twenty-four hours you would have become ill and died. We've used it before, but it wasn't so quick or sophisticated then."

"I know we have," Borisov said. "Why are you telling me this, Doctor?"

"Because I want to save my life," he said simply. "I will tell you who sent me here if you will promise I can go free and continue with my work."

Borisov didn't answer at once. He took out his cigarettes and lit one, taking his time. The stare didn't waver. What was the matter with the man? Didn't he need to blink like other human beings? "I promise you," Borisov said calmly, "that if you don't tell me, you'll wish you had by the end of this afternoon. My men are not scientists or psychiatrists, but they know just as much about the human body as you do about the mind. So take off your ring and after you have been searched for any other dirty tricks, you can sit down and tell me everything you know."

It was a magnificent funeral. The Moscow skies were a dazzling blue and the procession started out from the Kremlin to the deep melodious tolling of the city's bells. A phalanx of men who had been Keremov's friends, colleagues, and enemies all at the same time followed the coffin. Borisov was in the second line; Mishkoyan and one of the detentists, as they were called, headed the mourners. Nobody worried about the man who wanted closer cooperation with the West. He was window-dressing for the real successor. The marshal, Yemetovsky, walked behind Borisov. The troops marched to the beat of the Dead March from *Saul*. Crowds lined the route, openly weeping. The bells tolled again as they neared the final place of rest.

Flowers were laid against the walls of the tomb, including

homemade tributes from the Russian people who had never known his tyranny. Each member of the Politburo approached the open coffin, and bent to kiss the putty-colored face of the embalmed corpse. When Borisov kissed him tears dropped onto the icy face.

After the ceremony, there was a reception at the Kremlin for the members of the Politburo, the senior members of the Communist party, and delegates from all over the Soviet Union. The gathering was subdued; people talked in hushed voices, but already eyes were probing the candidates, whispers were circulating about who was going to be elected.

Igor Borisov made a slow progress round the party delegates, then to the senior party members. He spoke quietly to them, and they listened. He had planned a tribute to the dead president; and they were all invited to the headquarters on Dzerjinsky Square to watch a special film of his life and achievements after the official reception ended. Everybody was suspicious, but nobody liked to refuse. It would seem lacking in respect. And Borisov was not only a candidate, but could also still remain the second-most-powerful man in Russia after the election. Unless, of course, Mishkoyan had him replaced . . .

Borisov went ahead of them. He had arranged the conference room in the building. A portrait of Keremov draped in black had been hung over the screen.

At seven o'clock the room began to fill up. By seven-thirty everyone had arrived. Vodka was passed, and cigarettes. Borisov's men were also in the room, stationed near the doors. He called for silence and the lights were lowered. "Comrades," he said, taking position in front of the screen, "this is my personal tribute to a great patriot and a great leader. I believe it will affect us very deeply." He sat down and the screen came to life. There was a brief passage of solemn music.

But it was not Keremov's face that came into focus. The music suddenly died away, and there were murmurs from the audience. Borisov said aloud, "The man you see here is one of the most eminent psychiatrists in Russia, deputy head of the Semenov Institute. I would like you all to listen carefully to what he is going to say."

At first the audience was inattentive; they imagined they were about to hear a long, tedious tribute to the genius and humanity of their dead leader. His main contribution to human welfare in the field of medicine had been the authorization of the infamous psychiatric hospitals. But the words were not what they expected. Words like treason, and murder, and betrayal of the people of Russia. Words like ambition and insane impulses toward power.

There was not a sound in the packed room. Borisov sat like a statue, arms folded, listening to the doctor's monotonous, high-pitched voice.

Suddenly the silence was shattered. There were exclamations, and shouting from the auditorium. Then, without warning, the screen went blank. And once again there was silence. Heads turned toward one man.

Slowly he rose to his feet. "You have accused me, Comrade General," he said. "By trickery, you have accused me publicly before our comrades. Bring that liar before us, and let him repeat his lies to my face! I challenge you! Bring him here now!"

He had presence and courage, Borisov had to admit that.

"This is not the time or the place," he answered calmly. "The doctor will give his evidence before the Central Committee. If your plan had succeeded, I would be dead like Nikolaev, and Comrade Mishkoyan with me. All your rivals would have been murdered by an army of assassins, trained to further your political ends." He turned to face the audience. "Which is why, comrades, I called you here to listen to a tribute to our dead leader, Alexander Keremov. A tribute to his patriotism and his judgment. His dying wish was to stop this man taking control of Russia."

"Mr. Walden," Freda Young said, "there's a call from Brussels. Will you take it?" She knew he disliked being disturbed when he was in a morning meeting, but he gave high priority to this particular account.

"I'll take it in my office," he said. He made a joke to his executives. "I know what you're thinking, but Belgian Plastic isn't a beautiful blonde. I'll deal with this and be back in a minute."

He closed his office door. There was no sign of good humor when he answered. "Yes? Walden speaking." He had pressed a small button on the telephone; the conversation was being recorded. "No, I can't come over. It's impossible. You'll have to come here. I've got something important for you." There was a pause at the other end. He's tempted, Walden thought; the murdering bastard. He's tempted to come and see if I really have got something for them. He'll start to threaten for a minute.

"You must see me as usual," the voice said. "You could be in a difficult situation otherwise."

"I got the promotion you wanted in the trade papers," Walden countered. "It's not my responsibility if you couldn't get the orders through."

Walden must have damaged the bracelet mechanism in some way, he insisted, because they hadn't traced their agent. Moscow didn't consider he'd fulfilled his bargain. Which was exactly what Lomax and MacNeil had expected. He wouldn't be let off the hook, because they never gave up. And neither did SIS. That was the price he would pay for nearly getting Davina killed.

The officer from the Special Branch had done most of the talking. Colin Lomax said little. But Walden could feel his contempt without any words. "You got yourself into this mess," the man said. "And you'll stick with it now. You'll bloody well work for them and for us, Mr. Walden, for as long as we can use you. And if your friends on the other side find out you've been playing doubles, that'll be just too bad."

As they left, Lomax had paused and said quietly, "Just for the record, if I thought you'd known what that bracelet really was, I'd kill you. You didn't, so we'll leave it at that. But don't try seeing her again. Understand?"

Walden had opened the door for them. "I tried to get her out of it," he said to Lomax. "Which is more than you've done."

He had to persuade the Soviet contact to come to London. He didn't know why and he didn't care. For the rest of his life he would be subjected to pressure and danger by both sides.

"I'm so glad you could come down," Betty Graham said. "Isn't the weather lovely?"

Davina had lost a lot of weight, she thought, and she didn't look at all well. It was a relief to see Colin taking care of her. She had everything ready for them, Davina's old room, and the guest room for Lomax. She remembered how nice it had been when Davina was nursing him after the terrible wound he had gotten in Mexico. What a pity they hadn't got married then. All the misery that followed might have been avoided. . . . But there was no use regretting the past. Mrs. Graham had learned that a long time ago. No use missing her husband, because it wouldn't bring him back.

She had her little grandson permanently with her, since Charlie was fully occupied with her job and her new man friend in London. The house wasn't lonely, but she had known for the past few days that it soon would be. She was very thankful when she heard that Davina and Colin wanted to come down. She kissed them both. "I *am* glad to see you," she said. "Fergie's out in the garden; I've been so lucky, that nice girl said she'd look after him full time for me. He's growing up so rapidly. Let's put your things upstairs and then we'll have a drink outside before lunch. I've been very extravagant and got some help in while you're here. Otherwise I'd spend too much time in the kitchen."

Davina didn't come down till her mother and Colin were sitting outside. Mrs. Graham took the opportunity when they were alone to say, "Colin, dear, I'm worried about Davina. She doesn't look at all herself. Is she working too hard?"

"She has been under a lot of stress lately," he said. "But being here will do her the world of good. It's sweet of you to have us. And don't forget, I'm very domesticated, and I really would like to make myself useful. So give me some jobs to do, won't you?"

She smiled and patted him on the arm. "Thank you, Colin. You are very kind. I'm quite well set up, you know. Financially too. Fergus left me everything, including the house. With something to Charlie, of course."

She lowered her voice, "I was rather surprised. You know how much he adored Charlie. I expected to have a life interest and the rest to go to her."

"Well, I'm glad he didn't do it that way," Colin answered. "He didn't mention Davina?"

"No, I'm afraid not," her mother said sadly. "And she was so good about it. She never asked to see the will or even mentioned it. I shall put that right, of course. But don't say anything to her about it."

"I won't," he said. "Here she is. What can I get you, darling? White wine?"

"That would be lovely." She stretched out in the garden chair, resting her head against the cushions. It was very hot, but then the west side of the house had always been a sun trap. Nothing changed here, even though her father was dead. The old house and its magnificent garden breathed a life independent of the people in it. They died or moved but it remained, as the centuries ran on.

She half-listened to her mother; Colin was talking to her, all she had to do was say a word now and then. They got on very well. She thought back to their first meeting, and remembered thinking what an abrupt, chip-on-the-shoulder type he was. Her father and mother had liked him from the moment they were introduced. When he seemed to have only a few months to live, they had taken him in and cared for him as if he had been their own son. That was another thing her father never forgave her for; refusing to marry Colin and settle down. She didn't want to think of her father. It was easy for outsiders to say that people grew up and came to terms with the sorrows of childhood. Her only brother was killed after the war and there were the two girls left. Beautiful, winning Charlotte Graham and the shy, reserved Davina, always in her sister's shadow. Awkward, prickly and uncommunicative. No wonder he gravitated to the bright star that did him so much credit. He called his younger child by the nickname she used for herself, when she was too young to pronounce her own name properly. Charlie. But he never saw her as anything but vulnerable and feminine. He hadn't loved Davina, and whatever she did, he preferred what her sister represented. The clinging sex symbol; every man's little-girl ideal who had to be protected and adored.

Davina sat up. Charlie hadn't appealed to Ivan Sasanov. The memories were suddenly crowding back. She no longer heard the voices of her mother and Colin. Ivan had come to Marchwood with her. She had been in love with him, and accepted that as soon as he saw Charlie, that would be the end of it. His words came back to her too. Spoken in her bedroom upstairs after they had made love for the first time.

"I don't find her attractive. I want a woman who can give. She only takes."

Lomax hadn't been interested in her either. To be fair, she hadn't tried very hard. Just gone through the motions of flirtation, which were as natural to her as breathing. And also she was happily married. And Davina had destroyed that marriage. It was the first time Charlie had been really hurt or known what it meant to suffer.

Davina saw the little boy toddling toward them across the

lawns, holding the nanny's hand. Charlie had her child. Davina's had never had the chance to live. It died soon after its father, Sasanov, in Western Australia.

"Fergie?" Her mother called out. "Come to Granny, darling. Come and say hello to your Aunt Davina."

He was an enchanting little boy. Last time she had seen him was after her father's funeral. She took him on her knee; and he wound his arms round her neck and kissed her. She felt her face flush. It wouldn't take much to make her cry if she didn't stop this morbid reflection on the past. She glanced up and saw Colin looking at her. "Here, Fergie," she said defiantly, throwing the unspoken challenge back at him, "Go to Granny now." For a reason she didn't understand, Lomax grinned.

It was a lovely afternoon. She went for a walk, then settled into the swingseat Lomax had brought out and erected, and dozed till teatime. She still wore a scarf to hide the bruises. Her voice was back to normal, and the last check-up had said she was fit and there would be no lasting ill effects.

Humphrey asked for help from the Moscow embassy, and they were waiting impatiently for more than the usual rather pained acknowledgment of their request for information. Davina had added a note of her own to the ambassador, stressing that this could provide vital information needed to break an organization known as the Company of Saints. In the meantime, Russia was without an elected leader. Keremov's deputy stayed on as caretaker. He was an old man in his late seventies, a puppet who had done what Keremov wanted, someone who would be glad to step down and retire from public life. It was a time of hiatus, and ideal for Davina to take the rest she needed. Only for a few days, a long weekend at the most, she insisted to Lomax. She couldn't be out of the office when the new leader of Russia was elected. It seemed certain now that Mishkoyan would be chosen. And that meant a new and even more ruthless phase would begin in the Intelligence war between East and West.

Twenty-four people were arrested in the Semenov Institute of Psychiatric Medicine. Eight officers in the External Affairs section and three in the Internal Security division of the KGB were taken in to the Lubyanka for questioning. And in Moscow and

Leningrad, a number of men and women were removed from their offices and homes and sent to the main prison hospital outside Moscow. It was done with speed and without attracting attention. The disciples of Ma-Nang were gathered in, and Borisov reckoned at last that Russia was safe.

He was curious to know exactly how they had recruited his bodyguard, Alexei. He himself had called him a killing machine. And innocently given him the opportunity to murder Nikolaev by sending him to Poland. The Company of Saints. It was typical of the sinister cast of the founder's mind. A sick, cruel mind, poisoned in its contempt for the values that even Borisov considered essential to a civilized world. He would hold the trial in private, as soon as the election was over and the political situation stabilized. There would be no public exposure, no leak to the outside world. Borisov was a student of Roman history. He knew what penalty to impose. The destroyer would be forced to destroy himself. But there was one serious problem that had to be resolved. Thinking about it angered Borisov more than anything else he had discovered. And it had to be rectified, or there would be terrible repercussions. He had an idea that appealed to him. A very unorthodox idea, but it wouldn't be possible to implement it later. Also a chance to satisfy an old curiosity. For a long time now, he had wondered what Davina Graham was really like.

"It's unheard of," Humphrey exclaimed. "You can't possibly go."

"I agree," Tim Johnson said. "The foreign secretary may not be our favorite man at times, but I think he's right about this."

"Just because it's never been done before doesn't mean it shouldn't at least be considered," Davina retorted. "Look, I know what's getting to both of you. What happened at Welton isn't going to hem me in for the rest of my life. If they wanted to have a go at me again, they could do it any time. On my way here, in my flat—anywhere. I'm not going to give up on this. As for Hilton, he's so anti-Soviet he's practically paranoid. I've made up my mind. But I'll leave the final decision to the prime minister. If Number 10 says 'No,' then I can't argue. If they give me discretion, which I think they will, then I'm going to Stockholm to meet him. I shall try and get an appointment this afternoon. Now let's get on with the dull routine, shall we?"

When they had left her office she didn't get down to work at once. It was an extraordinary proposal. Unprecedented, as Humphrey had pointed out. An invitation, passed through the British embassy in Moscow and relayed direct to SIS, for Miss Graham to meet Igor Borisov in Stockholm. To discuss matters of mutual concern to their countries and their own organizations. He had offered full guarantees for her safety and asked for the same for himself.

"There is no way," Davina maintained, "short of a direct order from the prime minister, that I can refuse to go. And besides," this was to Colin Lomax, "I want to. I want to meet Igor Borisov face to face. And I have a feeling he feels the same about me. For the same reason."

"And what is your reason?" Colin demanded. "What possible good can it do you to compromise yourself with our NATO allies to make personal contact with the head of the KGB, a man who could even be the boss of the whole Soviet world in two days' time!"

"He had Sasanov killed," Davina said. "I've fought him in the dark for five years. Now I want to see him, just as I see you. Don't try and stop me, Colin, because you can't. You can come with me, but that's as far as I'll go."

They caught the ten o'clock flight from Heathrow. Two of MacNeil's men from Special Branch traveled with them. They went tourist on her insistence. No VIP treatment, nothing to draw attention. Ordinary passengers on a scheduled flight from Stockholm. The meeting had been arranged on neutral ground. The headquarters of the Red Cross.

The flight took just over two hours. They were met by an embassy car; not an official car but the privately owned Simka of the assistant to the second secretary. "Welcome to Stockholm," he said. He had been told he was escorting a group of officials from the British Red Cross. He thought they were unenthusiastic about the sights of the city that he pointed out. Glum and boring. He enjoyed his posting and liked Stockholm. The drinking laws were a nuisance but there were compensations. Like the Swedish girls. Beautiful was an understatement. And he wasn't a drinking man, as it happened.

"Well," he said, and he didn't hide his relief at getting rid of them. "Here we are. I'll leave you at the entrance if you don't mind. Parking is such a problem at this time of day."

Inside the building they were met by a member of the British embassy staff. Trade councillor was his official position. He was in fact the head of "C"—and responsible for Intelligence inside the embassy. Davina introduced him to Colin Lomax and the two Special Branch officers. He summed up all three with a look. The lady had brought protection. So had her Russian counterpart. "They're in through here," he said quietly. "Everything's been checked. If you'll follow me, Miss Graham."

They had set aside a pleasant ground-floor room that over-looked a garden. There were three men inside; one sitting, two standing close. When she came in the seated man got up. There had been a photograph of him on file, taken many years ago when he was attaché at a foreign embassy. She had studied it for some feature that would distinguish him from the other Soviet diplomat-spies, and found nothing. A round, unremarkable face with nondescript features. Nothing to fix in the memory.

He was taller than she had expected. Quite burly, as if his middle years were telling. Hair that had been fair and turning gray. Brown eyes, a wide mouth and a short nose. And wearing an over-padded Russian jacket and too-wide trousers.

For a long, silent interval they looked at each other.

And this, Borisov said to himself, is the woman who has caused me so much trouble for so long. This is the adversary who wrecked my operation in Mexico. The woman who got promoted for exposing the most valuable traitor we had in place since Philby. I got promoted for killing her husband, the defector Sasanov. She is not my idea of beauty. But she must have been for him.

"I am Igor Borisov," he said. He had a deep voice and his English came easily.

"And you know who I am," she replied.

He nodded. "I am pleased you decided to come. I will send my companions away. It is better that we talk alone."

"I'll do the same," she answered. She opened her bag and took out a cigarette. He lit it for her with a heavy American lighter.

"I have seen photographs of you," he said. "But they are not like you."

"I've only seen one of you," she remarked. "A very old one, when you were in Cairo. It's not like you either. General, I can't stay in Sweden more than a few hours. What is the purpose of our meeting?"

To her surprise he smiled slightly. "If I said curiosity about you, would you believe that?"

"No. You wouldn't waste your time, or mine."

"But I have been curious to meet you," he said. "Shall we sit down? People in our positions work against each other for years and never speak face to face."

"Perhaps it's just as well," Davina answered. "We can't afford to see the other side in personal terms."

"I don't agree with you. But I have had to see you in that way ever since the attempt to kill you. I have been very disturbed by it."

Davina said coolly, "It disturbed me too. I had believed you were responsible for these people until it happened. Afterward I wasn't sure."

"That's why I asked you to meet me," he said. "I want to tell you that I had no knowledge of it, and I would never have allowed it to happen. The people concerned have been arrested and will be punished. What have you done with the girl—'France' was her code name, wasn't it?"

You *have* arrested them, Davina thought. And broken them, if you know that.

"She went mad," she answered. "Completely lost her mind. Apparently she thought she was strangling her mother. You also know how it was arranged? About the bracelet?"

"Yes. An ingenious idea, but not new. And not infallible either, I'm glad to say. The principle is quite sound. The activities of all these people were based on one premise; a proportion of men and women are potential killers. Like human bombs they have a detonating mechanism that a skilled operator can identify and activate. In each case, the assassins were selected because they had the right kind of personality disturbance. There had to be a hate object, you understand, and preferably one associated with extreme guilt, like a parent or a loved one The aggression could be harnessed, like all energy, and directed against specific targets. With this so-called fail-safe—the programmed urge to kill anyone associated with the symbol. It was a mistake to choose the heart and the arrow, but then," Borisov shrugged slightly, "it was part of what you Christians call the cardinal sin of pride. Do you understand what it means?"

Davina said, "I understand what it meant to the village of Lu·

kina in the Ukraine. The heart and the arrow were used for murder. I felt we were getting near the answer before I saw the girl. And we'll have it soon."

He said, "The least I can do is to prove my good faith by giving you the answer. The Company of Saints was a private army of assassins, recruited to bring one man to power. A man as sick as the people who were sent out to kill. He saw himself like your Christian Lucifer, taking the throne from God. He parodied the Christian hierarchy in this organization. He even called the Soviet doctor who perfected the idea St. Peter. But like Lucifer, he fell. He will not be the next ruler of Russia."

"Can you tell me his name?" she asked. "I'd like to close the file."

"Marshal Yemetovsky," Borisov said. "A great hero in the Patriotic War. A loyal servant of Stalin. And lucky enough to outlive him. Perhaps Stalin's instincts were not so crazy as people said at the end. Perhaps he recognized the danger of Yemetovsky. You want to know the significance of the heart and the arrow?"

Davina nodded. She should have felt excitement, but she didn't. There was one question yet to be asked. She wondered whether he was expecting it. "What connected it with Yemetovsky? We couldn't find anything. Not through Commissar Rudkin or his relatives. We were trying to get the names of the Cheka squad."

Borisov said, "That would have taken a long time. Perhaps nobody would know. But it wouldn't have told you anything if you did learn who they were. Yemetovsky's grandparents came from Lukina. They were among the people killed. It was their own son who denounced the village. Yemetovsky's father."

"Thank you," Davina said after a moment. "Thank you for the information, General Borisov. But how did he think that killing all those people was going to help him?"

"He wanted to test the method," Borisov explained. "So his doctor protégé assures me. He wanted to divert attention from the murder of Nikolaev and from my murder, and from the death of his rival Mishkoyan, by letting both East and West think they were at the mercy of a terrorist group who struck down indiscriminately. A situation like that allows the army its chance to take power."

"And did they try to kill you?"

"No. The assassin decided to save himself instead. He hadn't been programed like the others. I hope that you have accepted my explanation, and my sincerest apologies."

Davina stood up. "I have," she said. "It wouldn't do, would it, General, if we started loosing off at each other?"

"No, it wouldn't," he said firmly. "That was my concern. I didn't want British reprisals coming to Moscow."

"But it doesn't matter if the underlings get killed?" Her tone was deceptive. It sounded innocent. Too innocent. He opened a platinum cigarette case. "Would you like to try one of these? They are a little strong."

"I got used to them once," she said. "My husband always smoked those."

He took one for himself, held out his lighter for her, and then inhaled deeply. "Yes," he said. "So he did. Again, I apologize for what happened to you. But it couldn't be avoided."

"I thought for a moment you were going to say you were sorry for what was done to him."

They faced each other. The truce was over.

"No," Borisov said. "I am not sorry for Ivan Sasanov's death. He was your husband and you loved him. Pretend that it was not so. Pretend that he was a traitor to your country. A defector who had gone over to the enemy. Like your brother-in-law, Kidson. You didn't spare him, did you?"

"I didn't kill him," Davina said fiercely. "I didn't send out a man to wire up his car and blow him to bits."

"No," he said. "But one day you may have to do what I did. And how will you behave then? I think you must ask yourself that question before you condemn me. We are the same, you and I, and the American at Langley. And the men in Peking and Tokyo. There is not much difference between us. A scruple here, perhaps. But underneath, we are a special type of human being. So are the ones who work for us. We are not part of the mass of the people. I don't pretend to be. You should not pretend either. Again, I am glad that we met. You will not kill me and I won't harm you. But that is the best we can offer each other. It doesn't apply to anyone else. You are going straight back to London?"

"Yes," Davina said.

He nodded. "I would like to see London again. It is a very charming city."

"I didn't know you had been there," Davina remarked. Somehow the meeting had been dominated by him from start to finish. Even at the last moment.

"I learned to speak English there," he said. "When I was a very junior filing clerk in our embassy. I'm surprised you didn't know about that! Ah—everyone comes back. Goodbye. I wish you a safe journey."

They didn't shake hands.

"Goodbye," Davina said. He stood back and she walked out of the room first. Lomax and the other two men joined her outside. The man from "C" hurried toward them. "I've laid on some lunch," he said in a rapid whisper. "Let's get them out of the way first."

"I don't want anything to eat, thank you. I want to get to the airport and away as soon as possible."

By the evening of the following day, it had been announced in Moscow that Igor Borisov had been elected chairman of the Central Committee of the Communist party. The title of president was only a formality after that. It was a historic moment. The KGB chief was the new ruler of the Soviet bloc. The media in the rest of the world poured out accounts of his career, mostly erroneous. Political assessments by people who claimed that he had been a vicious oppressor in his early days and others who called him a moderate with cultural leanings toward the West. His proficiency in western languages was cited as an example. He would be for peace and disarmament. He would be for an arms race and confrontation. He was cunning and heartless. Consumed by ambition. A fond husband and father in his private life. He had a sense of humor.

Nobody in the West knew anything about him compared with Davina Graham after only half an hour in the Red Cross building in Stockholm. She spent a long day putting down her impressions. They would provide a useful guideline for the future. She didn't know yet who his successor would be at Dzerjinsky Square.

"I don't think we should talk about anything until we've had some lunch," James White announced. She was looking much better, he thought; she had got her color back and lost that haggard look about the eyes. He had asked her to meet him at the Garrick Club after a personal plea from Downing Street. He had known Davina all her life. He might succeed in influencing her. He was determined to be patient with her. But it was a great effort.

"I love this place," he said. "I always feel at home here. You don't mind not being taken to some smart restaurant, I hope?"

"I much prefer this," Davina answered. "It's got a wonderful, peaceful atmosphere. You'd never think it was frequented by the law and the theater. And people like us." He watched her narrowly. He detected something critical in the last words—"people like us."

"It's age," he declared. "In the face of time, human antics die down to a murmur. That's what is so good about a club like this; the extroverts have to lower their voices and the introverts get a chance to speak up. I think that's rather good, don't you?"

"Very apt," she smiled and sipped at the glass of sherry beside her. "I don't think we should wait to have lunch before we talk. Otherwise we might get indigestion afterward. You know I'm resigning, don't you?"

"So I've been told," he said. "I couldn't believe my ears. I still don't. You've decided this at the most critical time for the Service, you realize that? There's a new man at the Kremlin and another new man heading the KGB. Couldn't you at least carry on for another year? Give yourself time to settle down?" He leaned toward her, "It's still shock, after what happened. You should have taken proper sick leave. If I'd been in charge I'd have packed you off somewhere for a month in the sunshine."

"I'm sure you would," Davina said. "But it's not the solution. If you asked me here to give me a long lecture you're only repeating what everyone else has said, from the Foreign Office to the prime minister. The words 'abdicating your responsibilities' have been very firmly said to me. And duty to my country, of course. I don't think I'll be on this year's Honors List."

"Davina," he interrupted, "for God's sake be sensible. If hard things were said, it's not surprising. You're too good at the job to lose without a fight. You ought to take it as a compliment."

"I do," she said seriously. "The point is, I *was* good at it. And I enjoyed every moment of it. But not anymore. If I try to explain to you, will you listen? I mean, really listen and see if you can understand?"

He sat back. "Of course. I might even be able to help in the end."

Davina lit a cigarette. She drew on it, and said, "I gave up smoking for quite a time because of Tony. I was in love with him, and I trusted him. Have you any idea what it meant to me to find out that he was dealing with the KGB behind my back? Don't misunderstand, Chief, I don't regret him anymore. I don't even want to think about him, because it still sickens me. At least I had my work; then Colin came back into my life and put the pieces together again. But I knew it wouldn't last either. It hadn't before and I wasn't nearly as dedicated then. On the way up I'd broken with my family because of what happened to my sister. It wasn't till my father died that I could go home. Remember that funeral? I couldn't even cry about him; all I could hide in was my work. We talked about it in the garden. You think I'm full of self-pity. I can see that. And maybe I am; maybe I've got to be sorry for myself first and then learn how to be sorry for other people all over again. I'm sorry for Humphrey, odd as it sounds. He was so bitter when I got the job. How often did he lunch with you to gripe behind my back? How often did you encourage him to make life difficult? No, please, don't say anything. I don't mind. I knew about it and I didn't care. Which says something about the kind of person I was turning into.

"I found myself being understanding about Ivan's death. I started to put myself in your place and accept your explanations. That was quite a change of attitude, if you think back a bit."

"What you're saying," James White said, "is that you felt the job was asking too much of you. What you've quoted are personal disappointments. But we've all had to suffer them in some form or another. You couldn't run the Service as well as you did and expect anything else. I warned you about that from the start."

"I know you did," Davina answered. "But you didn't warn me about the kind of person I'd become as a result. Would you like to know what really tipped the scales?"

"I would indeed," he said and sighed.

Davina said quietly, "When I met Borisov I faced him about having Ivan murdered."

James White glanced at her. "I wondered if you would mention that," he said

"You shouldn't have," she retorted. "And do you know what he said? 'One day you may have to do what I did. And what will you do then?' " She stubbed out her half-smoked cigarette. "I did ask myself that question, and I knew the answer. One day, I'd justify the murder of a human being and send someone out to kill him—or her. And that was the moment when I knew I had to quit. So, that's it. I feel much happier now that my mind is made up."

He said, "I don't know what to say to you, Davina. Except just once more—don't give it all up in a hurry. What you are frightened of may never happen."

"What I am frightened of is happening already," she said. "I am going to stop it before it's too late. Tim Johnson will take over. And he'll be every bit as good. I don't think that particular question will worry him."

Sir James stood up. "Well," he said, "I think we may as well go down to lunch. Do you know, getting you to resign is probably the biggest coup Borisov has ever brought off?" At the table he said, "What does Colin say?"

Davina smiled a little. "Oh, I don't think he'll mind."

"You haven't told him?"

"Not yet. I wanted to get everything tied up first."

"Have you got any plans? What are you going to do with yourself?"

"I don't know. I'd like to look after my mother for a bit anyway. Charlie's getting married next month and she'll be on her own at Marchwood.... The menu looks good, what shall we order?"

James White knew how to lose gracefully. He suggested smoked salmon and a bottle of champagne. He didn't say what it was celebrating.

"Isn't the country lovely at this time of year?" Lomax was driving; he had opened the sunroof and Davina's hair was flying in the wind. She looked young and happy. He thought, if only this could last. If only we didn't have to go back on Monday morning. "If I had a choice," he said, "I'd move out of London."

Davina looked at him. "Would you? But what about the ghastly commuting?"

"Depends where you are," he said. "Wiltshire, Hampshire, they're all dead easy with the motorway. Wouldn't suit you though, darling. Eight o'clock at the desk and all that."

They were near the turn-off for Marchwood. "Do you remember the first time you came here?" she asked him.

"Four years ago," he answered. "How the time flies—yes, I remember it very well. You were very stuffy and condescending, I thought. I didn't look forward to going on a job with you at all."

"And you were as prickly as hell," she retorted. "You drove off like a maniac and showered gravel all over the drive. I was furious."

He reached over and held her hand for a moment. "We had some happy times here, didn't we? I must say it's a beautiful place."

When he stopped the car in the drive, she said, "Colin, just a minute, before we go in. I've got something to tell you."

Mrs. Graham had heard them arrive, and came to the front door to welcome them. What she saw made her decide to wait for a few minutes.

"Darling, we can't sit here all day," Davina said when he let her go. They opened the car doors and came toward the house hand in hand.

"You know," Lomax said to her as they approached it, "I can't think of a nicer place to spend a honeymoon."

"I can't either," Davina said. They opened the door and went inside.